PRAISE FOR

Just a Summer Fling

"A heartfelt story set in a warm and wonderful small town, where love and laughter are around every corner. Readers are sure to fall in love with Lake Sullivan!"
—Shirley Jump, *New York Times* bestselling author of *When Somebody Loves You*

"A quirky, feel-good romance. I loved this book!"
—Jennifer Lewis, *USA Today* bestselling author of the Desert Kings series

"A happy escape into a lovely, heartwarming story."
—Alison Bliss, author of *Rules of Protection*

"A bright, warm, intelligent love story from a promising new voice in romance." —*Kirkus Reviews*

"Cameron's characters are complex and well crafted . . . [This is] a summer to remember." —*Publishers Weekly*

"A light-hearted, sexy romance that readers will not be able to put down . . . immensely enjoyable." —*RT Book Reviews*

Hometown Hero

CATE CAMERON

BERKLEY SENSATION, NEW YORK

BERKLEY
SENSATION

An imprint of Penguin Random House LLC
375 Hudson Street, New York, New York 10014

HOMETOWN HERO

A Berkley Sensation Book / published by arrangement with the author

Copyright © 2016 by Cate Cameron.
Excerpt from *Just a Summer Fling* by Cate Cameron copyright © 2015 by Cate Cameron.
Penguin supports copyright. Copyright fuels creativity, encourages diverse voices,
promotes free speech, and creates a vibrant culture. Thank you for buying an authorized
edition of this book and for complying with copyright laws by not reproducing, scanning, or
distributing any part of it in any form without permission. You are supporting writers and
allowing Penguin to continue to publish books for every reader.

BERKLEY SENSATION® and the "B" design are registered trademarks of
Penguin Random House LLC.
For more information, visit penguin.com.

ISBN: 978-0-425-28206-9

PUBLISHING HISTORY
Berkley Sensation mass-market edition / February 2016

PRINTED IN THE UNITED STATES OF AMERICA

10 9 8 7 6 5 4 3 2 1

Cover art by Jim Griffin.
Cover design by George Long.
Interior text design by Kelly Lipovich.

This is a work of fiction. Names, characters, places, and incidents either are the product of
the author's imagination or are used fictitiously, and any resemblance to actual persons,
living or dead, business establishments, events, or locales is entirely coincidental.

Penguin
Random
House

Thanks to my editor, Julie Mianecki, for the painless editing, and my agent, Andrea Somberg, for the painless contract negotiations. Publishing is EASY (when you work with the right people)!

Also thanks to the many people who helped me gain a basic understanding of MMA—all mistakes are mine, and credit for everything I got right goes to them.

❧ *One* ❧

"HE'S CALLED THREE times," Bonita said. "I'm your roommate, not your secretary. Call him back, even if it's just to
tell him not to call anymore."

Zara buried her head farther beneath the throw pillows on
their comfortably ragged sofa. If she could just stay there in
the soft darkness a little longer, maybe it would all go away.

But Bonita wasn't giving up. She lifted Zara's feet and slid
onto the couch, then let Zara's feet fall into her lap and started
massaging, her strong hands working through the calluses
and tension.

"Or if he really *is* stalking you," Bonita said softly, once she
had Zara nice and relaxed, "you should call Terry. The company has a security department for a reason."

Zara pulled her feet away peevishly at the mention of the
company's CEO. He'd been a Mixed Martial Arts fighter back
when the sport was just beginning, and he deserved a lot of
the credit for bringing it to the mainstream. But he was driven,

and expected his fighters to be the same. "I don't want to talk to Terry. And Calvin Montgomery's not a stalker," she grumbled into the cushions.

"Good, then," Bonita said. "So you can give him a call and deal with whatever it is."

"We've always e-mailed before." Zara pulled her head out from under the pillows and squinted through the late afternoon sunshine to see Bonita's face. "That's rude, right? If you set up a system of e-mailing, you shouldn't just switch over to the phone because you feel like it. Right?"

"Really rude. You should call him up and tell him so."

"I'm injured. When someone's injured, they don't have to talk on the phone."

"Actually, you're supposed to avoid looking at computer screens," Bonita corrected. "So the phone would be better than e-mail. Maybe your friend knows that."

"He's not my friend. And since when are you an expert on concussions?"

"Since my darling roommate keeps getting them. And if he's not your friend, what is he? He's got a pretty sexy voice. Nice and low . . . I bet I could get him to moan real nice. . . ."

"Yuck. Stay away from him. He's an asshole."

"Really?"

Bonita sounded like she was asking for the truth, so Zara took a moment to try to provide it. "I don't know. Probably. I mean, he definitely *was* an asshole. But he's been good ever since then. You know, good to Zane."

Bonita already knew that story, so Zara didn't have to explain what she meant. Except maybe an elaboration on just how very good Calvin Montgomery had been to Zara's brother. "He visits him more often than I do. He doesn't travel as much as me, and he lives closer, so it's easier for him. But still . . .

he really stepped up. And Zane says he was good during the trial and everything, too."

"So you're not returning his calls because . . ."

Because Calvin was part of Zara's old life in Lake Sullivan, and she needed to keep a bit of distance from that world. She'd moved on, she'd grown up, but it was still easier to deal with it through the remoteness of e-mail rather than the immediacy of a phone call. Besides, Zara had a pretty good idea of what Calvin wanted to talk about, and she didn't think she was ready for that conversation. Zane's impending release was exciting, of course, but also terrifying. What if he couldn't cope? What if Zara couldn't give him the help he needed?

But Bonita didn't need to hear all that angst. So Zara shrugged and said, "I'll call him. I just haven't yet."

And of course that was when Zara's phone rang. She made a face. She could just let it go to the message system, but then she'd have to either listen to the message or erase it without listening, and both options seemed a bit overwhelming right then. "One more time?" she said pleadingly.

Bonita sighed dramatically. "Absolute *last* time, you baby." She leaned over and pulled Zara's cell phone off the coffee table. "Zara Hale's phone." She listened for a moment, then said, "Oh, hi, Andre, it's Bonita. I think Zara's around somewhere . . . let me just try to find her, okay?"

She held the phone out to Zara, who reluctantly took it. Andre was her manager and, at least in theory, was in her corner. Not someone she should be blowing off. "Hey, Andre," she said, making sure she sounded chipper and bright. "You just caught me—I was on my way out for a run!" She ignored Bonita's raised eyebrow.

"Did the doctors clear that?" Andre sounded skeptical.

"Yeah, of course." They'd said she could start phasing in

her normal routine again. She was pretty sure they'd meant, like, taking showers instead of baths, and getting dressed in real clothes instead of wearing sweats all day, but maybe they'd meant exercise. She couldn't be sure.

"Well, okay," Andre said reluctantly. "But you're looking after yourself, right? You're not pushing too hard?"

"Nope. I'm pushing just hard enough."

"Okay, good. You need to come back strong and ready. You're a major investment and you need to make sure you act that way."

Funny, she'd thought she might be something that *wasn't* purely financial. How naïve. "Yeah," she said. "Strong and ready. Got it."

"Okay. So in the meantime . . ." Andre paused, and Zara could totally picture him leaning back in his chair, stroking his goatee, ready to drop the next line as if he was some sort of master of manipulation. "We have a new opportunity."

"Yeah? What? Not more modelling—that was a disaster."

"No. Not in entertainment, exactly . . ."

"Oh my God, Andre, do they want me to be an astronaut? That's so exciting! I mean, it's a surprise, sure, but I really think I can handle it!"

He gave her his best long-suffering sigh. It was more effective in person, and even there, it had long since lost its power against Zara. "No. Not an astronaut. But something almost as inspiring, really."

"Porn?" she guessed.

"No. You've made your feelings on that perfectly clear."

She shouldn't have *had* to make her feelings on doing porn clear to the manager of her Mixed Martial Arts career, but at least he'd finally gotten the message. "So . . . what?"

"You like kids, right? You've been looking for a chance to work with them more closely?"

"No, not really. Kids are pretty annoying, aren't they? I mean, I don't know that many, personally. But they don't seem good." She thought back over her very limited experience with people younger than herself. Loud, undisciplined, out of control. "Yeah, I think kids suck."

"No," he said with exaggerated patience. "You like them. You've been looking for an opportunity to give back to the community. You had a tough start and you still have some rough edges, but people have been understanding about that and given you chances, and now you want to help some other disadvantaged kids get a chance. Right?"

"Okay, first off, nobody *gave* me a damn thing. I *earned* my chances."

"Fine. You earned them. And other kids should earn them too. But they shouldn't have to fight quite as hard as you did. They should get a bit of help. A hand up, not a hand out. Right?"

"Maybe?"

"Work with me, Zara. You're at a crucial juncture of your career here. Two concussions is not good. Your opponents know to go for the headshot now. I know you're fast and you usually take them out before they can land a good hit, but obviously that's not always the case, or you wouldn't be injured right now. Right?"

"What's your point?"

"My point is, you need to take a break until your brain is solid in your head again. The company isn't going to let you fight anytime soon, even if we push for it. Their insurers and the PR department do *not* want their headlining female fighter pulling a *Million Dollar Baby*."

"She was a paraplegic, not brain damaged."

"Whatever. The point is, you're valuable healthy, and you're a damn disaster if something goes permanently wrong. So they're not going to let you back in the ring until their doctors say it's safe. So unless you want to be looking at a layoff, we need to find ways to improve or at least maintain your value while you're recovering. It can't be physical. But it can be PR."

"With *kids*?"

"Not just any kids. This guy hasn't contacted you? This . . . Calvin Montgomery? He said he'd get in touch directly."

Zara's grip on the phone got a little tighter. "What the hell does Calvin Montgomery have to do with anything?"

"It's his idea. And he's got the company on his side, too. I thought Terry was going to pass out he was so excited about it all."

"All *what*?"

"He really didn't get in touch with you. Damn, he said he was going to." Andre sounded a little disillusioned with Calvin Montgomery, but charged on anyway. "He wants you to help him start up a community center, back in your hometown. What's it called? Lake Sullivan? Whatever. They've already got the place built and mostly staffed, but they're looking for a few more people. He says there's loads of disadvantaged kids there and they need some hope and someone to inspire them, and he wants you to be that person, and I swear, Terry just about came in his pants. Thinks it's a good way to improve the MMA image. He's throwing serious funding at the project. Some for you, some for the facility. It's excellent."

Andre paused for breath, and maybe Zara should have taken the opportunity to interrupt, but she was a bit too dazed by it all. "Montgomery wants your brother involved, which . . . I'm not so sure about. But whatever, we can negotiate on that. But seriously, making you into some sort of Ripley character, like from *Aliens*? You're a fierce warrior woman with a soft spot for kids. It's brilliant. Just couldn't be any better. You work there for a while, you do whatever the hell people do when they start up community centers, none of it hurts your brain, you train enough to stay fit but don't bring yourself right up to the peak . . . I honestly can't think of a better way for you to be spending your time. Can you?"

The list of better things was so long Zara wasn't sure where to start. Should she organize the options alphabetically or in order of preference? Best to keep it simple, probably. "Anything but that." Anything but going back to rural Vermont and getting involved with the Montgomery family and dealing with a bunch of annoying children. "Maybe I could become a nun or something. They like kids, don't they? Some of them?"

"Nuns can't have sex, Zare. You still want to consider that option?"

"Maybe something else." Her sex life might be a bit slow, but she wanted to at least keep the option open. "I mean, there's plenty of messed-up kids in New York City! I can stay right here! And, you know, you can figure out photo ops or something, right? I don't have to spend a *lot* of time with them, do I?"

"People aren't as gullible as they used to be. It takes more than a few snapshots with some raggedy kids. We need testimonials from concerned locals, recorded tears from your protégés, poignant anecdotes about how much you've learned. We need more than a photo op, Zara."

"This is bullshit. We don't need any of that. I'm a fighter, not a humanitarian. I'm the MMA champion! I've got the damn belt—I'm looking at it right now. How is messing around with a bunch of kids going to make me fight better?"

"It's going to make you *look* better," Andre said, not entirely patiently. "You know how it goes. You get fights based on what the fans want to see, and right now . . . well, as long as you're defending the title, you're fine. But if you're out for too long and lose the title, or if you come back and aren't quite up to speed yet and lose it, you're going to need the fans on your side. And it'll do great things for your endorsements, too."

"I'm so tired of that crap. The men are allowed to just *fight*. They don't have to look pretty and flirt with reporters and work with damn kids!"

"Simple question, Zara. Because, I don't know, maybe I missed something. So let me just check . . . are you a man?" Andre paused, just long enough to pretend he was waiting for an answer. "Oh, no, you're not? Okay, next question. Do you live in a fantasy world of total equality, or do you live in this world?" Another pause for effect. "Oh, you live in *this* world? Then stop wasting my time with your whining and help me manage your career as a female fighter in the current universe. Okay?"

Zara was pretty sure she was out of arguments, but that didn't mean she liked the idea. "By working at a community center? Seriously?" She paused. "Why the hell is Calvin Montgomery interested in making me work at a community center?" And the worst part, "In *Lake Sullivan*? They don't want me in Lake Sullivan, Andre. They practically kicked me out."

"They want you now. Being on the cover of both *Sports Illustrated* and *Maxim* will change a lot of minds."

"This whole thing is stupid."

"Give it some thought," Andre said soothingly. "It'd be good for your career, and like I said, Terry's willing to pay for it all."

"What does that mean, exactly? How much money?"

"We'll have to negotiate the details. But it'll be a hell of a lot more than you'd make lying around on your couch feeling sorry for yourself. And I'll talk to your sponsors, too, see if we can milk some extra out of them." He waited for her next objection. When it didn't come, he said, "Okay, then. Think about it. I'll talk to Terry and figure out some of the details. And look after your brain, okay?"

"Okay," Zara said grudgingly. She hung up, then looked at Bonita, who'd been listening to Zara's half of the conversation with obvious interest. "Fine, you're right. I need to phone Calvin Montgomery. Did you write his number down somewhere?"

"MR. Montgomery?" Allison's voice stopped Cal on his way out the door. "Zara Hale is on line three for you."

It was tempting to keep walking. He'd called the little brat three times and she'd ignored him until he'd gone ahead and talked to her boss? Now she wanted to talk to him, but maybe *he* was too busy to talk this time.

Yeah, tempting, but not appropriate. He was the responsible one, after all. "I'll catch up," he told the people he'd been walking with. They were on their way to The Pier for lunch, so it wasn't like he was going to be missing a meeting or anything. "Order for me—whatever the special is."

That taken care of, he turned back toward his office. "Line three?"

Allison nodded from her desk outside his door. He hadn't liked the setup originally; Allison had been with the company since he'd been a toddler, and he was pretty sure she'd been assigned as his assistant largely to keep an eye on him. Having her stationed by his door made it feel even more like she was his sentry. His jailer. But he'd gotten used to her, just like he'd adjusted to the rest of it. And having her so intent on running his business life was actually a good excuse to delegate a lot of his work to her, so he'd started to think of her presence as a perk.

And there were other advantages to the job, he remembered as he sank back into his luxurious desk chair and swivelled around so he could look out the floor-to-ceiling windows toward the lake. Yeah, his work was boring and he had a babysitter assigned to him, but he made good money and worked in a pleasant environment. It could be worse.

He picked up the phone and said, "Zara? Thanks for calling back." He didn't bother to mention how long it had taken. No point in starting off with her on the defensive. "I guess you've probably been told about the plan by now?"

"Yeah, I've been told." It had been a long time since he'd heard her voice, but she still sounded about the same. Totally pugnacious and looking for trouble. "What the hell are you up to?"

"Zane's out in less than a month," Cal replied calmly. "He's going to need a job, and some stability."

"What? I mean, yeah, okay, but what's that got to do with me and a community center?"

"He can work there, too. He likes kids, and he told me he wants to find a way to start giving back."

"He's a convicted felon! You really think he's going to be allowed to work with kids?"

"His crimes had nothing to do with children, and there was only peripheral violence. I don't think there's any reason we can't trust him around young people. With adequate supervision, of course."

"Adequate . . . you don't expect *me* to supervise him, do you? He's my big brother! He's not going to listen to me. And it's not like I know anything about any of this!"

"No, not you. We've got a professional manager in mind. Good experience, relevant education, the whole package. She'll be in charge of supervising you and Zane."

"Okay, well . . ." He could practically hear her recalculating. "Okay, if this is what Zane wants and you can find a way to make it work, then, great, it sounds like a good plan. For him. But why am I getting dragged into it?"

"Because I *can't* find a way to make it work, not without some help."

"I really don't understand how I'd help anything."

"Two ways." Cal kicked his feet up onto the windowsill and leaned back in his chair. He was pretty pleased with himself on this one, but he tried not to let that come out in his voice. "One, you make the town more likely to accept Zane. You may not believe it, but you're a golden girl up here now. A celebrity. Local girl made good. Pick the cliché, and you fit it. So people who might object to *just* Zane working at the center will be okay with it if you're involved."

"You're right, I don't believe it."

"Well, if you ever came by, you'd know. As it is, you'll have to trust me."

There was no answer, not right away. Finally, Zara said, "That was one way. What's two?"

"Two . . ." This one was going to take a bit more finesse. "You being involved makes it easier for Zane to accept the job. He's a proud guy, Zara. You know that. He's never wanted to take favors from me, not if they involved money. So he won't want to take this job, not if he thinks it's me giving him a handout."

"You think he's going to be more willing to accept help from me? His baby sister? You're delusional."

"Well, no, I'm not. As a matter of fact, once I explained how you'd be involved, Zane agreed to go along with it."

"Bullshit."

Cal grinned. He wished this meeting could have been in person so he'd have been able to see the expression on her face, but at least a phone call was better than e-mail. "It's not bullshit at all. When I told him about his baby sister getting two concussions in one year and maybe facing permanent brain damage if she didn't stay out of the ring for a while? When I told him how you were pushing to get back too early because you had nothing constructive to do with your time? When I said I'd love to get you involved in this project, but didn't think I'd be able to persuade you if he wasn't involved?" Yeah, this had been a good plan. Cal was proud of himself. "He knew what he had to do. He's taking the job so that *you'll* take the job."

Damn, it would have been great if he'd been able to see her as she processed it all. Finally she said, "Okay, you don't know shit about my career, or my health. So you're lying, really. And you're playing us off against each other, *for* each other? You've set it up so he'll take the job to help me, and I'll take the job to help him."

"Exactly."

"Why? Why is this any of your business?"

Interesting that she was the one asking that question, when her street-smart brother hadn't. But Cal had the answer already figured out, ready for when he'd been talking to Zane, so it was easy to use it now. "Because I want the community center to succeed. I want it to target kids who need it. Sure, everyone's welcome, but you know what I mean. The middle-class kids getting dropped off by their loving parents for an afternoon of basketball or crafts or something? They don't *need* it. But there are kids who do. A lot of them. And I think you and Zane will be good at reaching those kids."

"Why, because we're poor, downtrodden trash? We can speak to our people?"

"You're not trash. But, yeah, because you grew up without money and without strong parenting. Because you struggled with finding your places in the world. I think Zane should be involved because he can be a good lesson on what goes wrong if you don't make the right decisions, and also a good lesson about it never being too late to change. And you? Obviously a success story. The kids need to see more of those. Probably the girls especially. You didn't get knocked up and start a family way too young because you didn't know what the hell else to do with your life. You broke free. The girls definitely need to see that."

He let her ponder for a moment, then said, "It doesn't have to be a long-term commitment. Just give it an honest try. See if it works for you. Okay?"

"I'll think about it. And I'll talk to Zane about it. This is my week to visit him."

"Are you safe to drive? With the concussion?" As soon as the words were out of his mouth, he knew they'd been a mistake.

"You don't know shit about my health," she growled. "Remember? And I can take care of myself."

"I know," he said quickly. "Sorry. I've been talking to Zane too much—you know how protective he is."

"How protective he wants to be, maybe. But he hasn't been able to do much for me for the last decade, and I've been just fine. I don't need him *or* you thinking you're in charge of my safety. No way."

"Absolutely," Cal agreed. And he did agree, at least in theory. A bit harder to convince his instincts about it, but his brain was certainly aware that Zara Hale could take care of herself, and then some.

"Okay," she said grumpily. "I'll talk to Zane about it."

"It's not that terrible, Zara. We've got a good facility, and the town has changed. Seriously, they love you here now.

There are posters of you all over the place, and they sold tickets and did a huge event at the bar for your last pay-per-view fight. It sold out fast."

"That fight lasted twenty-three seconds."

"And the cheering went on for hours. Every time they showed a replay, I thought the roof was going to lift off."

"You were there?"

"Of course. Everyone who's anyone was there. It was the social event of the season."

"Yeah, I'm sure your whole family showed up, furs and pearls and all."

Well, that was a good point. But he chose to ignore it. "You should come by," he said. "I think you'd be pleasantly surprised."

"I'll think about it. Maybe. After I talk to Zane. But if he's not really into this, there's no way I'm doing it."

"Fair enough."

They ended the call, and Cal sat and looked out his window. Zane and Zara Hale, back in Lake Sullivan. Back where they'd always belonged, before things had gone so wrong. He hadn't been able to save either of them then, but that didn't mean he couldn't help them out now. He'd been raised with every privilege, all the financial *and* the emotional support he could have ever wanted, and it had made him strong. It had also given him a pretty good dose of liberal guilt, and helping Hales *and* disadvantaged kids was a great way to soothe his conscience.

Yeah. He was doing the right thing. He pushed out of his chair and strode out of the office with the energy that always made Allison frown suspiciously. Things were coming together. It was about damn time.

⸓ Two ⸓

EVEN AFTER ALL these years, driving past the tall, windowless walls of the Clinton Correctional Facility still made Zara shudder. She'd first visited her brother here when she was sixteen, defying her aunt and hitchhiking all the way from the city in order to see him. He'd been furious, of course, frightened at the risk she'd taken; she'd been more intimidated by the prison than by the trip. Walking into the building with its cameras and protocols and armed guards felt like surrendering herself to the harsh authority she'd been fighting all her life. But she'd gone the first time and she'd kept going, every other week for the last decade. Once her career had picked up and she'd started getting bouts farther from home, she'd coordinated with Calvin, making sure he could fill in on the weeks she was travelling.

It had become routine, more or less. She'd gotten to know the system, figured out not to wear underwire bras or any jewelry that would set off the metal detectors, learned the names of some of the corrections officers, gotten friendly enough that they wouldn't be too uptight if Zane and Zara got into a particularly good card game and ended up going a few minutes over their allotted hour. Yeah, it was all fine now—everything but the long drive past the twenty-foot-tall white wall.

The wall was too big, too oppressive. And it was too hard to think of her brother stuck on the other side of it for so long, not even able to look out a window and see the life that was passing him by.

But she toughed it out this time just like all the others, turned into the parking lot, made sure she left her phone and any other contraband in the car, and headed for the visitors' entrance.

"Nice fight," one of the guards said as she signed in. "I had my money on you, but damn, I thought she'd make you work a little harder for it!"

Zara snorted. "It was hard enough, thanks." She thought about the fierce elbow strike that had rocked her head back just before she'd gotten her arm lock and ended the fight. She'd barely been able to see by the time the ref raised her hand in victory, barely been able to stand as her trainers had helped her back to the change room. Yeah, she'd worked hard enough for that victory.

"Got your next fight scheduled yet?" The guard clearly hadn't heard the concussion rumors that were starting to circulate. Which made Zara wonder how the hell Calvin Montgomery seemed to know so much about it.

She was glad to leave the guard in ignorance. "I'm taking a bit of a break. There's no one really worth my time, you know?"

"I hear ya," he agreed, and waved her through the metal detector. She made her way to the familiar visiting room and looked at the people around her. A lot of families. Kids here visiting their fathers, growing up thinking this was normal. Spending time at home with just a mom, who was probably too tired to give them the attention they deserved. What had Calvin Montgomery said? Something about kids needing to find their place. She hoped these ones wouldn't think "their place" was jail.

And maybe she could do more than just hope. Maybe she could do something to help these kids, or others just like them.

Or maybe she could mess them up even worse than they already were.

Zane was escorted in, then, moving easily beside the CO, giving Zara a terse nod when he saw her. He'd been nineteen when he'd come to this place, and he'd be pushing thirty when he left. The wild, laughing boy was gone, replaced by a man who'd never existed outside the high, windowless walls of the prison.

It struck her then what a gift the offer from Calvin Montgomery was. A chance at a stable job, doing something Zane wanted to do? How many other inmates were leaving this place with that kind of future ahead of them? Zane could have a life. It would be a late start, but he could do it. As long as Zara's stubbornness didn't get in the way.

"Just another couple weeks," she said as he sat down.

Zane nodded. "Yeah. Did Cal talk to you?"

"Yeah. You want to do it?"

"I don't know. Do you?" Typical dry, expressionless Zane. Even as a boy, he'd been volatile about all the little things, but stoic when something really mattered. As a man, he played his cards close to his chest for everything.

"I don't know. Do you—" How to ask this? Zane and Calvin had been best friends before Zane's trouble, and that connection had never faltered. Calvin had stood by Zane through the trial, tried to use whatever connections he had to help out, and he'd kept Zane in his life ever since, even though it would have been so much easier to walk away. But still, Zara wanted to hear the words from her brother's mouth. "Do you trust him? I mean, he's a *Montgomery*. He's—"

"He's a good man, and a good friend." Zane's tone left no room for disagreement. "You hating him because of his family is no different than them hating us because of ours."

"He left! Don't tell me that wasn't part of what set you off, seeing him get to go away and have opportunities while you were stuck at home. Trapped in that damn town—"

"He went away to school, Zare. That's pretty normal behavior. I messed up because I *was* messed up. Nothing to do with him."

"And you couldn't go away because you were stuck looking after your little sister."

"More because I barely graduated high school. Bad grades and no money do not lead to college, little sister or not." Zane shook his head. "You know all this. Seriously, you're still mad at him? At any of them? You've held on to it all this time?"

Well, yeah, she had, and she wasn't quite ready to let it go yet. If she wasn't blaming the Montgomerys for Zane's downfall, maybe she'd have to blame herself. "So maybe it wasn't his fault you did what you did. But it was his fault you got caught! He turned you in!"

Another head shake, this one combined with an expression of frustration. "He did me a huge favor, Zare. You never should have followed me; you should have been safe at home." He ignored her eye roll. "And when I needed someone to get you out of there, I called the one person I knew I could trust. I'm not going to blame him for doing exactly what I asked."

"You asked him to call the cops on you?" She could still

remember Calvin's strong arm around her waist as he'd dragged her away from the motel room where Zane had been hiding. The fear and anger at being forced away from her brother. And underneath it all, the relief at having an excuse to leave, a chance to get away from the raving, bewildering mess her brother had somehow become. But she'd never admitted to the last part, and she wasn't going to do it now. "He called them as soon as we were out of the parking lot. Told them exactly where you were."

"I know."

"He turned you in."

"Of course he did," Zane said levelly. "What else could he have done?"

"*Helped* you!"

"He did help me. He got you somewhere safe, and he did what he could to make sure I didn't get in more trouble." Zane looked at the ceiling for a moment, then cut his eyes back to her. "I can barely remember parts of that week," he said, his voice so quiet Zara had to lean in to hear him over the buzz of the crowded room. "Not just the parts when I was drunk or high . . . other parts. Parts where I was just . . . just gone. I don't know what I was doing when you got there."

She did. He'd been sitting in a ragged old armchair, staring at the duck painting hanging crookedly on the wall, holding a hunting knife. He hadn't heard her say his name, not for a long time. Not until she'd moved around and gotten between him and that stupid duck painting. She didn't want to think about that, not ever. "But once I got there, you got better."

He shook his head again, then shrugged. "I got—I got it under control. I held it together, so you wouldn't get hurt. I tried to, at least. Just like I'd been trying back home. But I knew I couldn't hold on. That's why I called Cal."

"And when he got there, he should have *helped* you."

"How?" The question was short and simple, but there was an intensity in Zane's expression that made it clear the answer would be much more complicated. "I still don't know what was going on with me, not really. And as soon as he got there, as soon as I knew he'd keep you safe, I let myself go again. You remember that, don't you?"

She made herself nod. She remembered it far too well.

"He called the cops because he was afraid I was going to kill myself. Or hurt someone else and then attack the cops and get shot. Something bad. Something I couldn't make up for just by doing some time in prison."

"Some time? Ten years, Zane!"

"He didn't know all the stuff I'd done, and he didn't know how they'd sentence me. But still—I'm still alive. And I don't have to go through the next fifty years of my life knowing I hurt somebody. Killed somebody. I don't have to do that, so, yeah, he helped me."

"You could have gotten shot by the cops right there at the motel. He took a huge chance."

"Yeah, he did. But he did what he could to make it safe. He called his dad first, did you know that? And got his dad to call a judge, and the judge to call the cops. Just so the cops knew there was someone watching them, someone who expected things to go peacefully. So they called in a psychologist and a negotiator and all kinds of crap they wouldn't have done if they'd thought I was just another backwoods hick going crazy. Cal did what he could. And he helped at the trial, too. Being in New York meant his family didn't have much pull, but he was there, every day, and he testified for me at the sentencing."

"Lot of good that did you. Ten years?"

"Could have been worse," Zane said dully.

It was probably the longest conversation Zara and her

brother had ever had on the topic, or on much else, really. Zara wasn't absolutely convinced that Calvin was innocent, but she supposed it didn't matter what she thought. This wasn't about her. And it was the present, not the past. So without holding a grudge, and thinking about what Zane needed *now*, what made sense?

"I think maybe I want to try it," she said. "The community center thing. It might be interesting. If it works with your plans."

"I can fit it into my schedule," Zane said dryly.

And that was that. It was decided. Zara would e-mail Calvin the next day to let him know.

She'd committed. She was going back to Lake Sullivan. Summer vacation spot for the wealthy, claustrophobic hellhole for Zara Hale. Yeah, she was going back. But it was strictly temporary, and Calvin Montgomery had better understand that.

"I hope you know what you're doing," Michael said. He was Cal's older brother, the favored son, the responsible one who was committed to his family and ready to contribute to the dynasty. Normally he was fun to torment, but on this occasion Cal was a bit too tense about the situation to really enjoy himself.

"I hope so, too," he replied.

"You'll need to keep a close eye on things," their mother said sternly. She'd been against the idea to start with, but now that Cal was committed, she wanted him to succeed. "The challenge of opening a new center is enough without having to worry about a convict on parole and a . . . what is she again?"

"A savage?" Cal's father suggested dryly. He'd also been

against Cal's plan, and he didn't seem to have changed his opinion as completely as his wife had. "That was certainly my impression of the young lady when she lived here. She was completely out of control."

"Well, she's got a lot of control now," Cal said. "It's called Mixed Martial Arts, Mom, and Zara's known as one of the most disciplined fighters in the business. Intense, focused, driven, smart. No mistakes."

"Well, maybe she gets the mistakes out of her system *outside* the ring," his father suggested. "Now, Michael—we need to talk about the golf tournament. Have we contacted all the sponsors from last year?"

Cal let the conversation wash over him. He wasn't much of a golfer. And while the tournament was an important annual event, raising funds for the local hospital and officially closing out the season at the local golf club, there really wasn't much that needed to be discussed. The town was full of money in the summer, tourists and cottagers pumping cash into the local economy, and a lot of them were happy to come up for a weekend in the autumn to enjoy the foliage and play a little golf. They weren't hard to recruit. Michael was chairing the committee this year, but he'd passed almost all of the responsibility on to his very capable assistant. Cal would make his donation and show up and play eighteen holes, just like everyone else in the family, and that would be that. There wasn't much to talk about. At least for him.

But his family clearly disagreed, so while they chattered, he ran the community center business over in his mind one more time. The ribbon cutting the next day, the plans for ongoing fund-raising, the staff and volunteers they'd already found, the people they still needed to recruit. And, of course, the Hales. The wildcards in all this. He thought back to the kids he'd known. A bit rough, both of them, but not a mean bone in either of their bodies.

But now that it was too late to change anything, Cal had started having second thoughts. Zane had spent the last ten years in a maximum security prison. Even if half the stuff Cal had seen on TV was true, Zane had surely been living among animals for a decade—would they have driven the goodness out of him?

And Zara? Cal had seen her fight. Every one of her pro bouts, mostly on pay-per-view but twice in person, without her knowledge. She was . . . his father wasn't wrong maybe. There *was* something savage about her. She was a fighting machine. What had she done to turn herself into that? When she'd gained all that strength, what had she lost?

Damn it. Cal had seen this as an opportunity to help two people he cared about. But what if he was about to mess this up just as badly as he'd messed things up ten years before?

❧ *Three* ❧

ZANE WAS TREMBLING, and Zara had no idea what to do about it. She'd been ignoring it for a while, hoping the problem would solve itself, but that didn't seem to be working, and really, "ignoring it" seemed like a pretty shitty way to deal with her brother's emotional—whatever this was. But he'd already said he didn't want to go anywhere to celebrate his release, just wanted to get home, so she was doing her best to give him what he wanted.

"Okay, we're almost there! Not much farther!" Even to her own ears she sounded like a demented cheerleader. Still, she'd started, so she kept going. "I've only seen the place online, but it seems pretty nice. There's two bedrooms upstairs, two bedrooms in the basement—it's a walkout, so it's not dark or damp or anything—so we can both have some space when we need it, and then we'll share the main floor. Kitchen, dining room, living room, a pretty nice deck . . ." What else, what else? "There's no view or anything—well, there's trees. I don't know if that counts as a view, really. But there's lots of them. Lots of space. It might be a bit too quiet but it's just a rental. Just temporary."

He nodded jerkily. "Sounds good," he managed.

"It's close enough to town that we can get pizza delivered. So that's good. But we can pick up some groceries today, too. Or I can. You know, if you don't feel like it." If he'd rather stay at home and shiver. "You could make me a list. And you'll need clothes, too. I just bought those things for you to start with, but obviously you'll want to pick out your own stuff. We can go into the city—not New York maybe— well, we can go there if you want—but I think you'd have to get permission from your parole officer, right? We could just go over to Burlington maybe—whatever works for you. Or we can order stuff on the Internet. You can order everything on the Internet now. I know you don't like computers, though. Wait, do you still not like computers? I'm not crazy about them, but they've gotten a lot better. We could get you a tablet, if you want. They're like—I don't know, you just poke the screen and things happen. You don't have to type. That might be—"

"Shut up," Zane finally said, and it sounded more like a plea than an order.

Zara swallowed her next words. They'd been pretty stupid anyway. There was no need for her to say anything, she just—damn it, she really wanted Zane to stop shaking. She wished he'd committed his crimes in Vermont instead of New York State so the drive home wouldn't be so long, but if she'd had the ability to make wishes come true, she supposed she'd use it to wish he'd never committed the crimes at all. Never felt so alone, and so desperate. She'd wish she'd been a better sister and given him the support he'd obviously needed.

She reached over and turned the heat up in the car. It was a beautiful early fall day, still warm enough not to need a jacket, but maybe Zane was used to a different temperature. Maybe behind that cold white wall, the prison had been hot as hell.

But Zane reached over and turned the dial back to the left. "I'm fine," he said through gritted teeth. "You don't have to boil us alive."

"Okay. Do you want—" She stopped herself before she could start on some new, random speech about places they could go to eat. "Are you hungry?"

"I'm fine."

They drove silently for another few miles, Zara fretting, Zane still shaking.

It wasn't like she'd never gotten the shakes herself. Adrenaline was both a friend and an enemy, and sometimes your body just had too damn much of it with no way to burn any off. "Do you want to get out and walk around maybe?"

"Jesus, Zara, I'm *fine*."

"You're shaking like a junkie! You're acting like something's wrong, but nothing's wrong! Everything's finally right, after way too damn long, and you're acting like you're scared!"

"Leave it alone! I'm—"

"Fine. You're *fine*. I get it." They drove quietly for a while longer. As they left the interstate, Zara said, "I'm driving through the McDonald's in St. Albans. If you want something special, let me know. Otherwise, you're getting a Big Mac meal."

He didn't answer right away. Finally, though, he sighed. "Aren't you, like, an elite athlete? Are you allowed to eat that crap?"

"I'm an elite camp counselor, from the sound of things.

When I get cleared to fight again, I'll get in shape. For now, though, a little fast food won't kill me."

He was quiet for another moment, then asked, "The menu about the same?"

Shit, she hadn't really thought about that. "I don't know. They have more salads now. Wraps. They're trying to be healthier, you know?"

"You going to get a salad?"

"I'm getting a Big Mac and fries."

"Okay." He leaned back into the seat and relaxed at least a little. "That's good. That's what I'll get, too."

She wondered when he'd last had a choice about what to eat, and wished she'd found somewhere better for his first meal as a free man. But there'd be many others, she reminded herself. Start small, build to something better.

"Cal said he might come by tonight," Zane said. "We might go out for a bit."

Now it was Zara's turn to tense up. "Is that okay? I mean, for your parole?"

"Yeah. I can't get shitfaced or anything, and I've still got to go see the probation officer—got to 'report'—tomorrow. But I can go out for a bit. That's kind of the point of not being in jail anymore."

She wanted to ask more. Wanted to demand details about who he'd be seeing and what he'd be doing. Maybe she could set a curfew, or maybe she could creep along after them, spying and supervising and protecting.

But probably none of that was a great idea. He was going out with Calvin, so Calvin would have to be the babysitter. Not ideal, but better than Zane being on his own.

"Great," she made herself say. "I got my credit card company to give me an extra card, with your name on it." She'd hated herself as she'd done it, but she'd asked them to put a thousand-dollar spending limit on the card. She wanted to help, but she didn't want to be stupid. She wasn't worried about losing money as much as about giving him the resources to get himself into serious trouble. But that seemed petty now. "I can give you some cash, too."

Another long silence. Off the highway, into the small-town traffic that was somehow more intimidating than the more intense hustle of the city. Because there was less anonymity here, Zara supposed. She couldn't pretend the cars were just metal boxes to dodge; she had to admit that there were people inside them, people watching her. Judging her.

As they sat in line at the drive-through, Zane quietly said, "I'll pay you back. I kept track of how much you gave me when I was inside, and I'll keep track of how much I take now, too. I'll pay you back. All of it."

She wanted to tell him not to worry about it. She made good money, especially with her endorsements and bonuses, and she was happy to share. But she knew that wouldn't go over well, so she shrugged casually. "When you get around to it. No rush."

"Yeah, 'cause you're a big shot now," he said, and his voice was teasing, full of that warm fondness that she'd been missing for too long. "Easy come, easy go, spreading cash around, no worries."

"I've got an extra car waiting for you at the house," she said grandiosely. "They like to give them to me after a good fight. I've sold a couple, of course. I've had a lot of good fights, and a girl can only drive so many cars." She waved her hand through the air, fingers spread as if they were being pried apart by her imaginary bling.

"Seriously?" Zane asked. "They give you *cars*?"

"I make them a shitload of money," she responded. "And

they pay MMA fighters a hell of a lot less than they pay other professional athletes. If I get a car here or there, I earned it."

"A car here or there," he echoed.

"I'm trying to be smart with the money," she said quickly. She wasn't sure if she wanted her big brother to respect her, or if she wanted her jailbird roommate to know she wasn't easy pickings. Almost all the first, she decided. But maybe a tiny little bit of the second. "I mean, it's not a long career, you know? Women haven't been pro for long enough to have reliable numbers, but most of the guys are out by their mid-thirties at the latest. Your body just can't take the abuse forever."

"But you're going back this time? I mean, two concussions. Don't you think maybe that's a sign?"

"It's a sign that I got sloppy and let some crazy bitch get a hit in when she shouldn't have. I came in too strong, didn't keep my defenses up. It won't happen again." Now she was the one jittering around a little, and she thought about blasting the horn to hurry up whatever was taking so long at the drive-through window.

"It won't happen again? It's already happened twice!"

"The first time wasn't my fault! I didn't know! It was just a regular fight, a regular punch—"

"Jesus, Zare, I'm not saying any of it's your fault." Zane shook his head, took a deep breath, and turned to stare out the front windshield. "I'm so proud of you. I see you fight— no pay-per-view, obviously, but they let me watch some clips on the Internet—and it's like I'm in awe. I look at this fierce, strong woman in the octagon and try to see my bratty baby sister somewhere in her, and . . ." He trailed off. "You've had an incredible career. You're a force of nature. Absolutely. If it did end now, you'd be going out on top."

They pulled up to the order post then, so she was able to keep herself from screaming at him. This was a happy occasion, she reminded herself as she talked to an invisible person about hamburgers. Her brother was free. His life could begin now. She needed to focus on that, not on his insane ramblings on a topic he knew absolutely nothing about.

Everything would be fine. Zane's life was starting. And hers wasn't over. She wouldn't let it be.

CAL looked at the house, then back down at his phone where he'd entered the address from Zara's e-mail. They matched. This was either the right place or he'd miscopied the address. He thought about calling up the e-mail and double-checking, but headed for the front door instead.

It wasn't like he was looking at a mansion. It was just a nice middle-class family home. But that was about the last place he'd ever expected to find either of the Hales.

He rang the bell and thought about the trailer the Hales had been living in when he and Zane met, in first grade. Cal hadn't really understood about poverty then. He'd just found a funny, smart, tough kid who was really good at playground games, and they'd become friends. It had taken a while before Zane trusted Cal enough to let him see his home, and it had taken a while after that before Cal realized that it was really where they lived. Really *how* they lived.

After the trailer the Hale family had moved to an apartment in town, then another apartment, then a townhouse, and then, after Mr. Hale left for good, back to a trailer. Not even in an official park. Just an old wreck parked in someone's backyard with an extension cord running to the house. Zane and Zara had been allowed in the house once a day to shower, and that was it. The trailer had been boiling in the summer, freezing in the winter. It had been their home for three years, until Zane had finally lost it and gone on his spree.

"Spree." Such a light, whimsical word. Not right for what Zane had done. What would be better? His explosion? His meltdown? Breakdown? Crisis? What was the word you used when someone who'd followed the rules his whole life took off across the state line, stole a gun and a baggie of pills from a random drug dealer, then robbed three stores in three different towns, led the police on a high-speed chase and drove well enough to actually evade them, then holed up in a closed-for-the-season motel for three days until his sister and then his best friend found him? No, "spree" definitely wasn't the right way to describe all that.

The door opened then, and Cal's mind lost the ability to consider words, or much of anything else. He'd seen Zara on television, in interviews and magazine shoots. He'd known that the angry duckling had turned into a beautiful, though still angry, swan. But the images from his memory were nothing compared to the warm, breathing, three-dimensional woman standing in front of him. No makeup that he could discern, blond hair pulled back into a sloppy ponytail, wearing sweats and a beat-up Ramones T-shirt, and still the most perfect woman he'd ever seen.

"Zane's in the shower," she said, obviously not nearly as impressed by him as he was by her. "It's his third one since we got here. If he's in there for another two minutes, I'm sending you down to check on him."

"Okay," Cal managed. Yeah, she was beautiful. But she didn't want anything to do with him and he needed to remember that. "Should I wait outside?"

She squinted at him as if trying to decide if he was setting a trap or just stupid. "You can come in," she finally said.

He stepped inside, schooling himself to go straight ahead

and not give in to the feeling that his entire body was being pulled magnetically toward her.

"You want a beer while you wait?" she asked as she strolled toward the back of the house, her perfect, strong, round ass drawing his gaze so powerfully he was pretty sure his eyes were actually bugging out of his head.

"Sure," he heard himself saying. Apparently a tiny part of his brain was still functioning, more or less. He stumbled after her, scolding himself as he went. *Zane's baby sister. Zane's baby sister. Off-limits.* When that didn't calm his libido, he tried, *Thinks you're a douche. Thinks you're a douche*, and had slightly better results.

The beer was on the top shelf of the fridge so she didn't have to bend over much to reach it, and that was probably just as well. She used the lower half of her shirt to protect her hand as she twisted the caps off two bottles, giving him a tantalizing glimpse of toned belly, then handed one to him and moved over to perch on a stool at the breakfast bar.

"You're okay to be drinking?" he asked. "You know, with your head?"

"My head is none of your business," she replied, and took a healthy swig of her beer. They sat in uncomfortable silence for a moment, and then she sighed as if physically releasing her grudge. "You're going to take care of him, right?" She waited, apparently realized that he had no idea what she was talking about, and impatiently said, "Zane? You're going to keep an eye on him? Not let him get in any trouble?" She took another swig of beer while he struggled for words, then blurted out, "He's not . . . he's still adjusting. Obviously. It's a big change. I get that. It's totally natural, or whatever. All part of the process." She paused, apparently hoping Cal would have something to say, then shook her head. "This had better not be some big piss-up tonight, is what I'm saying. He's still on parole. They can drag him back if he messes up. And it's more than that. It's not just about them, but about *him*—he needs this to work. You know?"

"I do," Cal finally managed. "We're not planning anything big tonight. Just going into town for a beer or two, probably. You can come if you want."

"I don't think Zane wants that." She sighed. "And I have to trust him out of my sight, right? I mean, he's a grown man. He's not stupid. But—"

She broke off, taking a deep breath to regain her control, and Cal wrapped his fingers around the counter in front of him, using its solidity to anchor himself in place. His body knew what it needed to do. He was a man, and she was a woman . . . a goddess . . . damn it, whatever she was, she was upset and he should be over there, wrapping his arms around her and giving comfort and protection.

He wondered how bad she'd hurt him if he tried. Just pain, or would she go for an actual maiming?

"You need to take care of him," she finally said.

It may as well have been a royal decree. "I will," he vowed.

Zane arrived then. He was wearing loose jeans and an even looser T-shirt, as if the clothes had been bought for him by someone who thought he was larger than he was. His hair was wet, his face a strange mix of anticipation and anxiety.

"Hey," Cal said quietly. He stood up, moved forward, and stopped. He wasn't much of a hugger normally, but somehow he'd found himself tempted to embrace twice in the last few minutes. This time was less likely to result in bodily harm, though. And after he'd spent a decade sitting across a counter from Zane with a strict no-contact rule, a hug seemed like a good way to emphasize that things were now different.

Unless Zane wasn't ready for that. Cal half lifted his arms, ready to convert the hug into a shoulder slap as needed.

But Zane was there. Strong and solid, he stepped forward and wrapped his arms around Cal, held on just a moment longer than might have been strictly casual, then let go before it was awkward. "Good to see you," he said.

It had only been a week since their last visit, but Cal couldn't disagree with the sentiment. "Good to see you, too." Maybe there was more that they could have said, but they didn't need to. Zane was free, and his best friend was there for him. That was all that mattered. The world had been upside down for far too long, and now it was finally turning itself upright again.

That was when Cal noticed Zara. The smile was frozen on her face, and her fingers gripped her beer bottle so tightly the knuckles were turning white. What the hell? Had Cal screwed up already? Was he not watching Zane according to her specifications?

"You're sure you don't want to come with us?" he asked, trying to sound casual.

He wouldn't have thought her smile could get any tighter, but she managed. "No, Zane wants some time without his baby sister in his hair."

And Zane, damn him, didn't disagree. He just shrugged, his eyes fixed on the air somewhere over her shoulder and said, "We'll be working together starting tomorrow, right?"

"That's the plan," she agreed, and took a big swig of her beer. "Okay, then." She jerked her head in dismissal, but she was the one who started moving. "I'm going to unpack some stuff." She sent a look in Cal's direction, a strange sort of pleading glare. A reminder of his promise to look out for Zane, he figured. As if he needed to be reminded.

"We probably won't be late," he said. A bit awkward,

trying to calm her down without making Zane feel like he was being dictated to. Well, it wasn't like he hadn't known there'd be some challenges.

"Let's go," Zane prompted, and Cal left his half-finished beer on the counter. This was Zane's first night of freedom; Zane was in charge.

❧ Four ❧

THE TOWN HAD shrunk. Not its actual boundaries . . . there were actually a few new buildings sprawled out on the edges of the place. But the buildings. They were smaller than they used to be.

Rationally, Zara knew that was nonsense. A mad scientist hadn't used a shrink ray on the place. But the red brick bank with its white roof and columns . . . it loomed huge in Zara's memory, an imposing shrine to everything she hadn't had. Now it looked like a toy.

She kept walking, past the post office, which also seemed like a child's model, along the patch of grass by the war memorial, which had always seemed small, past a small storefront with a cheerful-looking woman placing some pottery in the window—and Zara stopped in her tracks when she got to the corner and looked down the side street.

There had to be a mistake. There was simply no way that could be—she took a few steps closer, as if it would make a difference. *That* was the school? It wasn't just smaller than she'd remembered, but also so much dingier. Mrs. Brady, who'd accused Zara of stealing the field trip money when the whole class knew it had been that other kid, Aaron somebody-or-other . . . that woman had been working in *this* building? When she'd marched Zara down to the principal's office, her hands gripping Zara's shoulders so tight, the hallway had seemed endless—but how long could it possibly have been?

Zara craned her neck to see if the building had some sort of strange addition not visible from the street, but she knew it didn't. She wasn't sure if the hallway had been stretched by her fears at the time or by her anger over the years since, but clearly the scale of it was all in her mind. She looked around the little town. Clearly a *lot* of things had been expanded in her mind.

She made herself start moving again. She'd spent the morning at the shiny new community center, getting trained on safety procedures and how to use scheduling software and fifty other things that weren't even remotely interesting, so when she and Zane had been given a lunch break, she'd practically sprinted for the door. Zane had decided to stay behind and practice on the computer, which was just plain masochistic, but that was his problem. She'd needed out.

Of course, being outside wasn't as easy as it should have been, not with all the memories, and the confusion about what was real and what wasn't.

She found the café the trainer at the community center had recommended and ducked inside as if she were escaping a bitter winter wind. This place was new. She couldn't remember what business had used the space when she'd been younger, but it didn't really matter. New was good. No memories to worry about.

She stepped back out of the way and took a look at the

chalkboard behind the counter. That was when she became aware of the man standing by the register, squinting in her direction.

"Zara Hale?" he asked. He was youngish, fit looking, maybe a bit too ruggedly handsome for her tastes; he looked *wholesome*, and in Zara's experience that meant trouble. Wholesome men didn't tend to think much of women like her.

She moved one of her legs back a little into a balanced stance and made sure she had room to swing her arms, if she had to. "Yeah?"

He smiled then. "Welcome back." He waited a second, then prompted, "I'm Josh Sullivan. Went to school with Zane? I heard he was back, too. That's good."

She relaxed a little, but not completely. "Josh Sullivan?" The last name was familiar obviously, but the first? She'd heard it certainly, but in what context? Everyone in Lake Sullivan went to the same school; being classmates wasn't the same as being friends.

He nodded, then looked at the woman beside him. She'd been joking with the server, but was smiling at Zara now. She was wearing casual jeans and a thermal shirt, but she looked more like someone *pretending* to be working class than someone who actually was. Zara couldn't quite figure out what was giving that impression until Josh said, "This is Ashley Carlsen. She's spending the winter up here."

"Ashley Carlsen," Zara repeated, and did a little squinting of her own. "You're an actor."

"And you're Zara Hale," Ashley responded with a smile. "MMA. I've been seeing your posters all over town. I admit it, I'm too much of a wimp to watch the fights, but I love that women are making names in it. Way to go!"

Zara felt like she'd been braced for a blow that clearly wasn't coming, and she was a bit off balance as a result. What the hell was Ashley Carlsen doing in Lake Sullivan? And she'd actually heard of Zara? It was way too surreal, and knowing she was gaping like a fish pulled out of the lake didn't actually make it any easier for her to collect her thoughts.

Josh seemed to take pity on her, turning away, but then he was back, having reached behind the counter to grab a pen and pad of paper. "If I give you my number, can you give it to Zane?"

"And we're having people over this weekend." Ashley looked up at Josh with a sickeningly adoring smile. "We're just back in town and Josh has about five million people in his family, so it seemed best to say 'hi' to everyone all at once. It's supposed to be sunny on Saturday, so we're grilling." She leaned a little closer to add, "But they're all going to be Josh's gang. I don't really know that many people up here yet. It'd be great to have someone who was at least neutral, you know? Someone who hasn't known Josh since he was in diapers, with all their in-jokes and family stories."

"It's not just family," Josh said quickly. "Pretty much everyone's invited. You should come, and bring Zane. Everyone would love to see him."

"Saturday for dinner," Ashley said. "But come midafternoon and hang out if the weather's good. Josh, write down directions, too."

Josh did as he was told. Zara blinked hard. She felt like she'd just been sent through a strange carwash and been buffed with friendliness from all sides. It was way too much.

"How long are you in town for?" Ashley asked.

"Uh . . . I don't really know. A couple months maybe?" Zara managed to add, "You?" before falling back into her confusion.

Ashley beamed as she said, "Forever. We live here now . . . we just might have to leave town for a few months to work now and then."

"You're living *here*," Zara said flatly. "Lake Sullivan. You live here now. Voluntarily."

"Yeah," Ashley said, her smile faltering just a little. "Are you not happy to be back? You don't like it here?"

Somehow, Zara didn't have the heart to rain on this woman's parade. "I'm just getting used to it," she said. Lame, but true enough, and it was nice to see Ashley's beam go back up to full wattage.

Josh handed her the slip of paper and the couple finally left. Zara took a deep breath and tried to remember what she'd been doing before being caught up in it all.

The woman behind the counter gave her a sympathetic grin. "They're a bit much," she said as if agreeing to something Zara had actually said out loud. "Too damn happy all the time." She shrugged. "But it's kinda cute, really. Josh has always been so quiet."

Why was Zara hearing about this? Why was the woman telling her *anything*? "I need two sandwiches," she said, trying to get the conversation back to somewhere approximately where it should be. She had no idea what food Zane liked these days, so maybe she should just ask the server for whatever their most popular sandwich was, but even that level of personal service suddenly seemed like too much. "Both turkey and bacon, I guess."

The woman nodded and got to work, letting the conversation flow back to questions about types of bread and choices of condiments, and Zara started to relax. But as she was heading out the door, the server called, "You should come Saturday. It's going to be a lot of fun," and Zara's shoulders tightened again.

She didn't answer, just made a noncommittal sound and got the hell out. It was a bad sign when the community center she'd been so happy to escape from was now seeming like a sanctuary, a place to get away from all this invasive friendliness.

Still, she kept the scrap of paper with Josh's phone number and directions on it, and she passed the invitation along to Zane when she saw him.

"Yeah?" he said, frowning. "I don't know. It's a big thing? I'm not sure if I really want to go to some big thing."

It would have been so much easier to ignore it. Zara certainly didn't have any interest in the event. But Josh had sounded genuinely interested in seeing Zane again; and Zara might just be visiting Lake Sullivan, but Zane was back to stay. He needed to make some friends besides Calvin Montgomery. "We could stop by," she said tentatively. "And then if it's too much, we could leave."

Zane shrugged. "Maybe. Let's play it by ear."

"Sounds good," Zara said, and they ate their sandwiches in companionable silence.

"I'VE been getting phone calls," Cal's mother said. Claire Montgomery was impeccably put-together, as always, but the frown that creased her forehead was unusual. "A little worse than we anticipated, actually. My circle contributed significantly to this project, because they trust me, and they're feeling as if that trust is being abused. They point out that the community center is a *community* concern, not a make-work project for your childhood friend."

Cal snorted. "The sponsorship money we're getting from the MMA guys is significantly more than we're paying Zane Hale. We wouldn't be getting that money if Zara wasn't involved, and Zara wouldn't be involved if Zane wasn't. So if all your friends are worried about is their money, they can stop worrying." He gave her a chance to respond, but when she just kept frowning at him, he nodded. "But they're not really worried about the money, are they? They're worried about how it looks."

There weren't that many women in his mother's "circle," not that many ladies of leisure in their corner of Vermont. The women were gathered from a radius of about an hour's drive, with Lake Sullivan close to the middle; they donated money and time for fund-raising, but they weren't daily visitors to the community center. They didn't really know what was going on. Still, they felt qualified to judge. "After twenty years of working his ass off to deal with his absent mother and useless father and to look after his baby sister, Zane hit a wall. It was too much for him. If he'd been one of 'us'? If he'd had a family monitoring his behavior, ready to step in if he got out of line? If he'd had the money to go away for a while, take a break, get some support? If any of that had been there for him, things would have been different. But nobody helped him." Cal had tried, he told himself. But he'd been a kid himself, away at school for the first time, and he'd let himself drift away from his best friend when that friend had needed him most. But now he was making up for it. "After *twenty years*, he lost control for less than a week. He still didn't hurt a fly. But, yeah, he broke some laws. Wrecked some stuff, stole some stuff. It was wrong. He gets that. He spent ten years getting that. Jesus, isn't that enough?"

"Oh, spare me your speeches." His mother sounded impatient rather than angry. She'd been raised working class before marrying into money, and her experiences had left her practical, but not hard-hearted. "Nobody's trying to punish him more than he already has been. But what's his job exactly? What will he be doing?"

"He's just sort of a jack-of-all-trades right now. Filling in as needed. The center's open to kids for the first time today, so everything's still in flux. We'll figure things out more once it all settles down."

His mother raised an eyebrow. "Yes, because he must have a very versatile skill set after ten years in prison."

"Mom . . ."

She stood gracefully. "I'm just telling you what people are saying. You need to be aware of it. But you don't necessarily have to do anything about it."

Well, that was an easier end to the conversation than he'd expected. He walked her to the door of his office and she stretched up to kiss his cheek. "You have a good heart, Calvin. There's nothing wrong with using it. But we need to make sure it stays balanced with your head."

She left then, and he stayed behind and wondered why "we" needed to make sure of anything to do with his heart *or* his head. Working for the family business was part of it, he supposed. He'd done his time in higher education, gotten his MBA from Columbia, so he was more than qualified for his job, on paper. And he'd spent his summers working at all different levels of the company, getting practical experience. Furniture manufacturing wasn't glamorous, but it had kept the family comfortable for generations. And they'd diversified under his father, moving into real estate and tourist developments. The family had owned half the lakeshore by the time the area really took off as a summer destination, and they'd been selling off parcels ever since, at fairly ridiculous prices. Yes, the family was comfortable indeed.

Maybe too comfortable. His mother wasn't officially employed by the company, but it was a rare day she wasn't in the office, working on whatever project had caught her attention. His father ran the place, his older brother was in line to take over; Cal mostly filled in as needed. Nothing too intense, and plenty of time for other pursuits. Most of which were social, he admitted. Some might say frivolous.

But for the last year, the community center had been taking up a lot of his free time. He'd been happy to take advantage of his mother's contacts when he found himself elected chair of their board. And he'd solicited corporate and private donations from his family members and their friends. So, damn it, the center *was* their business. Without their support he probably wouldn't have gotten it off the ground. He couldn't ignore them now, just because they were saying things he didn't like.

No, he couldn't ignore them. But they'd only contributed money; he'd put money and a lot of heart into the place. And he wasn't going to let them dictate how it should be run, or who should be hired.

He quickly scanned his schedule on the computer, then grabbed his jacket and headed for the door. "Allison, I'm heading out for the afternoon. Can you call Simon and tell him I'll meet with him sometime tomorrow?"

He could sense her curiosity and disapproval, but he'd never let that slow him down before, so there was no reason to start worrying about it now.

Besides, he had other responsibilities. Other concerns. He smiled to himself as he jogged down the stairs toward the parking lot. He had to balance out his heart with his head, as his mother had said. That was his number one priority.

⇝ Five ⇜

THE PLACE WAS *crawling* with kids. The daycare had been bad enough, and Zara had been happy to escape it after they'd done a quick tour of the rooms. But now, back in the main gym, all the kids who'd just gotten out of school were running around, screaming in excitement, acting like animals that had been caged for their entire lives and had finally gotten some freedom. It was bewildering and intimidating.

At least, it was for Zara. Zane was in the middle of it all, holding a clipboard, ticking off names for—for something, God knew what, and he looked more relaxed than he had at any point in the week since she'd picked him up at the prison release center. Hell, he looked more relaxed than he had for the last decade. *She* was the one about to start shaking.

"Good turnout," a familiar voice said from over her shoulder.

"They're insane," Zara said as she turned, and she was pretty sure she meant it.

Calvin just grinned. "It'll probably settle down once the novelty wears off. But for now? They're pretty excited."

Zara tried to imagine how she would have reacted to something like this when she was a kid. She supposed it would have depended on where she was living. If she'd been in one of the apartments or the ragged townhouse, she'd have been thrilled. Somewhere to go after school instead of sitting around staring at the walls or bugging Zane. But if she'd been living in the trailers, out in the boondocks . . .

"What about kids who take school buses home?" she asked Calvin. He gave her a blank look, and she said, "If their parents can come pick them up later, that's great. But you said you wanted *all* kids to come here. You wanted to focus on the ones who need it most. What about the kids who have to go home on the bus because there's no one to pick them up, or because their parents don't have a car or don't have money for gas?"

He frowned thoughtfully, and finally said, "Damn. Yeah. We should have thought of that." He looked out at the sea of children, now being divided up into different groups for the various activities the center had planned. "We're flooded right now as it is. I probably won't get a lot of support for a program to recruit even *more* kids. But you're right, those guys need us. Let me think about it."

He was nothing like she'd remembered. Zara should have been focusing on the conversation, worrying about the kids, but at least half of her brain was trying to figure out Calvin Montgomery. He'd always treated her like a nuisance. A tagalong brat. Four years younger was a whole different world when you were a kid. And she guessed she'd assumed he'd still be treating her that way.

But he wasn't. He'd heard her concern, and appreciated

it. He was treating her with respect. And the respect was for what she could do with her brain, not with her body. It was throwing her off a little, but she liked it.

He'd grown up. And he was treating her like she'd grown up, too.

"Thanks," she said quietly.

He looked a bit startled. "For what?"

"For helping Zane." For helping her, too, but she didn't think she was going to go quite that far. Instead she nodded her chin toward her brother, who was distributing basketballs to a pack of kids who looked like they were junior high age. "He's loving this. And he's good at it."

"But you aren't," he said quietly. "You're standing over here on the sidelines."

"They said they didn't have a job for me right away! They said I could just watch and get a feel for things!"

He held up his hands in quick surrender. "I meant you aren't loving it, not that you aren't good at it. I just—I was feeling a bit guilty for dragging you into all this. You don't seem all that comfortable with it."

"Comfortable?" She shrugged. "I'm a big girl. A little discomfort isn't going to hurt me."

"You're actually smaller than I thought," he said, and then looked embarrassed, as if he hadn't meant to say the words out loud. But he clearly realized he couldn't leave them hanging there without an explanation. "Not such a big girl, I mean. From seeing you fight, I expected something different. Well, I know the stats . . . Five foot six, a hundred and thirty-five pounds. But you seem bigger when you fight. You seem bigger from a distance."

She had no idea how to take that. Was it demeaning? Was he calling her puny? It didn't really seem that way, but—what the hell? "That's my fighting weight," she said. "I'm actually heavier than that now. From any distance." She briefly thought about mentioning that she wore a compression bra with a chest protector during her bouts, but she couldn't think of any reason that having more obvious breasts would make her seem smaller. And she didn't want to give any Montgomery more reasons to think she was uncouth, so she probably shouldn't start talking about her boobs. She needed to get this conversation back on track, and then get away from it entirely. "So I'm fine, Zane's great, and the country kids will be in here soon. Everything's good. Right?"

"Seems like," he agreed cautiously.

"Okay. The office said there'd be loads of registration forms to sort through today, so I'll go help with that. See ya."

And that was that. She wasn't sure why talking to Calvin made her uncomfortable, but it did. Probably because he knew too much about her, or at least her history, and she didn't know a damn thing about him. She couldn't say what made him tick, what he cared about, *who* he cared about. Did he have a girlfriend? Or a wife even?

She had no idea, and that was fine, she reminded herself. He was none of her business. She was in Lake Sullivan for Zane, and maybe a bit for herself. Calvin Montgomery wasn't important.

But damn, the man looked good in a suit. She'd never really been with someone so polished, but it was kind of intriguing to think about it. Fun to imagine all the different ways she could muss him up . . .

No. Bad thought. Bad.

She scolded herself as she headed for the office. She'd keep busy, and he'd go away, and everything would be fine. That was her plan, and she was known for following through on her plans.

*   *   *

"IT'S kind of hard to enjoy my beer with my sister staring at me like she's about to tear me apart," Zane said, and Cal glanced at the life-size cardboard cutout across from their booth at Woody's, the town's only bar. Cardboard Zara was dressed for a fight, with gloves on her hands and a fierce glare on her face. Cal tried to focus on her face, and not look at the rock-hard abs displayed just below her tight sports bra.

"We could switch tables, but there's a poster of her over there, and there, and that huge one by the door. And you'd better brace yourself, because Hugh said he's been trying to get her to come by in person, and if she does, I'm sure he'll take a lot more pictures and splash them up all over the place."

Zane sat still for a moment, then nodded reluctantly. "She did good for herself, huh?"

"She did," Cal agreed. It certainly wasn't what he'd been thinking of ten years earlier when he'd tracked down her aunt in Queens and told her Zara needed somewhere to live. She could have stayed in Vermont if she'd gone into foster care, but he'd been convinced that she needed a fresh start. She'd needed to get the hell away from Lake Sullivan, where everyone thought they knew her just because they knew about her parents, and knew about Zane. He'd been convinced she could be more than another lost soul, if she just got the chance.

But his imaginings had involved the smart, pretty girl going to college and finding a nice office job somewhere. Apparently he wasn't quite the master manipulator he'd imagined himself at twenty, judging by how far reality was from his plans. Which was a damn good thing, his thirty-year-old brain reminded him.

"This concussion stuff," Zane said thoughtfully. "How serious is that?"

Cal frowned. "Well, I don't know exactly. I've heard rumors, and I talked to the head guy at the organization about it, when I was trying to set all this up. But I haven't seen doctors' reports or anything. You haven't asked her?"

"Not really." Zane made a frustrated face. "Not at all. It's kind of weird between us. I mean, you and me? Things have changed, yeah, but not that much. You're still the rich golden boy, I'm still the poor screwup." He didn't give Cal a chance to object to the characterization. "But Zara? I used to be her *hero*. Sure, she was an idiot for thinking that, but whatever, she did. I looked after her, looked out for her, backed her up when she got into whatever stupid trouble she could find. That's how we got along, you know?"

"And now you feel like she's looking after you?"

Zane sighed. "Feel like it? I know it. I'm living in the house she rented, driving her damn car, working at a job I wouldn't have gotten without her, borrowing cash from her . . . she gave me a credit card, for Christ's sake. It's like I'm her kid. *She's* looking out for *me* now. And the scary thing is, she's doing it a hell of a lot better than I ever managed with her."

"She's older than you were," Cal pointed out. "You were still a kid yourself when you were trying to take care of her. And you did a great job. You're the one who put her in a place where she *could* be as successful as she's been."

"I don't know about that." Zane thought for a moment. "Maybe I helped. I hope I did. But that's not what we're talking about. The point is, however it happened, she's a totally different person now. She's not my baby sister, and I'm sure as hell not her hero."

"She's still your baby sister," Cal said quietly. "She always will be. And you being her hero? Maybe you're not. Maybe she doesn't need one anymore."

"Because she's one herself," Zane said with a look at the cutout. "As long as this concussion thing doesn't get in her way."

"She's the three-time MMA champion. She's never lost a pro or amateur fight. She's blazed a trail, and she's shut up a hell of a lot of people who said women didn't belong in the sport." Cal shrugged. "Even if she never fought again, she'd still be a hero. A legend."

"I don't think she'd agree with you about that."

"Well, maybe we need to make her agree."

"When's the last time anyone made Zara do anything?" Zane finished his beer and shook his head. "She's a big girl now. She makes her own decisions."

"Have you seen the stats on concussions? Do you know how serious they can be, especially repeated ones?"

"You think she's in bad enough shape that we could have her declared mentally incompetent and take over her decision making?" Zane barely paused before saying, "No? Me neither. So it doesn't matter what I've seen or what I know. It's Zara's decision, not mine."

Apparently Zane was having less trouble adjusting to Zara's new status as an independent adult than Cal was. "Yeah," he agreed reluctantly. "But you could persuade her, couldn't you?" Zane looked at him skeptically, so Cal tried, "You could at least make sure she has access to all the relevant information. Right?"

"Yeah, I'll teach her to Google things. Oh, wait, she already knows how to do that. She's the one who showed me."

"So you're just going to sit back and let her do something stupid?"

"Jesus, Cal, how is this any of your business? Did I miss something when I was away? Why are you so worried about Zara?"

"I'm just . . ." What? What the hell was he thinking? "I'm trying to figure out why you *aren't* worried about it."

"I guess I'm just a shitty, don't-give-a-damn brother. Is that what you're thinking?" There was a definite family resemblance between Zane's glare and the expression on the face of the cardboard cutout.

"No! Absolutely not." Cal wished this whole conversation would just go away. His intentions had been good, but his execution obviously sucked. "I don't know what I'm saying. I just—she's a good kid. I don't want her to get hurt."

"You're not hearing me, and you're not seeing her. She's not a kid, Cal. Not even close."

No, she wasn't. Damn it. He wondered why he kept trying to see her that way.

Maybe because the alternative was to see her as a woman, strong and beautiful and desirable. And intimidating, and with too much baggage between them, and with a complete lack of interest in him as anything other than someone who might help her brother.

Yeah, it'd be a hell of lot easier to go back to seeing her as a bratty tagalong kid. But he wasn't sure he'd be able to.

♁ *Six* ♁

ZARA STOOD IN the little room beside the main gym, staring at the newly installed equipment. For the first time since she'd come back to Lake Sullivan, she almost felt at home. Free weights, punching bags, mats, protective equipment for sparring . . . It would have been perfect if only the gear had been a bit more ragged and if there'd been a bunch of sweaty, swearing men working out all around her.

Instead, she was surrounded by members of the center's board of directors, headed by Calvin Montgomery. "It was a generous donation," he was telling the others. "In addition to their cash support."

Yeah, Terry had come through. Zara wasn't sure just why he was pushing this so hard. She supposed it wasn't much money, really, compared to what the company was making. But it was a lot for a town like Lake Sullivan.

One of the directors, an older man with a comb-over, leaned forward and poked at the heavy bag with one finger.

"Seems like good quality," he said grudgingly. "I'm just not sure what use we'll have for it."

"It's a fast-growing sport," Calvin said calmly. "And we've got a world-class athlete working for us. We want to set up classes—Maxine will take the lead on the children's classes, with Zara there to assist, and they'll reverse that structure for adult classes."

"And you're going to be around long enough to follow through on that?" the older man asked Zara skeptically. It was the first time any of them had addressed her since they came in the door.

"No promises," she said. She was tempted to leave it at that, but this was Calvin's baby, and he'd been good to Zane. She owed him, at least a little. "But there's a guy down in Burlington who's interested in driving up and doing classes here, if you need him. So the equipment won't be wasted."

The board members nodded carefully, and a few more of them stepped forward and started investigating the equipment. One of them, a middle-aged woman with a permanently concerned expression, said, "And what will these classes be about? Self-defense, or—"

"No, not self-defense. I'm not qualified for that. If you're in a real situation, you'd fight differently than you do in the ring. More running away, probably. I do sports MMA. Like—like any sport, I guess. It's not real life."

The woman nodded. "Fitness?"

"Well, kind of. But, like, just as it happens. Really it's—it's a *sport*." She didn't know how else to explain it.

Calvin stepped in smoothly. "Like if you played soccer, you'd get fit from running around, but that wouldn't really be the point of it. The lessons would be about technique and strategy and so on."

Zara nodded. "Yeah. Like that."

The woman looked thoughtful, then smiled. "I'm going to sign up for a class. My daughter's fifteen. She could be in the same class as me, if she's interested?"

"I guess," Zara said. She had no idea what age divisions should be. She had no idea about most of it.

"Great." The woman nodded. "I'm glad you're here. I'm looking forward to it."

Zara had never been good with this sort of thing. The overblown reactions from fans? People screaming that they loved her as she walked out of the tunnel before a fight? It was strange, but she could handle it. But a simple, genuine expression like this? She wanted to crawl under the pile of gym mats beside her. "I hope I don't disappoint you," she muttered.

The woman wandered over toward another pile of equipment, leaving Calvin and Zara standing together.

After a short silence, Calvin said, "You're going to get Zane out to Josh's this weekend, right? He said he wasn't sure about going, but he should be there."

It was that simple for him? He just knew what other people "should" do? Zara shrugged. "We're going to play it by ear," she said. That was all he was getting from her.

He didn't seem completely satisfied, but the other directors were clearly done playing with the new toys by then so he herded them out of the room and back to whatever the hell boards of directors did at their meetings, and Zara was left alone in the room.

She ran her hands over the heavy bag again. She'd visited her doctor before leaving the city and been cleared for moderate activity. Not hard workouts. But it wasn't like the bag was going to be punching back, and Zara had too much nervous energy. She needed to take the edge off. And the best way to do that was definitely training.

It would be a good way to test out the equipment, she told herself as she started moving. It would be irresponsible for her *not* to work out. Yeah.

She grinned in anticipation. It was going to feel really good to hit something.

And it did feel good, once she got going, but it was strange to be working out alone. At home she'd have been surrounded by other people, mostly men. Her coaches had always been men, her trainer was a man, and she generally sparred and grappled with men, except for the few occasions when she could find a woman who could keep up with her. She liked being one of them, accepted into their loud, sweaty world.

This place was too *nice*. She worked at the heavy bag, the sounds of her strikes clearer and more isolated than they would be at home. The air was cool and dry, the room bright. It was hard to find her determination here. Hard to feel driven, inspired.

But she dug inside herself and found what she needed. Enough grit to leave the bag behind and begin her calisthenics. She pushed hard, trying to find out how much conditioning she'd lost during her layoff. She usually took a week or two off after a fight, but it had been more than a month this time. Sit-ups and push-ups, with all the variations of each. She was still fit, but she could feel herself dragging a little. She could do weights the next day. And there was enough room in the main gym for short sprints, and maybe she could get her trainer to send up one of the huge elastic bands he tied around her waist and made her run against. And . . .

And suddenly she was on the ground. What the hell? Her head pounded and her stomach churned. She looked up at the ceiling, and it took her a moment to remember where she was. What she'd been doing. She struggled to sit up, and a wave of dizziness forced her back down flat.

First she fought back the confusion, then the fear, and then the anger. She was so used to obedience from her body that this rebellion was bewildering and felt like a betrayal. Had she honestly just passed out? Was that what had happened? Her brain was—what the hell was it?

The doctors had warned her about post-concussion syndrome, and given her lots of lectures and brochures.

But that was for weak people, not for her.

She sat up again, a little more slowly, and refused to acknowledge the blackness trying to creep in from the sides of her field of vision or the dull throbbing deep in her skull. She'd let her diet go to hell since she'd been on break, and she probably hadn't eaten enough that morning. That was all. She'd been stupid to ignore proper nutrition. She knew better.

She rolled to her knees. She was okay. She'd do some stretches, cool down properly, and she'd remember to eat more the next day.

Everything was okay. But as she slowly leaned over to reach for her toes, her hands were shaking. And she had to shift her head a bit to the side to make sure her tears fell onto the dark fabric of her shorts, not onto the mat, where someone might see them.

THAT Saturday was a beautiful fall day, and Josh's party had a great turnout. Cal ended up parking halfway down the long drive and hiking the rest of the way with a bottle of wine in one hand and a case of beer in the other. It ended up taking him about half an hour and two beers just to get to the house, not because of the distance but because of all the people he had to stop and visit with on the way.

That was the way with the Lake Sullivan world. Over the summer, everyone put their heads down and worked their asses off dealing with the influx of tourists. Even the Montgomery clan worked harder at that time of year, although not nearly as hard as some of the other locals. There was a brief break in the middle for The Splash, a weekend-long festival celebrating all things summer, and then it was back to the grind until fall.

Now tourism was dying down. Still steady, with people driving through to appreciate the fall foliage, but not nearly as intense. So the locals finally had time to do a little catching up.

Josh enjoyed the conversations, but he knew he wasn't giving them his full attention. He was too busy looking around, trying to see who was there. Well, if he was being honest with himself, he was trying to see if the Hales were there.

And if he was being completely honest? No, he decided. He didn't need to go that far and decide which Hale was of more interest to him right then. After all, it would be good for both of them to get out and meet people.

He was on the steps of the house, adding a few of his beers to the big tub of chipped ice, when he felt someone bump against his side, too hard to be accidental. He looked up and saw Zane watching him expectantly.

"You came," Cal said, and he forced himself to look at Zane instead of peering around to find his sister.

"Making an appearance. Could bail at any moment." Zane's voice was light, but his eyes were moving more quickly than usual, darting around as if he was searching for danger.

"Not having fun?"

Zane shrugged. "It's a bit intense."

Cal tried to see the gathering through the eyes of someone who'd been in jail for the last ten years. Kids running around, screaming and laughing and crying. Women everywhere, chatting and being beautiful and smelling good. That would all be unfamiliar. And the men? Zane should be used to being around lots of men, but maybe a crowd like this, in prison, would have been potentially dangerous.

Cal reached down and pulled two bottles out of the tub he'd just been refilling. "Want to go down to the barn, check on the horses?"

"You don't have to babysit me," Zane said gruffly.

"Okay, I won't. Want to go down to the barn and check on the horses?"

Zane frowned at him for a moment, then finally, grudgingly nodded. "Yeah. Okay."

They opened their beers on the way, and Cal could see Zane's body relaxing as they moved. He wasn't thinking about Zara anymore, not until Zane looked over his shoulder almost guiltily and said, "Zare's going to kick my ass."

"What? Why?"

"The whole point of coming to this was to see people, and now I'm running away."

"You're seeing *me*," Cal tried.

"I've already seen you. Lots."

"So we'll take a barn break, then go back up. Or hey, can Zara drive us home? We could get sloppy drunk and drool all over everyone and then she'd *want* us to go hide in the barn."

"Nice plan, except we left the beer up at the house."

"That's our timer, then. We get one beer down here, then we go back for another, do a little visiting, and run away again if we have to. Lather, rinse, repeat."

Zane was relaxing. It was all good. They looked at the horses and scratched the ugly brown one's neck while he rolled his eyes in appreciation, and they finished their beers and headed back to the house.

Cal felt good about it. He was being useful. Wasn't bird-dogging his best friend's baby sister. Well done. Then he saw Zara on the porch of the house, standing next to Ashley, laughing at something Josh's shaggy dog was doing. The two of them were radiant, full of strength and beauty and youth, and Cal's breath caught a little.

Okay, so he wasn't totally pure when it came to the Hales. He could accept that.

ZARA was pretty sure she was glad she'd come, but the whole situation was weird. "These people all hated me when I lived here," she said quietly to Ashley.

Ashley raised an eyebrow at her, then shook her head firmly. "No," she said. She glanced over at a trim woman carving up wedges of a late-season watermelon. "I don't believe it. There's no way Aunt Carol hated you. I don't think she's ever hated anyone."

Zara frowned over at the woman. "I don't think I know her."

"And most of them probably didn't know you, either," Ashley said. She wasn't quite scolding, Zara decided, but she was pretty close. "I mean, you were a rough kid? Is that the problem? Big deal. Did you kill anyone, or . . . I don't know, torture their pets or anything? Did you do anything really worth *hating* you for?"

"No, I didn't." Zara felt like that proved how mean the townsfolk were, but apparently Ashley wasn't going to take it that way.

"So they probably didn't hate you," she said calmly. "I mean, there are assholes everywhere, sure. But I don't think there are more of them in Lake Sullivan than elsewhere. I'd actually say there might be a few less."

Zara gave her a skeptical look, but Ashley just beamed

back and said, "And here come two definite non-assholes now!" She stepped forward and reached her hands out to an elderly couple making their way through the throng. "You made it!" Ashley said.

The man nodded. "Of course. I had to check in on my fishing buddy. We still have time to catch a few bass before the winter, if you're tough enough to handle a little cold. And then there's ice fishing . . . if you're going to be around for The Slide, that could be your first derby."

"There's an ice fishing derby?" Ashley demanded. She sounded genuinely excited by the idea, although Zara couldn't see why.

"Oh, my," the older woman said. "I was worried that helping you might make his fishing addiction flare up, Ashley, but I never guessed it was *contagious*."

Ashley grinned, then half turned to include Zara in their conversation. "Mr. and Mrs. Ryerson, this is Zara Hale."

"Hale," Mrs. Ryerson mused. "Why does that name sound familiar?"

The signal was subtle, but Zara made her living by reading body language and knowing what people were planning. She saw Mr. Ryerson's tiny head shake, saw Mrs. Ryerson's blink, and she knew the warning had been exchanged. *Don't press for more*, Mr. Ryerson had told his wife. *You won't like what you hear.*

Zara straightened a little and ignored the old man. "Might be because my dad was the town drunk for about twenty years. Might be because my brother just got out of jail. Might be because I make a living as a professional fighter."

Another blink from Mrs. Ryerson. "It was your brother," she said slowly. "He's working at the community center, isn't he? I heard about him from Andrea Thompson. She said her son's taken a liking to . . . Zane, isn't it? Taken a liking to him, and it's the first time little Scotty's come out of his shell since his father died."

Oh. Zara nodded a little jerkily. "Zane's good with kids," she said quickly.

"And you're a professional fighter?" Mrs. Ryerson looked . . . damn it, she looked *interested*. "What does that mean exactly? You make a living at it?"

Mr. Ryerson poured his wife a glass of wine and listened as Zara explained her job. She was a bit tentative at first, waiting for the first look of disdain on the woman's face, but it never came. Mrs. Ryerson was interested in the training, and the business side of things, and she loved it when Zara and Ashley discovered they had the same favorite photographer for promo shoots.

Everything was just so easy. When Ashley had to go help Josh with the food, Zara and Mrs. Ryerson tagged along and were put to work, setting out huge vats of various side dishes, running around to find rocks to anchor napkins against the cool breeze that had sprung up, and whatever else needed doing.

It was strange to be part of something like this. Something . . . wholesome, she supposed. Family-friendly, judging by the number of kids who were swarming around the place. There was a bonfire being lit, and a guy with a guitar behind him and a plate of food on his knee, clearly fueling up before producing some music. It was nice.

She stepped back a little, away from the table and into the shadows around the house. Nice. Too nice. This place wasn't for her. She wasn't one of these people. They were being polite, but they didn't really want her there. Not her. And she didn't want them!

A napkin blew by at her feet and she bent over to catch it. And just like that, she felt the darkness coming. She caught herself with her free hand on the ground, crouched down, and forced her vision back with just her will. She would *not* get dizzy here. Not with all these strangers ready to stare at her.

She rolled backward until her back was braced against the wall of the cabin and pushed herself upright, well-trained muscles responding as ordered.

She stood there for a few breaths, making sure she was okay, and trying to think of her justifications. It had been a weird angle to bend at. She'd had a couple beers. She hadn't eaten enough protein that day. It was almost certainly the protein. Her body was used to getting a lot of it and she'd been slacking off. She'd have a burger and everything would be better.

But she wasn't quite brave enough to move over toward the grill yet. She'd just take another moment and make sure she was okay. And then she'd forget all about this little glitch.

THERE were a few picnic tables set up, but they were mostly taken up by older folks, or else parents trying to get their kids to eat something without spilling the food all over the ground. Most people were sitting on blankets around the bonfire, or on fallen logs and boulders a bit farther back in the trees. Calvin saw Zara perched on the back steps of the house, staring at the bonfire from a distance, and wandered over with his plate of food.

"Warmer near the fire," he said. The day had been beautiful, but the evening air was cool.

"I'm fine here," she replied shortly.

"Mind if I join you, then?"

"Won't you be cold?" She didn't sound like she actually gave a damn about his comfort.

He sank down onto the lower step. "I'm tough. I can take it."

She didn't respond. He took a bite of potato salad and said, "How are things going at the center? You settling in okay?"

"It's fine," she said.

"You're finding things to do?"

"Yup." She had no expression in her voice or on her face, but still somehow managed to convey a complete lack of interest in him.

He raised an eyebrow. "Are you mad at me about something?"

And she raised an eyebrow right back. "Why would you think that?"

"Well, you're not exactly . . . you're not acting *un*-mad."

"I'm not *acting* at all." She raised a hand as if she was going to rub her temples, then frowned and jammed the hand back onto her lap.

He could have been sitting anywhere else on the whole property having a perfectly pleasant time and yet he'd chosen to subject himself to this. But, damn it, he could break through whatever was bothering her. He was a friendly guy, widely considered both charming and handsome. He was a good conversationalist, genuinely interested in others. Zara was a bit of a challenge, sure, but he was up for it.

"Zane seems to be doing well," he said.

And Zara turned toward him like a flower seeking the sun. "Yeah? Really? He's not telling me much. I mean, I see him at the center, and he looks happy enough. But they've got him on the evening shift now, so I don't see him too often. And we don't really. . . ." She frowned, then shrugged as if deciding to be honest. "We don't talk at all, not about anything real. But he's talking to you? You think he's okay?"

Well, now Cal felt like an asshole, using her brother as a way to get her attention. But at least he could honestly say,

"Yeah, I think he's good. We've gone out for beers a few times, and he seems to be adjusting. And he's here tonight—a bit slow to warm up, but look at him now."

They both turned and saw Zane sitting on one of the blankets by the fire, chatting to a young mother who was juggling a toddler and a plate of food.

"Is he meeting people? You know—making friends?" There was something awkward in her voice, something strange.

Was Zara Hale asking him if her brother was getting laid? Judging by the stricken expression on her face, the way a lovely tinge of pink was blossoming on her cheeks, he was pretty sure she was.

"He's met a few people," Cal said cautiously. Zane had left Woody's with a woman the other night, but maybe he'd gone back to the Hale house afterward, or maybe he'd spent the night and Zara hadn't noticed because they were working different shifts. Or maybe he'd walked the lady home like a true gentleman and then returned to drive himself back to the country. It was none of Cal's business, and probably none of Zara's, either.

Because she wasn't really interested in her brother's sex life, he didn't think. At least, he hoped she wasn't. Her curiosity was just a symbol, a small part of her larger concern. "He's doing okay," Cal reiterated. "He's meeting people, settling in. I'm sure it's a—I don't know, a challenging transition. But he's making it."

"And you'd tell me if he wasn't?" She sounded almost pleading. "If something goes wrong, I can help! I can—I can do whatever I need to. I *will* do whatever I need to. As long as I know it's happening, I can fix it."

It was a strangely distorted version of the conversation Cal'd had with Zane. Cal wanted to protect Zara, Zara wanted to protect Zane. And Zane was probably doing okay all on his own. "He's a big boy, Zara. He can take care of himself. I really think he's doing fine." And then he added, "But, yeah, I'll let you know if I see something to worry about."

She nodded, and her shoulders lowered a little. "Thank you."

He felt almost bashful, like her thanks had been a gift and he was a schoolboy too shy to know how to receive it. Which was just stupid. He needed to get control of himself, so he changed the topic a little. "And you? I know, the center's 'fine.'" She had the grace to look a little sheepish at her previous lack of engagement. So he pressed a bit further, giving her a warm smile and leaning in just a little. "But what about your head? The concussion? Is it—"

The transition was quick. Her face shuttered again as she said, "My head is (a) none of your business. And (b) just fine."

So much for sheepishness. Before he caught up to whatever had just happened, Zara had turned away from him. "You were right. It's cold over here. I'm going to the fire."

And she was gone, leaving Cal looking after her. What the hell? He pushed himself to his feet. He had no idea what the problem was, but he was going to find out.

ZARA made her way around the fire, practically stalking Zane, willing him to eat faster so they could get the hell out of there. She stopped walking when she heard him laugh. It was free and easy and relaxed; she hadn't heard him laugh like that in ten years.

He was having fun. Making friends. He needed to stay.

She took a few steps backward then turned, though she wasn't sure where she was heading.

She almost collided with Calvin Montgomery. "I'm sorry," he said quickly.

"I wasn't watching where I was going."

"No, not about that. About before. For what I said."

Damn it, she was too on edge for this. She turned to him and stared, the same gaze that told her opponents they were in over their heads. "What did you say? What are you sorry for?"

He paused before saying, "For being nosy maybe? I'm honestly not sure. But whatever—I don't know. Whatever made you decide to leave. I think it was me, and I'm sorry for whatever it was."

It was so easy for him. He could just expose himself like that, make himself vulnerable with such a wide-ranging apology, because he was confident he wouldn't be attacked. Not him. No, he was safe from all that. But she wasn't, and she wasn't going to be stupid enough to take off her armor just because he was able to. "Yeah, you were nosy. You should back off. But it's no big deal." She turned away, and felt his hand on her shoulder. Not holding her, not really, but more contact than he had any right to be making. She knew just how it would feel to turn around and drive her fist into his solar plexus.

But he was going to help her with Zane, so he was an ally. *Not a friend*, her inner voice reminded her, *not someone you can trust*. But she hadn't needed to hear that. She knew it well enough already. So instead of hitting him, she demanded, "What?" and gave him another glare.

He leaned against a nearby rock, lowering his head so they were on the same level. She wondered if he was deliberately trying to appear submissive and nonthreatening or if it was all instinctive for him.

"What?" she demanded again.

He said, "I feel like we keep—I don't know. I guess mostly *I* feel like I keep pissing you off. And I just want you to know that it's totally accidental. This isn't like some juvenile 'tease the girl you like' scenario. I'm not trying to banter with you, or flirt or whatever. I don't know what you don't like, but I want you to know that I don't do it on purpose."

Her laughter surprised even her. "You aren't trying to— Jesus, of course you're not trying to flirt with me! I mean . . ." She laughed again, more relaxed this time. The surprise of it all had taken the edge off her resentment. Off her fear. "Why would you think that? Seriously, are you that bad at flirting? You do it and women take off? Is that your history?"

"No," he said, and he was laughing a little himself. "I'm not bad at flirting. I'm pretty good at it, really. I was just trying to figure out why I keep making you angry, and that's all I could think of. I thought maybe you were feeling sexually harassed or something."

"Did you think that through at all? I mean, you know how I was raised, you know I work in an almost all-male environment with some guys who are pretty damn rough, you know I get my picture taken when I'm wearing a sports bra and tight shorts, you know I was in *Maxim*, for God's sake, all tarted up and presented for the viewing pleasure of every pimply fifteen-year-old on the continent. And you think I'd get all worked up about someone asking me how I was feeling? Seriously?"

"Okay, when you put it that way, it does sound a bit stupid."

"A bit?"

He grinned again, casting his eyes sheepishly toward the ground. Then he looked back up. "It sounds really stupid. It was just the only thing I could think of."

She sighed. Why the hell was she getting into this, and with

Calvin Montgomery of all people? But apparently her judgment was taking a short vacation, so she said, "What would your interpretation be if I was a guy? If you couldn't just flip to your 'wow, women are so delicate and sensitive' bullshit?"

"I guess maybe I'd think you were a delicate, sensitive guy?"

"Or?"

He stared at her for a moment, then said, "I might think I'd hit a sore spot. Something you didn't want to talk about."

She should leave it at that, but she wasn't going to. "But it's not your fault, right? It was just an innocent question. No way you could know I don't want to talk to you about my head. It's not like I . . ." She trailed off and looked at him expectantly, waiting for him to fill in the blanks.

Which he reluctantly did. "Not like you've told me to mind my own business every other time I've asked about it."

"No, of course not. I mean, if I was a guy—or, hey, just for fun, let's say I'm a woman. But one that you actually respect, rather than just steamrolling over whatever she says—if I was someone like that and I'd told you repeatedly to leave a topic alone, and you just kept coming back to it? Damn, what would that make you?"

"An asshole?" he guessed glumly.

And now she *really* should leave it, but the killer instinct that made her strong in the ring wasn't easy to turn off in other situations. "And what would a polite response be, for someone dealing with an asshole in a public place?"

He nodded as if accepting his medicine. "It would be totally polite and reasonable for a person to leave the area in order to get away from the asshole."

She looked at him then. Really looked. Not at the kid she remembered, the one who'd treated her like an unwanted hanger-on. Not the teenager he'd been, abandoning his best

friend at the worst possible time. And not her stereotype of
who he was now, pasted together from what she remembered
of his family, the town, and other men who were big fishes
in little ponds. She looked at *him*. Too handsome, still. Too
preppy and proper looking. And the way he carried himself
was too confident, too secure in his own status and strength.

But here he was. He was looking up at her with humility,
listening to her with real attention, and seemingly taking
her words to heart. How did that fit in with the kid she'd
known *or* the stereotype of who he was now?

It didn't fit, not at all, and she needed to think about that.
But not right then.

"Okay," she said quietly. "So that's why I left. It's not a
big deal, but it's not any of your business, either."

"Come over to the fire," he suggested. "I'll leave you
alone. I promise."

She was tempted. She knew better, but there was something drawing her in. Not him. No, that couldn't be it. "It's
been a long time since I've sat around a fire," she said slowly.
"I used to really like them. But in the city—I guess rich
people have fireplaces. But there's nothing like this."

"No," he agreed quietly. And then he just stood there,
waiting.

The guy with the guitar set his plate down and picked up the
instrument, and he strummed gently. Not loud enough to disturb
anyone's conversations, just a quiet backdrop to the party.

"That's Theo, one of Josh's cousins," Calvin said. "He
usually plays in a band at Woody's but he took the night off
to be here."

She nodded, and took a half step forward. The sun was
almost down, and in the dim light, people didn't look as
strange as they had earlier. They weren't staring at her; most
of them were looking at the fire, or at each other.

A little kid, maybe four or five, was walking around the edge of the bonfire and stumbled over something on the ground. For a moment, he wobbled, and Zara drew in a quick breath. The fire was a hazard. The kid was going to fall into it. But an adult hand reached out and steadied him, and the boy smiled at his rescuer and let himself be pulled away from the flames.

"Come sit down," Calvin said, still quiet.

Zara wanted to. That was the scariest part. "I'm going to go help tidy up," she said, and as soon as she said the words, she knew they were right. She needed to keep her mind sharp, and Calvin Montgomery was not good for that. Yes, it was a good decision.

Still, as she headed toward the long tables set up by the house, she waited to feel his hand catch her shoulder again to stop her from running away. She could almost feel its warmth, and its gentle weight.

And when it didn't come, she was disappointed.

Seven

"SO YOU HAD a good weekend?" Michael's voice was casually neutral, but he was watching Cal too intently for the illusion of relaxation to be convincing.

"I guess, yeah." Cal waited for his brother to clarify whatever point he was trying to make. They were in Cal's office and Michael had come all the way down the hall from his own space for something more important than chitchat. They weren't the sort of brothers who just hung out.

"You were spending time with the Hales, I hear."

Was Cal supposed to be impressed with Michael's spy network? Half the town had been at Josh's barbeque and it wasn't like Cal had been sneaking around. So he just shrugged.

But Michael clearly wasn't ready to let it go. "Ten years ago, Zane Hale called you for help, and you turned him in to the police." Michael's voice was still calm and conversational. If anything, he sounded pleased with Cal's decision in the past. "Maybe Zane was so desperate for visitors while he was in prison that he made himself forgive you, but Zara? She's just forgotten it all?"

Cal wanted to react. He wanted to explain, justify, say that Zane had actually thanked Cal for turning him in because it had kept him from getting in more trouble. He wanted to insist that he'd thought Zane would get help, or a slap on the wrist, not be locked away for a decade. He'd been naïve, sure, to think Zane would be treated like Cal would have been. Zane's father didn't golf with judges and Zane hadn't been in school or been able to afford a good lawyer, and had been too proud to let Cal pay for one. Cal hadn't known the consequences of his decision would be so horrible.

But Michael wasn't the one Cal should be offering explanations to, and he didn't want to give his brother the satisfaction of knowing he'd gotten a reaction. So he just shrugged. "I don't know. She's never mentioned it." He smiled blandly. "Did you look at that report from Lawrence? I'm inclined to go along with his ideas, up to a point, but I really think he's being a bit alarmist in some of his projections."

Michael waved a hand dismissively. "Lawrence is always looking for a reason to panic. Ignore him." He leaned forward in his chair and said, "Don't you think that's a potential problem?"

"Ignoring Lawrence?"

"No. The thing with Zara Hale."

"We're at work here, Michael. Do you think maybe we could have a work-related conversation?"

"We've already had the conversation. You should ignore Lawrence. Now, for other matters . . ."

"I don't think we *should* ignore Lawrence. He's got a lot of good analysis in there."

"Okay," Michael said easily. "Put a memo together, outlining what you think we should do, and you can use Lawrence's analysis as support if you want, just as long as you're careful with his conclusions. Now, on to other matters. Zara Hale—"

"Is none of your business."

Michael raised an eyebrow. "You don't think so?" He shook his head in disappointment. "You keep forgetting that you're a Montgomery, Calvin. And that Montgomery Holdings is a *family* company. Whether you're at work or out on the town, you represent this company and this family."

"Oh, come on," Cal said. "Are you serious about this?"

"Dead serious. Look, you get away with a lot. The younger son, without all the responsibility . . . it must be nice. But you don't get away with everything. And spending time with a convicted felon and his prizefighter sister? It's going too far."

"Too far for what?"

"For your role in the family." Michael sat back in his chair as if he had this all thought out and was ready to educate the ignorant youngster. "Dad wants to retire, you know."

"Mom wants Dad to retire," Cal corrected.

But Michael shook his head. "No, Dad, too. He's told me so. He's said he's getting tired, and he wants to hand the company over. But he sees it as a sacred trust. Great-grandfather Montgomery started the company, it's been handed down through the years, getting stronger with each generation. Dad wants to be sure it's strong when he passes it to us, and he wants to be sure it stays strong."

"You are not telling me that hanging out with the Hales threatens the strength of this company."

"Because a company's reputation means nothing?" Michael asked sarcastically. "All that fancy education and you somehow missed the importance of branding?" He shook his head. "Montgomery Holdings is branded as a conservative family company. We sell real estate to conservative people, provide

vacations in our conservative, family-friendly resort proper-
ties. Even the furniture we make is conservative. Ex-cons and
prizefighters?" Another head shake. "Not conservative."

"What about valuing people for who they are? Is that not
a 'family value' we could be promoting?"

"You tell me, Mr. Bigshot MBA. If this was one of your
case studies, would you say it would be good for the company
if one of the two heirs presumptive was cavorting with"—he
stopped and wrinkled his nose with a show of fierce
distaste—"with people who would not appeal to our target
market?"

"No one's 'cavorting,'" Cal said lamely. He had no other
response. It wouldn't be good for the company for him to
be publicly linked to either Hale. He could see that. But he
didn't want to admit it, and not just because he didn't want
to give his brother the satisfaction of being right.

"Dad can't retire until we're stable," Michael said. His
voice was quieter now that he knew he'd won. "And doesn't
he deserve to take a break? He's worked his ass off for the
last forty-five years, Calvin, building this company into what
it is today. He's done all that for us. Shouldn't we be trying
to repay the favor?"

He stood up then, but his mercy was coming too late for
Cal's peace of mind. "Think about it," Michael said as he
left, shutting the door quietly behind himself.

Cal leaned back in his chair and stared out the window.
Yeah, he was going to think about it. Damn it.

❧ Eight ❧

"ZARA! ZARA! WATCH me kick!" Donny Black was so excited he was hopping.

Zara crouched down. She hadn't been working with kids for long, but she'd already figured out that it was hard to really understand their movements from above their eye level. "Yeah, okay, buddy, let me see it."

The six-year-old started from a good position but lost his balance partway through, ending up with a sort of splat of his foot against the heavy bag, after which he stumbled backward and fell down. But he was immediately on his feet again, beaming at Zara. "See that?"

"I did, yeah. That was—you were really balanced at the start. That part was good!"

"Yeah!" Donny roared, and lined up for another kick.

Maxine, the manager of the center and instructor for the children's MMA program, wandered over and watched Donny's next attempt. "How's he doing?" she asked Zara softly.

"He sucks. They all suck." She grinned. "It's great."

"Great?"

"Yeah. They're just having fun. It's nice." She was talking mostly to herself when she added, "I'd forgotten it could be like that."

"Kids are good at reminding you of all the different ways to do things," Maxine agreed. Then she clapped her hands. "Okay, guys, circle up!" And she found her place at the front of the room, ready to teach the moves Zara had helped her to refine.

Zara stepped back and watched. After a few hours of observing an expert, she was grateful she wasn't the one in charge of the kids' program. The techniques of martial arts were one thing, but they didn't have much in common with the tricks of teaching, especially not with children. Max had everything broken down into kid-sized bites, a few minutes of one thing followed by a few minutes of something else, with lots of chances for messing around in between. The kids were learning discipline, sure, but they weren't getting drowned in it. Zara was pretty sure she would have sent most of the students home crying and shaking after their first class if she'd been put in charge.

She caught movement out of the corner of her eye and looked toward the door of the gym as one of the girls from the office stepped inside. It wasn't too unusual for the office staff to tour around; most of them gave classes part time in whatever their fields were. But there was something about her expression this time that didn't seem right. And sure enough, when she spotted Zara, she made a face and beckoned her over.

"I'm really sorry," she said as Zara arrived. Then another grimace before she blurted out, "The police are here. They want to talk to you. I convinced them to wait in the conference room, but they seem pretty impatient. I don't think they're going to stay there for long. Can I cover for you down here, and you go up and see them?"

Zara's brain had stuttered to a stop at the word "police." It thawed out enough to allow her a jerky nod of agreement to the plan, then froze again as her body started moving toward the stairs. *Police, police, police.* Nothing good came from police. Whatever this was, it was bad. Zara herself was safe, but Zane? Was this about him?

The door of the conference room was open and a deputy looked out and saw her as she approached. She tried to read his expression. He smiled, happier than he would have been if he was bringing her news of a death or something, but his eyes stayed on her, cold and assessing. So it was going to be *that* kind of a meeting.

"What's going on?" she asked as she stepped into the room. She'd mostly gotten over her shock, and the fear was turning into frustration. And that could too easily shift to anger, so she needed to keep herself under control.

"I'm not sure if you remember me, but I'm Deputy Marshall, this is Deputy Garrett. We'd like to ask you a few questions."

She vaguely recalled Marshall coming by to deal with her father a few times, arresting him or giving him warnings. She squinted at the younger cop, noticed his pale skin and white-blond hair and said, "You related to Donna Garrett?"

"She's my younger sister," he said easily. "You two went to school together, right?"

Well, the "together" part could have been argued, but they'd definitely been enrolled in the same school at the same time, so that was probably enough for this conversation. "Yeah." Probably Zara should have asked how Donna was doing, but she didn't actually want to know and didn't feel like pretending. "What do you want to ask me about?"

"Well, first," Deputy Marshall said with a smile that she was pretty sure was supposed to be sweet and fatherly, "we'd just like to confirm some basic information. Can you tell us your name, please?"

"You don't know my name?"

Deputy Marshall's smile got a little tighter. "We'd just like you to confirm it for us."

Zara fought the urge to make something up. "Zara Hale."

"And do you have family in the area?"

Yeah, that was what this was about. She fixed him with a steely glare. "My brother, Zane Hale."

The officer nodded as if he'd proved a point. "Thank you. And, Miss Hale, could you tell us where you were last night? Say, from four in the afternoon until the next morning."

"Why do you want to know?"

"We're just running an investigation, Miss Hale."

"Into what? My whereabouts?"

"It's a general investigation." He smiled again, like a kindly uncle waiting for a child to stop being silly. "So, last night?"

Zara wanted to object. She could call lawyers, make a big deal out of it, force these assholes to fight for every drop of information. But maybe that wasn't the best way to help Zane. "I worked until about six thirty. Here. Then I went home."

"So you were at home from about six thirty until the next morning? Anyone who can corroborate that for us?"

And there was the trap, Zara decided. She knew they weren't asking about her, so they must be interested in Zane. But they didn't want to come right out and say it, hoping to catch her unaware. And Zane hadn't been home the night before. She had no idea where he'd been. But if the police were here, talking to her, chances were good they'd already talked to Zane, and then they'd come to her to confirm something he'd said. She took about a quarter of a second to think it through, then confidently said, "Yeah, my brother was home. He can back me up." And as casually as she could manage, she added, "So what's this all about? What happened last night that you think I was involved in?" *That you think Zane was involved in*, she corrected in her mind.

They confirmed her suspicion when Deputy Garrett leaned back into the conversation, his face just as pointy as his sister's. "It was just you and your brother? And you were with him all night?"

"Ew. He's my brother . . . we didn't share a room or anything." Her mind raced, trying to figure out what they'd believe, and more important, what Zane might have already told them. She remembered his old instructions about lying to authority, rules that had been pretty damn important when the two of them were trying to stay together despite neglectful parents. Keep the story as close to the truth as possible. Try to pick another event that was almost like it, and pull any needed details from that event. So in this case? When had they spent time together in their new house, at night? . . . "We were doing some unpacking, putting together Ikea furniture, that sort of thing. Puttering, you know? We made a late dinner, and by the time we ate it and finished all the jobs, it was probably . . . I don't know, probably one in the morning? Maybe later."

"And then what?" Deputy Marshall asked. His smile wasn't so sweet now, and she took satisfaction in that. Whatever they'd been looking for, she hadn't given it to them.

"And then . . ." She'd better still pretend she thought this was about her. "I went upstairs to bed. Zane probably would have heard me if I went out. But maybe not. My room's right above the driveway, so I would have heard him, for sure. But he might not have heard me." There. Acting like it was all about her, but still letting them know he hadn't gone anywhere. Damn, she was doing pretty well.

Deputy Marshall exchanged a look with his partner, then said, "And you'd be willing to swear to all of this under oath?"

"Under oath?" That was her cue. "Look, I've told you where I was, and you've told me nothing. Now you're trying to . . . to what? What is it you think I did?" She shook her head. "No. I'm not willing to do anything else for you until I've talked to a lawyer or until you start talking to me. What's all this about?"

Marshall sighed as if she had disappointed him. "We're trying to keep this as informal as possible, Miss Hale."

"By asking me to swear an oath?" She shook her head and stood up. "No, that's not informal. I've told you where I was. If you want anything more from me, you can contact my lawyer."

"And your lawyer is . . ."

The deputy clearly thought he was calling her bluff; he was still thinking she was poor little Zara Hale, spunky but completely without resources. Old Zara would have been bluffing if she'd started spouting off about lawyers, but new Zara? New Zara took a fair bit of satisfaction from being able to say, "Will Doughton at Doughton and Associates in New York handles my business. I haven't had any need of a criminal attorney, but if I need one now, they're a full-service firm so I'll probably go through them. You can contact Will and he'll refer you to the appropriate member of his staff."

And with that, she nodded to each of them in dismissal and swept from the room, as well as she could sweep wearing a T-shirt and yoga pants.

Her adrenaline got her past the curious secretary and out of the office area, but she could feel it fading as she moved and knew that she needed to get somewhere private in a hurry.

There was trouble with the police. Not for her, so it must be for Zane. It seemed like she'd told them the right thing, what Zane had wanted her to say, but she couldn't be sure. And why had she needed to? What the hell was going on? She headed toward the staff locker room, where she'd left her cell phone. Had he been calling her all morning, needing help and unable to reach her? While she'd been putzing around with little kids, pretending she knew anything about teaching, had he been desperately calling her? Was he with the police, or was he somewhere worse? Was it only his freedom in danger, or was it his life?

She made it into the change room and fumbled with her locker, glad there was no one around to see her. When she finally got the door open, she scrabbled for the pocket of her jacket, yanked her phone out . . . and looked at the screen, displaying no messages.

Zane hadn't called her. Zane didn't have a cell phone. She hadn't bothered to get him one. Damn it, she'd been thinking about buying him one so she could track him, but really he'd needed one so he could call for help! What if he was hiding somewhere, and had no way to reach her or anyone else? What should she do, what *could* she do—

The knock on the locker room door startled her and she stared at it as it pushed open an inch or so. Not enough for anyone to see anything, but enough so she could hear. "Zara? Can I come in?"

She leaped for the door, yanking it open so fast Calvin stumbled a little. "Have you heard from Zane?" she demanded, pulling him inside and then locking the door behind them.

"Do you know what's going on? I think he's in trouble, but I don't know what for! I don't know where he is!"

"He's at the police station," Calvin said. His voice was calm, his gaze steady. "He called me and I arranged for a lawyer. They haven't pressed charges yet, but they're investigating him for an armed robbery last night."

"Armed robbery? Why? Why do they think it was him?"

"Description matched."

How closely did the description match? she wanted to scream. Had her brother, her sweet, desperate brother who'd made mistakes but was trying to start over, had he done this? "Was anyone hurt?" she asked, and the universe froze for a moment before Calvin answered.

"Not seriously. The victim was pushed to the ground, it sounds like. Scraped up a little, but he's okay."

"No. Zane wouldn't do that. He doesn't need money, and he's not violent!"

"I agree," Calvin said calmly. "I'm sure it wasn't him."

Zara had no idea how it happened. One moment she'd been standing there, more or less stable, and the next she was sagging, not quite falling, but she could see the blackness trying to creep in again from around her field of vision, and she felt her consciousness backing away from her body.

And then there was a strong arm wrapping around her, catching her under her shoulders, and a warm, solid body snug in beside her, guiding her over to the wooden bench in the middle of the aisle. "Okay," Calvin whispered, "everything's okay," and Zara really, really wanted to believe him.

UNDER other circumstances, Calvin might have been more than happy to have his arms full of Zara Hale, but as it was, he was mostly bewildered. "Shh," he tried, since his chant of "okay" hadn't really gotten him anywhere, but it wasn't as if Zara was actually making any noise. She wasn't crying. It honestly seemed more like she'd been about to faint, but a woman like Zara Hale surely didn't faint just because she'd had a scare.

Still, it was all he had to work on, so he went with it. "Zane's going to be fine. I've got a lawyer with him, and we both know he couldn't have done it, so they'll just—I don't know, they'll just let him go. He'll be fine."

Then he stopped to think about it. A recently released convict who matched the description given by the victim? He was sure Zane would be exonerated eventually, but it might take some time. "I don't suppose he has an alibi? For last night about ten o'clock? Do you know?"

"Yeah," Zara said. "That's what they were asking me about. The police. That's what they wanted to know." She seemed stronger now, less shaky, but she wasn't moving away from him and he just couldn't make himself retrieve his arm before she asked him to. "I told them he was at home, from the time I left work until morning."

"Well, that's great, then! I mean—it's great, right?" Why was she staring at the floor so intently?

"It's what I told them," she repeated, and his stomach fell.

"Shit. He wasn't there?"

"His car wasn't. I didn't go downstairs and search around for him, but—no. I don't think he was there."

He tried to catch up. "Shit. Why'd you lie? If he told them he was somewhere else, it's going to look bad! For him, maybe, but for you absolutely. Interfering with a police investigation . . . I don't know what else, but, Zara, this is not good. Think about how it's going to look when he tells them where he really was and the stories don't match."

And now she pulled away from him, and he had to let her go. "Or maybe I should have just turned him in, right? That's what you'd do. What you've *done*."

He froze. "You know why I did it. Because I couldn't get him under control and I thought he was going to hurt himself or somebody else. I thought he was going to hurt *you*. I didn't want—"

She cut him off. "Yeah, fine. That was then." She wasn't interested in his story, his excuses, not when she had more pressing concerns. "But now—the stories will match. I'm pretty sure. He must have told them he was with me, right, or else why'd they come talk to me? They asked me about it right off. I mean, they tried to sneak up on it a little, but they're not all that smooth, really. So I—we had a system, Zane and me. When social services or something would come nosing around and we'd have to cover for—whatever. Like, if we hadn't seen Dad for a long time and they asked us when we'd seen him, we'd say it was the night before, and we'd bounce back to whatever the real last night we'd seen him had been, and we'd tell them about that night as though it was the night before. You know? So that's what I did, I told them about the last time Zane and I spent much time together at night. From the way they reacted, I think it matched what he told them."

Zara had been fifteen when she'd left Lake Sullivan. She'd been doing all that, working out cover stories and lying to the authorities, when she was just a child. And now she was still doing it, and, damn it, maybe Zane was, too. "Well, that makes it messier," Cal admitted. "Shit. I wonder where he really was? Why wouldn't he have just told them the truth?"

She swallowed hard, but didn't answer.

"You don't honestly think he did it, do you?" He wasn't sure whether to be angry or sad. "There's no way!"

"No!" she said quickly. Then, more slowly, "But why didn't he tell them the truth, then? Why'd he send them to me? And he hates taking money from me, and I was so stupid, I rented that house because I thought it would be good for him to have somewhere nice to come home to, but he's not making much at the center and he insists on paying half the rent, so most of his money is gone just paying that! So he really needs money, and he won't talk to me! I have no idea what he's thinking or feeling. No idea what he's *doing*—"

"We'll figure it out," Cal promised. He had no idea how exactly, but he knew he was committed to working it through. "I'll call his lawyer and see if he's being released. If he is, we'll sit him down and talk to him. You and me together, okay? We'll find out where he was, we'll talk to him about money and make sure he's doing okay. We'll figure it out."

She nodded slowly, then took a deep breath and nodded again, more forcefully this time. She was psyching herself up, he realized, putting away the anxiety and replacing it with determination. "Yeah," she agreed. "Okay. But, damn, I'm sorry for dragging you into this."

"You didn't. Zane did, when he called me for help."

"Called *you*," she said slowly. "Not me. He called his friend, not his family."

"He wouldn't want to bother you with something like this. He still thinks he needs to be your hero. He'll get over it sooner or later, but he's had a lot of adjusting to do."

She didn't look completely convinced, but she didn't argue. She just sat there while Cal dialed, then listened to his side of the conversation with the lawyer. "Being processed for release," Cal repeated for her benefit. "But the charges are still pending? This could still be a problem?"

"They're releasing him based on the strength of the alibi,"

the lawyer said. "But they'll be looking for more evidence. Probably a lineup, once the victim is able to come in. And there's some physical evidence to be processed, as I understand it."

Cal decided not to repeat that part of the conversation. "But for now, he's free."

"He will be shortly," the lawyer confirmed, and they ended the conversation.

"You ready to go pick your brother up?" Cal asked.

Zara frowned at her watch. "I've still got another two hours of work. I don't have any more classes, but I'm still supposed to be here, right? And did you take off work, too?"

"Zane's my friend," Cal said firmly. And then, feeling a little daring, he added, "And I'd like to think you're my friend, too. I don't mind skipping out of work. There have to be some benefits of a family business, right?" Of course, that made him think of Michael and the tantrum he'd throw over this latest problem, but he'd worry about that later. "You want to go see if you can get off early? If you can't, I can pick him up, give him the initial grilling, and you can tag team in when you get ready."

"You think it's going to be that bad?" she asked.

He smiled. "No. I think it's going to be fine. We'll make it be fine."

She nodded as if she believed him. "Okay, yeah, I'm going to go ask if I can leave. But unless there's a crisis, I'm going to leave anyway." She flashed a quick grin, and he was so grateful to see her back to her normal spunky self that he barely picked up on her mimicry as she said, "There have to be some benefits of a job you don't really want, right?"

She unlocked the door and jogged down the hall, and he followed a little more slowly. It occurred to him, now that it was too late, that it might have made more sense to talk to Zane before Zara was involved, just to figure out what had happened. If Zane had actually done this . . . damn it, it would break Zara's heart.

And Cal really, really didn't want to see that happen.

THE two of them had ridden in near silence on the way to the police station, and now the three of them were riding in complete silence on the way back out to the house.

Zane was in the backseat, staring at the floor, and Zara had no idea what to make of his body language.

No, that was a lie. She knew just what to make of it but she wished she didn't. She didn't want to accept that her brother was sitting back there looking guilty.

She slammed the car door a little harder than was necessary and then led the way into the house. Calvin had fallen back so Zane was between them, and maybe it was just Calvin being polite or maybe he'd seen the same thing in Zane's behavior and wanted to make sure the bastard didn't bolt away from this conversation.

They made it inside, walked into the kitchen, and Zara turned to stare at Zane, making the challenge as clear as possible without saying the words.

"I'm sorry," he said. "I screwed up."

Zara's stomach sank. It couldn't be true. He couldn't have been that stupid. "Why?" she almost whispered.

He shook his head and gazed fiercely out the window behind her. "I panicked, I guess. There's just . . . you don't know what it was like. Ten years, Zara. Ten years in hell, and then they think they're going to send me back there? No. No way, I can't do it. I won't do it."

"But before that! I mean, why did you . . . wait. What are

you talking about?" She stared at him, then at Calvin, who was looking almost as confused as she was but then seemed to find a little understanding.

"You're apologizing for lying about your alibi," Calvin said, and Zane nodded miserably.

"I can't believe I did it." He finally made himself look at Zara, and there were tears in his eyes as he said, "I'm a damn coward. I just . . . I lost my head, and I dragged you into this, and I knew you'd remember and you'd back me up but it's not what I should have done." He turned to Calvin. "I should tell the lawyer, right? He can get her out of this? I mean, if she says . . . she could just say she was confused about the dates." Back to Zara to say, "You told them about the night we put the Ikea stuff together, right? That's what I figured you'd pick. You could just say you got confused."

"Wait." Zara needed a minute to catch up. He hadn't done it. It sounded like he hadn't done it. But she needed to know. "Where the hell *were* you last night at ten o'clock?"

For a moment, Zane looked like he wasn't going to answer. But then he sighed and looked back out the window. "At the old trailer."

"The . . ." Zara turned to Calvin to see if this made any more sense to him.

"The one in the Richardsons' backyard?" Calvin said. "They don't even live there anymore, do they? They moved to the city a few years ago."

"Yeah." Zane sounded resigned to his confession. "The house is deserted. But the trailer's still there, and . . . I don't know. I've been going there sometimes. You know how small that back bedroom is? Just a bed and a couple feet of floor. Sometimes everything else feels too *big*, you know? Too open. So sometimes I go there, just to relax a little."

Because the trailer bedroom felt like a jail cell, and he liked that. Because her brother was overwhelmed by his freedom and was trying to find a way to re-imprison himself. Zara blinked hard to keep the tears from falling. "And you were there last night?"

"Yeah," he said quietly. "I went out after work. I slept there, came back here about four in the morning."

This was about Zane, Zara reminded herself. Not about her. She needed to ignore her own feelings, at least temporarily. If she freaked out, it would make him feel even less comfortable in the house, even more in need of a safe shelter. "We should sort through some stuff," she said, trying to sound calm about it all. "Your parole says you're supposed to live with me, right? Is that mandatory? Do you want to talk to your PO about getting your own place?"

He looked like a kicked puppy.

"Jesus, Zane, not because I don't want to live with you anymore!" And she did what she'd been wanting to do for too long. She took the few steps to him, wrapped her arms around his strong shoulders, and squeezed him tight. And he let her. After a moment, he even lifted his arms and hugged her back.

Her eyes were wet again when she finally pulled away. "I feel like I screwed up. I rented a place that's too big for you, where you don't feel comfortable spending the night, and where you have to pay more rent than you want to. Not that you have to pay the rent, though—I chose the place, I'm happy to pay for it. And if your PO says we have to live together, that's okay, we can move somewhere else. Seriously. This is just a rental. I don't care." She took a deep breath. "I don't care about the house or the car or any money that you want to spend. I just care about you."

"It's a nice house," Zane said. "I like it. And I can afford the rent. I just . . . sometimes I just need to be somewhere else." He stopped and looked at her for a moment, then said, "Not because of you. I'm not trying to get away from you, Zare. Not at all."

She took a breath that was only a little shaky. "Okay," she said. And had no idea where to go after that.

Luckily, Calvin was there, and he stepped forward from where he'd been leaning against the sink. "Has your probation officer suggested any counseling or anything? Any support groups, or people who could help you with your adjustment? I mean, there should be something like that, shouldn't there?"

"I don't know," Zane said reluctantly. "There's lots of stuff for how to get a job, but I've got that covered. As long as this mess doesn't get in the way . . ."

"How could it?" Zara looked to Calvin. "It can't, can it? Or mess up his parole? It can't do that! I mean, okay, we lied about where he was, but that's just because they wouldn't have believed us if we'd told the truth. And they don't know we lied, so we're okay, right? And they can't find any more evidence because he wasn't there. They can't find evidence of something that didn't happen, right?"

Calvin blinked hard, apparently a little surprised by Zara's vehemence. "That sounds right," he said carefully. Then to Zane he added, "But you should talk to your PO. And seriously, we should try to find some counseling. There's got to be other guys going through similar stuff, right? It's a big adjustment." He grinned quickly. "When I travel overnight, I take my own pillow with me, that's how much of a princess I am about change. So I can't really imagine going through something this much bigger."

Calvin leaned back against the counter and Zara wanted to hug him. He was making everything so much better, so much easier for both of them. She'd been a bitch earlier, bringing up Calvin's decisions from the past. Whatever had happened back then had been between Calvin and Zane, and Zane was obviously fine with it. And now Calvin was here, helping, just because he cared about his old friend, and by extension, his old friend's sister. He saw her looking at him and smiled at her, and she smiled back, and for a moment, everything made sense again.

⤞ *Nine* ⤝

WHEN CAL HAD returned to Lake Sullivan after getting his MBA, his parents had seemed to think he'd be moving back into his old bedroom at their house. He'd quickly disabused them of that notion but then they'd assumed he'd be eating dinner at their house most nights. He'd worked that down to every other Sunday. When he'd been visiting Zane regularly, he'd arranged it to be alternate weeks with the dinners and told himself he was visiting one prison one week and a different prison the next. Then he'd scolded himself for being so melodramatic.

But standing there in the front hall with his father glowering at him and his mother looking disappointed, he definitely felt trapped. The door he'd just entered through might not be locked, but it would be breaking a lot of rules if he used it to escape. Still, he was tempted, especially when his father jerked his head toward his study and said, "We should talk before dinner."

Cal thought about objecting, but he knew it was pointless. And Michael hadn't arrived yet, so if they could get this little chat wrapped up before he was there, at least Cal wouldn't have to deal with brotherly smugness on top of everything else. So he followed his father into the study, settled himself reasonably comfortably in one of the leather club chairs, and accepted the drink his father offered him.

"Scotch already?"

"Absolutely," his father replied, sinking stiffly into the chair on the other side of the fireplace. "Now, what's this nonsense with you and the Hale girl?"

"There's no nonsense. She's a friend, her brother's a friend—"

"Her brother's a criminal!"

"And a friend." Cal waited quietly as his father digested that.

Finally the older man said, "You've always had a soft spot for them, and I've never understood it. I used to think it was just your little rebellion, but it's more than that, isn't it?"

Cal frowned. "Do you ask Michael why he's friends with the people he's friends with?"

"Michael is friends with people that make *sense*! People who share his background, his values—people who will contribute to his future."

"I don't like his values," Cal said. He hadn't really thought about it before he spoke, but once the words were out, they felt right. "I don't want his future."

"What *do* you want, Calvin?" It was an expression of frustration, not a real question.

And that was just as well, because Cal had no idea how to answer. He had a fuzzy image in his head, something with a bonfire and a guitar and the smell of burgers and the sounds of laughing children. Something with a strong woman speaking truths he needed to hear. In his imaginings, of course, the woman didn't walk away from him after she spoke. No, she stayed, and leaned back into him and they soaked it all up together.

But he wasn't going to get into any of that with his father. "I just want to live *my* life," he said quietly. That was close enough.

"But you want to do it while working for *my* company."

Cal couldn't quite believe it was coming to this, but apparently his father was willing to push. So he shrugged. "At your company or somewhere else. I don't remember ever applying for the job with the company. It was just assumed that I'd be working there. If you don't think it's a good fit anymore, let me know. I can find something else."

And that was true, he realized. Sure, a job somewhere else would probably be more demanding. He'd have to prove himself rather than just coasting along. But maybe that wouldn't be a bad thing. Maybe it was time for him to stop doing what was easiest and start doing what was best.

He was almost disappointed when his father shook his head. "There's no need to get carried away. I don't want to fire you over this. No, Calvin, I want you to start taking responsibility for your place in the family, not give you an excuse for running away."

"My place in the family," Cal mused out loud. "As determined by you and Michael?"

"You want to have a voice in it?" His father pushed himself to his feet with a sudden burst of energy. "That would be wonderful." He set his glass down on the mantel and turned to face Cal head-on. "If you wanted to actually engage in what we're trying to do with the company instead of fluttering around the edges with your community center or your other special projects, I think both Michael and I would be thrilled."

"How did we go from talking about the family to talking about the company?"

"They're the same thing, Calvin!"

Cal stared, and then stood up himself. "No. Not to me they're not." He took a few steps toward the door, then stopped and turned. "And I wouldn't be so sure about Michael wanting me to be more a part of the company. Because I'm not much of a follower, Dad. You're right, I've stayed on the edges of the company. I haven't dived right into it. But if I did dive in? If I made the place my life, like he has? I wouldn't be interested in being his loyal second-in-command. You know?"

It was a long time before his father responded. Too long. It made Cal realize that his father wasn't upset by the idea of his sons fighting against each other for control of the company. His father *liked* the idea. "Healthy competition is a good thing," the older man finally said.

"Good for a business maybe. But good for a family?" Cal waited for an answer, but didn't get one. "I don't agree that the company and the family are the same thing," he said quietly. "And if I have to choose between them, I'll do what's good for the family."

"And you think it's good for the family for you to be spending time with these people?"

Cal snorted in surprise. He'd forgotten they were talking about the Hales and had to pull his mind back to that nonissue. "I don't think it's any of the family's damn business," he said firmly.

His father frowned as if he didn't like that answer, but he didn't reply. At least, not with words. Instead, he turned toward his desk. "I've got a little more work to do before dinner," he said. "You run along and keep your mother company."

It was clearly supposed to sting, the casual dismissal from the more important realm of men and business, but it was nothing Cal wasn't used to. It was in no way upsetting to be banished, but it was a bit frustrating to realize that after almost thirty years as his father, the old man still didn't know his son well enough to even insult him properly.

Cal found his mother in the living room, accepting a glass of wine from the new housekeeper's tray. "Something for you?" the woman asked him.

Damn, he should know her name. Lenore had taken care of the house while he was growing up but had retired a few months earlier. This new woman . . . "I'm fine," he said, although he wouldn't have minded another scotch. It just didn't seem right to accept anything from someone until he could remember her name.

"Thank you, Cleo," his mother said. Just that tiny bit of extra emphasis on the housekeeper's name, just enough to let him know he'd been caught. His father might not understand him, but his mom knew all his tricks.

He sank into an armchair next to the couch she was perched on. The furniture in this room wasn't really made for slouching, but he did his best anyway. His mother reached over and flicked his knee. "Sit up. And tell me what's going on between you and your father. It's not going to ruin dinner, is it?"

Mother code. She wasn't all that worried about the meal, she just wanted to know how serious things were. If it was bad enough that the two of them wouldn't be able to put on polite faces to get through Sunday dinner, she needed to intervene.

"I think we'll be okay," Cal said. "As long as Michael doesn't start stirring it up."

His mother was quiet for a long moment before she surprised him with a decidedly unladylike snort. He stared at her, and she said, "Well, really, what are the chances of Michael staying out of it?" A moment for him to realize she was right, and she added, "You'd better tell me about it. We can figure things out from there."

∻ Ten ∽

ZARA HAD THOUGHT it would be safe to offer an adult women's MMA class, assuming no one would be interested. But when she'd gone to check if the program had been cancelled, she'd been told it was at capacity. Twenty students for women's MMA in Lake Sullivan?

Now, looking at her prospective students, Zara began to understand. Ashley Carlsen was there, probably just being supportive, and a couple other women who seemed relatively young and athletic. But the rest of them? "I think there's been a mistake," Zara said firmly. "We've got a self-defense course offered next month—that's where you can learn about, like, how to break a hold and what kind of situations to avoid and all that. I think they're even bringing in one of those big padded guys so you can practice hitting him. This is about Mixed Martial Arts. Like jiujitsu or karate or . . ." She stared at them, trying to find the words that they would understand. "Like *boxing*," she said. "This is like a boxing class."

The director from the previous visit was there, with a girl Zara assumed was her daughter, and she said, "Not just boxing, though, right? We'll be kicking, as well?"

Mrs. Ryerson, who was somewhere in her mid-seventies by Zara's guess, nodded enthusiastically. "I want to kick people!" she said. Then she looked at the other women sitting around her and smiled not-quite-apologetically. "None of you personally. But we'll be wearing padding, won't we? Nobody will get hurt?"

Zara scanned the crowd, waiting for them to shrink away in horror, but they just looked back at her expectantly. "Well, nobody *should* get hurt," Zara said lamely. She'd certainly had lots of bruises in her time, along with the regular injuries that came from pushing her body to its limits, but that was when she was fighting against the best in the world. These women? "We'll spar at partial strength," she said. "But you can hit the bags full strength, once I've taught you how to do it safely."

"I'm looking forward to it," another older woman said. It wasn't until Zara heard the voice, the tone that managed to be quiet and authoritative all at the same time, that she realized who was sitting on the mat in front of her. Mrs. Claire Montgomery, pillar of the local community, lady who lunched, mother of Calvin and Michael. Mrs. Claire Montgomery wanted to learn Mixed Martial Arts?

"There's grappling," Zara said desperately. "That's like wrestling. This is all the different ways of unarmed fighting, mixed together. That's what we're talking about."

"That seems very efficient," Mrs. Montgomery said approvingly.

"It's hard work," Zara tried.

"So let's get to it." Another familiar voice, and Zara looked over to see Ashley grinning at her. "We're excited! Mold us into warriors, Zara Hale!"

Ashley, at least, seemed physically fit, although Zara wasn't sure a pampered Hollywood star was really going to enjoy getting punched in the face. "You've all gotten the medical clearance?" she tried, one last attempt to get out of this. The office had told her the paperwork was all in place, but what kind of quack would tell Mrs. Ryerson she should start MMA at her age?

"My doctor was a little surprised," Mrs. Montgomery admitted in what must have surely been a huge understatement, "but he said I'm healthy enough to try it."

"Mine said not to push further than what's comfortable," Mrs. Ryerson said. "Then he remembered that was what he told me when I wanted to start running a few years ago." She beamed. "He was there to cheer me on when I finished my marathon last spring."

A marathon. Okay. So the woman was tougher than she looked. Zara took a deep breath. She'd come in with a plan, and she might as well stick to it. "Okay, well . . . we want to start every workout with a warm-up. Some people do meditation at the start and the end, but I've never liked that because I'm no good at it so I can't really teach you that part." *Way to inspire confidence, Zara. Nice work.* But she pushed on. "We should just do some basic exercises and some stretching. So shoes off—no shoes on the mats, ever— and let's start with some push-ups."

Most of the women obediently rolled over into push-up position, but Zara saw two girls by the door exchange dubious looks with each other. One of them was so thin she was practically invisible, the kind of thin that suggested illness. And her friend was about the same age, round and soft, her body sort of melting into the mat rather than resting on it. Zara could tell they were mentally heading for the exit, and would go physically as soon as they got up the nerve.

She should let them go. A smaller class would be easier to teach, and those two clearly weren't athletic, or interested in sports at all. The smart thing was to let them quit.

So Zara wasn't quite sure why she found herself easing over toward them, stepping around the other women on the mats. "You're warming up, not wearing yourself out," she said as she moved. "Try for three sets, but don't push yourself right to trembling on any of the sets. Count as you go, go until your arms are tired, and then give yourself a break. Keep track of how many you can do today, and work on doing more next time."

She got to the two girls, both of whom had clearly seen her coming. The fat girl reached behind herself and grabbed her sweatshirt, either getting ready to leave or looking for some sort of armor, no matter how flimsy.

"You don't want to try?" Zara asked softly as she crouched next to them.

The skinny girl shook her head. "This was stupid." Her voice was quiet, but there was a jagged edge to it. "We thought it would be . . . I mean, we knew it would be . . ." She shook her head, clearly frustrated.

"I can't do push-ups," the fat girl said. "Not even one." She said it like a challenge, like a dare for Zara to have a problem with it.

Instead, Zara grinned. "That's fine. It's not about doing a push-up." She stopped talking as she realized the truth of her words. It felt important somehow, and she stood up.

What was she doing? She wasn't sure, but she thought she needed to at least try.

"Guys?" she said, loudly enough to catch everyone's attention. The push-ups stopped and faces in various shades of exertion red looked up at her. "Sorry to interrupt. I just wanted to start the class a bit differently. Sorry. I have done some teaching before, I promise, but it was in a different sort of class." She'd taught elite athletes, not retirees and couch potatoes.

She moved back to the front of the room, keeping a bit of attention on the two girls to make sure they didn't try to leave.

"I just wanted to clarify a few things about MMA," she said. She hoped this was a good idea. "I wanted to explain that it's a new sport, and it's made up of all different martial arts. I mean, you knew that. I already said that, right?" Yeah, she was making a fool of herself, but she'd started, so she kept going. "The thing is, that makes it really versatile. It means that each athlete—each participant—can play to their strengths. Does that make sense?"

She wasn't sure it did, judging by the expressions on the faces in front of her. "So, like . . ." She took a chance and waved toward the thin girl. "I'm sorry, I don't know your name."

There was a long pause before the cautious "Melanie."

Zara nodded. "Okay. Melanie. I don't know her at all, I haven't seen her move, I could be totally wrong. But I look at her, and I see that she's very thin. And MMA is a weight-class sport. You fight other people who are the same weight as you. So Melanie, if she competed, would be in a class with other really light people, and a lot of them would probably be shorter than she is. So with Melanie, I expect I'd recommend she do a lot of striking, ways to use her reach to get to people before they can reach her. That's playing to her strength. We should also work on her weakness, which seems like it might be . . . well, weakness. So we'll want to get her stronger without putting on a lot of weight."

So far, so good. No one was leaving. Zara pressed on. "And then Mrs. Ryerson runs marathons. So she's really fit.

That's not essential for MMA, but it never hurts. She's probably tough and she can outlast an opponent, so I'd want her to learn a good defense and find ways to tire the other fighter out. I'm not sure what her weaknesses will be, but once we find them, we'll work on them."

Zara knew what she wanted to say next, but realized she was doing it wrong. She should have asked permission maybe, or made up some imaginary person . . . she should have been *better* at this. She kept going anyway, even though she wasn't sure she should.

She looked over at the fat girl. "I don't know your name, either."

The girl sat up straighter. Tough. Yeah, she'd have to be. "Anna," she said, again as if she was daring Zara to object.

Zara nodded. "Okay. Anna. Hi." She took a deep breath. She was doing it. "Anna's carrying some extra weight around, and that means she's probably really strong. I mean, I go to the gym and lift weights for an hour a day maybe, but if someone's carrying extra weight all the time, they're getting a hell of a workout. The problem is that you can't just take the weight off and leave it outside the ring, go inside and kick ass, and then come back out and strap it on again. So I think Anna's strength is going to be that she's really strong, but the weakness, probably, will be that she can't use that strength against an opponent while she's using it to carry herself around. So that's what we'll work on for Anna. Basic technique, but also a way to use her weight to her advantage—grappling probably. And if we had more time, we'd work on keeping her strong but probably getting rid of some of the weight that's just sitting there, not being useful for anything."

Anna was squinting at her, clearly trying to figure out if all this was an insult or not, and Zara really wasn't sure which way the decision was going to go. She decided to leave it behind, at least for just then. She took a deep breath. "So the best part about MMA is that it's flexible. We can pick and choose different techniques to fit different strengths and weaknesses. The next best part about it? You win MMA based on what your body can do. So what I think we need to do in this class, if you're all cool with it, is to really focus on figuring out our different bodies, seeing how to use them, how to improve them . . . but improving them based on what they can do, not what they look like. Does that work for you all?"

There were some thoughtful looks, but no objections, so Zara continued. "Push-ups are good exercise. But the thing is, they're just good exercise because they use your muscles to lift a weight. If you can't do them, that's okay . . . the point is to try. I don't mean that in some little-kid, everyone's-a-winner-if-they-do-their-best way." No, she didn't mean that at all. "I just mean it's okay because it's the trying that makes you strong. Your body doesn't care if you bounce up and down off the ground a few times—it cares that you used a muscle, even if it's just for pushing into the ground and not going anywhere." Slight oversimplification maybe, but good enough for right then. "So we want to *try* to do push-ups. But that just means we want to use our biceps to push our hands into the floor while using our core muscles to keep our bodies straight. If doing all that means that your body rises away from the floor a bit, that's fine. But it's not the main point."

There was a bit of nodding now, and when Zara glanced over at Mrs. Ryerson, the woman smiled at her as if she approved. Strange how good that made Zara feel.

"Let's call them floor pushes," Ashley said. "It's not the 'up' that matters, it's the 'push.'"

God, if the guys at the gym could see Zara now, they'd laugh their asses off. But that was their problem, not hers. "Okay, good," she said. "Let's start with some floor pushes.

Don't slack off. Really try to push that floor away. But don't worry about whether you make it or not."

So they did their floor pushes, and then did some "stomach closers" instead of sit-ups, and then started working on their breathing. But Zara could sense the class's growing impatience. "You guys just want to hit things, don't you?"

Sheepish grins from some, wide smiles and nods from others. There was a right way to do things, a proper order to training that would efficiently lead to the best result. Except the best result for these women probably wasn't going to be a career in the martial arts. They just wanted to try something new. "Okay. We'll fast-track a little. There's some safety stuff you need to know—I don't want anyone breaking their hands or anything. But after that, we'll do some striking."

"Yeah!" someone cheered, and Zara found herself smiling, too. It *was* fun to hit things. When had she forgotten that?

CAL had spent most of the day at the furniture factory hearing about problems with the new suspension system they'd moved to for their upholstered pieces. "You pay this kind of money for a sofa, you don't want a spring in your ass," the foreman pointed out, and Cal couldn't disagree with him.

"Is there a way to make it work?" Cal wasn't an expert, but he was willing to learn.

So they discussed the options, came up with a solution, and then the foreman said, "And it's okay for me to go ahead with this on just your say-so? I don't have to run it past your dad or your brother?" He sounded skeptical.

Cal sighed. The furniture manufacturing wasn't his main area of interest, but it wasn't his brother's or his father's, either. "Go ahead with it," he decided. "I'll let them know."

Via e-mail, because he was still trying to avoid talking to both of them as much as possible.

"And it's okay to come to you with future problems, if they come up?" The man looked cautiously hopeful.

Cal forced himself to nod. His father wanted him more involved in the company, and Michael wanted him occupied in a way that didn't threaten his own status. So Cal taking responsibility for the furniture operations, no matter how boring he found them, would make everybody happy. "Yeah. You can come to me," he said. It felt like one more link chaining him to a life he wasn't sure he wanted, but he said it anyway.

He was on his way back to the office when his phone rang. He checked the call display, then pulled over and answered. It was the lawyer he'd found for Zane, and it didn't take long to get the update on the case. Once he hung up, he pulled back out into traffic. But he wasn't going back to the office anymore. He had something more important to do.

ZARA felt good. The women's class had gone well, she was doing okay with the kids, getting to know her way around the office; everything was coming together. She was heading down the front steps of the center when she looked up and saw Calvin Montgomery coming toward her.

She couldn't help herself; she smiled at him. She was in a good mood, and apparently wasn't looking to hide it.

And he smiled back. "Having a good day?"

"I'm an awesome teacher, and maybe even a good human being."

"Nice." Then he raised his eyebrows a little, voice almost teasing as he said, "Can you handle a bit more good news, or will your head explode?"

"I don't know." She gave him a cautious look. "Try me."

"They caught the guy," he said triumphantly. "The mugger. He tried to rob someone else last night and there were people nearby and they caught him. He's under arrest, the victim from Thursday picked him out of a lineup, and he's already writing out a confession. Zane is totally in the clear."

She stared at him and for a moment it seemed like he may have been right about the risk of head explosion. She had no words, and barely any thoughts, just relief and excitement and a feeling that anything in the universe was somehow possible.

And Calvin was smiling as if he completely understood. It seemed so natural to dart forward, to squeeze him tight in a celebratory hug and feel his chest move as he laughed. And then, somehow, it seemed completely natural to stay there, his arms wrapped around her as their energy changed, became something calmer, deeper. . . .

And Zara made herself push away. Damn it, what was she doing?

"Does Zane know?" she asked, fighting the urge to straighten clothes that really couldn't be all that mussed.

"The lawyer called him before he called me," Calvin said.

And Zane hadn't bothered to let Zara know. Things had been better between them since they'd had their kitchen powwow, but their relationship was still far from perfect.

Calvin shook his head at her. "Worry about it later," he said softly. "For now we should celebrate, right? Zane's freedom and you being an awesome teacher."

"I guess 'awesome' might be a little strong," she started, but he raised his hands as if he wasn't going to hear it.

"Nope. 'Awesome.' That's what you said, and that's what I believe."

"I've only really run one class so far. There's still lots of time for me to screw things up."

"Then we should celebrate now, before things go bad."

It was hard to argue with his logic or with his clear, persistent cheerfulness. "Okay," she agreed. "Yes."

"I'll drive so you can drink," he said as they headed away from the building. "You want to hit Woody's? Or we could go to The Pier, but they close every winter and they're not really ordering much fresh stuff anymore. Probably better food at the bar."

Zara'd been having trouble keeping to a sedate speed as they moved, letting her excitement out by throwing in little skips and jogs and bounces. She was even happy enough to accept the idea of letting Calvin Montgomery be in charge of a vehicle she was riding in. But the ultimate location slowed her down a little. "Woody's. I don't know. I heard it's a bit . . . done up?"

Calvin snorted. "The place is like a shrine to you. It'd probably be kind of creepy, but it has to be an ego boost, right?"

"It actually usually works in reverse for me," she admitted before she remembered it was a bad idea to open up too much. He stood with his fingers wrapped around the passenger door handle of his car and squinted at her thoughtfully, clearly waiting for an explanation. Well, she might as well get it over with.

"It makes me think of all the things about me that would ruin the illusion," she said, trying to laugh it off. "Like, oh, they think I'm tough but they don't hear me whining at my trainer when he wants me to do more core work. Or they think I'm pretty but they don't know how much makeup I was wearing for that shoot and how many pictures the photographer had to take before she got one that was good enough to use." She shrugged. "That sort of thing." Then she looked pointedly at the door handle. He could either open it or get his hand out of the way so she could do it herself.

He opened the door. Then he jogged around to his side and slid in next to her. He'd reversed out of the parking spot and was heading for the main road when he quietly said, "For the record? I think you're tough, and pretty. And it's going to take a hell of a lot more than a little whining or a lot of makeup to make me think differently."

He was kind of calling her crazy, but he was doing it in a really nice way. For once, she decided to let herself focus on the nice. Still, there was no point in getting carried away. "Let's try The Pier. It might be nice to be somewhere less crowded."

"Yeah, of course. And if they haven't got anything good on the menu, we can go somewhere else."

Or call it a night maybe. Her excitement about Zane and teaching had gotten her this far, but now it was morphing into something more like nervousness. What the hell had just happened? Was she going out to dinner with Calvin Montgomery? Was this a date? Damn it, was she on a date with Calvin Montgomery? That seemed like something that should have been thought over a bit more carefully, and then been avoided at all costs.

But Calvin was apparently unaware of her sudden hesitations, driving calmly through the light off-season traffic, heading toward the edge of town.

Zara risked a glance in his direction. If only he'd been a little less good looking. Or else, just as good looking but not quite as kind. Or damn it, he could be *both* of those things and it wouldn't be a problem, if only he wasn't Calvin Montgomery. Patronizing, superior golden boy representative of the mighty Montgomery clan. *That* Calvin Montgomery.

So she decided, for that night at least, he wasn't. He was someone else, just a guy. "Zane calls you Cal," she said. She hadn't really known she was going in that direction, but okay, it was a good question. "Do you prefer that? More than Calvin?"

"Strangers and my family call me Calvin; my friends call me Cal."

Well, that was unexpectedly easy. Maybe her subconscious was better at this than she was giving it credit for. "Cal," she said experimentally. It sounded okay.

And judging by the look on Cal's face, it sounded okay to him, too.

❧ *Eleven* ❧

"SO SCHOOL IN the city and then straight back here to work for your dad? You weren't tempted to stay down there?" Zara took a bite of her wood-oven pizza as she waited for Cal's answer.

And Cal found himself actually having to think before he gave it. "I think I was, kind of. Or maybe not staying in New York, but going somewhere else? Europe, or China, or even just the West Coast. I thought about that, for sure."

"But you just couldn't stay away from good ol' Lake Sullivan." She sounded skeptical about that, and he supposed he couldn't blame her.

"The family business," he said. The words felt heavy in his mouth. "Not much point in having a family business if there's no family involved."

"Your brother wasn't enough?"

"Heir and a spare."

"Really? You're the spare? Just because your brother's a few years older? That doesn't bother you?"

"It never used to," Cal said honestly. "Michael loves the company. He went to school nearby so he could still work at the company evenings and weekends. He didn't do an MBA or anything, just started working full time as soon as he could. He's tied to the company way more closely than I am. So it only made sense he should take over."

"And that's enough for you? You don't really seem like the sort who'd be content to . . . I don't know, to sit back and watch someone else run the show. You seem like you'd want to be—"

"World champion?" he asked lightly, and he shook his head. "Michael and I have never really been that competitive."

She was quiet for a moment as if trying to reconcile herself to that idea. "What about being challenged by your work, though? If you're already a VP, there's not really anywhere else for you to go, is there? Maybe the work's interesting now, but is it still going to be in thirty years when you're doing the exact same thing?"

Good question. And she was so beautiful and sincere as she was asking that he couldn't really shut her down. "I don't know. But I feel like I have to try, you know?" He shook his head. "My dad hasn't taken more than a couple days off in a row since I don't know when. I can't remember him ever taking a full week's vacation. It drives my mom crazy, but he says he has to be there in case something goes wrong. And he's doing all that for Michael and me. So the company we inherit will be strong and profitable. So when he wanted me to come back and share some of the load?" He shrugged. "It seemed like the thing to do."

"And are you going to keep the same schedule, and pressure

your kids into coming back to keep you from working yourself to death?"

He frowned out the window and down toward the water, saw the moonlight glinting off the gentle waves. He could see the dock, and the sandy beach, and he knew every path through the forest that surrounded the town. Then he turned and looked around the room. He'd been right that The Pier was winding down for the season and it was quiet that night, but a few tables had customers at them. People he knew mostly, or people who knew his people. "It's not a bad place to live," he said quietly. "I like it here."

"You could live here without working for the company, though. Couldn't you?"

He frowned. Could he? "I'd never really considered it. I mean, there's not a lot of work obviously. I'd never find anything that paid what I make working for the family, not without going to the city." But maybe that didn't matter. He had stock in the company, got dividends and had investments and otherwise made quite a bit more money than he ever managed to spend. "It might seem like an insult. To the family, you know? If I moved away, I could say I didn't like the town. But if I stayed here and didn't work for them . . . that'd hurt, I think."

She nodded slowly. "In a way, that's nice. I mean, that they want you to be part of what they're doing."

They sat quietly for a moment, then she made a face. "Sorry, was that kind of nosy? I'm not good at casual chatting."

"We could talk about your health," he suggested with a grin. "Post-concussion syndrome, that sort of thing. I hear that's always good for small talk."

Damn it, she even looked good when she was rolling her eyes. He wanted to be closer to her. Wanted her snuggled in next to him with his arm around her so no matter what direction she looked, she'd still be looking at some part of him. And he wanted to touch her, tweak her chin when she was teasing him, and, oh, God, he wanted to leave his hand there, stretch his fingers out along her strong jawline and tilt her head just right. . . .

"Sports it is, then," she said brightly. "Except I don't really follow any, except MMA. Which I haven't been following lately. So . . ."

"How'd you get into it?" he asked. "The MMA stuff. You weren't doing any of that when you lived in Lake Sullivan, were you?"

"No, I started in the city. I mean, Zane showed me how to throw a punch, just to defend myself. A few other bits and pieces. But nothing serious. But when I moved, there was a judo gym down the street and my aunt wanted me out of her hair, so I took a class there, and then they let me hang around and work out in exchange for doing chores. I was already fit and pretty strong from—I don't know, just from *life*—and I'm naturally flexible and balanced. So I just needed to learn technique. I got a job at a place a bit farther away that was moving away from pure judo toward MMA, and I picked that up there." She shrugged. "It just kind of happened. And then once I found out there was maybe money in it? I worked pretty hard."

"Never tempted to go to college?" *Because that was the plan I had for you.*

She snorted. "No. Not at all. I'm not really school-oriented, I don't think." She squinted at him. "You did, what, six years of school after high school? Didn't you want to, like, *do* something? Something real, not just sitting there learning stuff?"

"I was too busy partying to really notice, for my first degree," he admitted. "Getting away from my parents, all the way to New York City? I went a little nuts." Especially after his childhood friend had gone off the rails and been sent to jail, but he didn't think he'd mention that right then. "I did most of my learning in mad cram sessions right before exams. And then my MBA? It was a lot of case studies. So not necessarily real, but at least not straight theory. We got to apply what we were learning. I liked that."

"Case studies?"

"Yeah, like . . . well, the idea was that we were learning enough to manage all areas of a business, without really diving into any one area. So for accounting, we learned enough to be able to manage accountants, and to use the information they gave us. And then they'd give us a set of books, either made up or sometimes from a real company that was willing to share their information in exchange for ideas, and we'd go through and look at the real numbers and figure out what we could about the company, what their strengths and weaknesses were—that sort of thing." And he knew he should stop there, but there was something pushing him on, making him dare what he shouldn't. "For a marketing course, I actually did a case study on female athletes."

He waited for her reaction, and got only a cautiously raised eyebrow. So he pressed on. "I looked at MMA. It's a new sport to begin with, and then female fighters are even newer, so it was really interesting. I looked at a lot of other fields—other sports, but other entertainment industries as well—and tried to decide what ideas could transfer and what couldn't."

"And what'd you find?"

There was a new tone in her voice, one that told him he needed to tread carefully.

"Well, from a business standpoint—" Damn it, he was an idiot for bringing this up. But he kept going. "I found that it would likely be effective to market fighters as sex symbols. It would be best to have them look pretty even in the ring, but I did some surveys that showed the women still had to be effective fighters in order for the interest to be maintained. The men who were susceptible to marketing in this area needed to feel that the women were tough and strong, but also feminine and pretty. I did some work that suggested it could be effective to play up the contrast between the two personas . . . instead of trying to make the women look soft and pretty as they fight, let them look tough, and then contrast that to their soft, pretty looks in real life."

She wasn't eating anymore, just frowning at him. "There was a poster," she said. "Three or four years ago, maybe. It had me, like, split-screened. One side the way I look in the ring, and the other side . . . well, *not* like I look in real life, but with makeup and my hair done and everything, wearing a sexy dress. That poster was my top seller. It's still selling really well, I think. And the company uses that image for all their promotions."

"Yeah," he admitted. "I know the poster. I—" Well, he'd brought himself to this precipice. Time to throw himself off and see if he could fly. "I worked with the promotions team on that idea. As part of my MBA. That's how I heard about your concussion this time around; I'm still kind of in touch with Terry."

"Terry, the president of the company?" she asked. He couldn't figure out how she was reacting, but it certainly wasn't anything joyful.

"Yeah. He actually offered me a job, after I graduated. I came back here instead, but we've stayed in touch."

She nodded slowly, and he tried to keep his mouth shut, tried to give her a bit of time to absorb the new information. He was leaning forward, intent on her face, and he barely even noticed as she picked up a dry chunk of pizza crust. But he definitely felt it when the pointy end of the crust bounced off his forehead, and he jerked back in protest.

"Hey!"

"I hate that poster! I look fake on both sides of it!"

"But do you like the money it makes you? You get a cut of that, right?"

She frowned at him for a few breaths and then grudgingly said, "Yeah. I like the money."

"Well, settle down, then." He was still feeling cautious, but he was pretty sure this was going to be okay. "No more food throwing. My mom's friends with the owners here. If I get kicked out, I'll never hear the end of it."

She had another piece of crust in her hand and looked down at it thoughtfully. He braced himself as she lifted her arm, and then he relaxed as she popped the food into her mouth.

"I'm sorry you didn't like the poster," he said. "I was thinking of it as a marketing tool, not, like, an expression of your true self."

She was still giving him the evil eye, but she was back to eating her pizza, so he was pretty sure he was okay. "So what *would* you want your posters to look like?"

She frowned, tilted her head as she thought, then smiled ruefully. "I don't think I want posters. I mean, you're right, I want the money. But if I'm made up, I'd feel fake, and if they were too real, it would feel like an invasion of privacy."

"So what do you like about it? The whole career. Just the money, or is there more to it?"

"The money's good," she said readily. "Other than that?" Another pause as she thought, and he was pretty sure this wasn't easy for her. She was being honest, opening up, and it made him feel flattered, and also a little protective. "I like being good at it, I guess," she finally said. "You know. Being good at *something*. Being the best, even. I know, it's just a small sport, and it's not like it's important or anything. I'm not curing cancer or promoting world peace. But . . . I'm good at it."

He nodded. He could understand that.

Then her smile changed from tentative to something wild and fierce. "And I like punching people," she added. "Kicks are fun, too, but a good punch? So hard and clean you can feel it all the way to your spine? I'd almost forgotten about it until this afternoon, but it's a good time."

"Okay," he agreed. He supposed he could understand this, too. "Being good at something and punching people."

"Yeah," she said. "Makes the furniture and real estate business sound a bit boring, right?"

"It does," he agreed, and he meant it.

FOR an evening that was almost certainly a mistake, Zara was having a really good time. Cal was easy to talk to and easy to look at. It was a bit awkward that practically every person in the restaurant seemed to be one of Cal's friends or acquaintances who needed to say hello and give Zara curious stares, but he got rid of most of them pretty quickly.

When he insisted on paying the bill for her celebration dinner, she didn't argue too hard. She was used to paying her own way, but this was okay, too.

And when he took her hand as they walked out of the restaurant, she let it happen. She could tell herself that she'd just been too surprised to resist, but that wasn't really true. She liked holding his hand. Liked being near him.

She hadn't had much to drink, so he drove her back to the community center parking lot and pulled in a few spaces down from her car. Then he got out and walked her those few feet, like he was afraid she might get mugged or something in just that distance. In Lake Sullivan.

He stood and waited as she unlocked the door. She turned back to him to say good night, and found him watching her in a not entirely casual way.

"What? Is there food on my face?" She gave it a quick swipe.

He laughed. "No. No food. I just . . . can we do this again? Not a celebration next time, just dinner? Or something else?"

"Something else? Like . . . fishing?"

"Do you fish?"

"Not if I can help it."

"Not fishing, then. But maybe you like movies? Or hiking, before the snow comes? Or, I don't know, horseback riding or antiquing—"

"Ooh, antiquing! That sounds exciting!"

"Okay, brat, maybe one of the other options. We can just sit around and watch TV if you want."

"Just to be crystal clear." Zara had no idea why she was feeling so confident, or how she'd managed to forget her many reasonable objections quite so quickly. But she didn't care, not right then. "This is a date we're talking about, right? You're asking me out, like, in a romantic way? Not just hanging out as friends?"

"Right," he said.

He was tall enough that she had to stretch to reach his lips, but it was worth the effort. Just a quick peck, surprising herself almost as much as she surprised him. "Okay," she agreed, and she leaned back.

Or at least, she started to, but she ran into the strong obstacle of his arms. He'd moved quickly, catching her, not pulling in tight, but not letting her back away, either. And they stood there like that for a moment, frozen.

She could break free. She knew it, and she knew he knew it. And somehow that meant she didn't have to. Didn't want to. She let herself relax, and felt him relax, too, and she slid her fingers inside his open jacket, along his waist, and rested her hands on his hips. It was kind of nice, standing there, wrapped up together against the chilly night air. But it got a hell of a lot nicer when he lowered his lips to hers.

It wasn't a peck this time. It was something slower and sweeter, and Zara could feel it from her lips to her toes. Her fingers tightened, grabbing hold of the fabric of Cal's shirt and then releasing it, stretching her hands out to feel the lean strength underneath it.

Cal pulled away before they even needed to break for a breath, but he didn't go far. His lips hovered there, a couple inches from hers, and then he leaned back in for another quick, light kiss. "Okay," he said. "When?"

"When what?" When would she have his babies? Anytime, really.

"When can I see you again?"

He was still seeing her now. What was the rush to start planning the next time, when they could have more *now*? But maybe this was how things were done in Lake Sullivan. A bit slower, a bit more old-fashioned. They were supposed to kiss like that, and then, just . . . go home, alone. Hell, most of her hookups in New York had skipped the *first* dinner and gone straight to the bedroom. But really, she'd never been all that impressed with any of that, so maybe this different approach was worth trying. "I don't know. Tomorrow? Oh, no, not tomorrow, I'm supposed to do something with Ashley tomorrow. Maybe the next day? Or not until the weekend, if you want. I don't know what your schedule is like." Or what his expectations were or what the rules were or much of anything else.

"Day after tomorrow," he said thoughtfully. "I think I can wait that long."

Zara wasn't sure she could. But now that she'd cooled down

at least a little, she thought maybe she liked the idea of not rushing into anything that night. And she definitely wasn't going to blow off a friend, even a new one, just to hook up with a guy. Ashley might understand, but that didn't make it okay. So Zara nodded her agreement to the plan, and this time when she turned to get into her car, Cal didn't stop her.

She drove home, her mind spinning and hopping over all the excitement. She was doing something worthwhile at her job. She was maybe starting something with a sweet guy. She could ignore their history and his family and the rest of it, at least for right then.

Zane's car wasn't in the driveway at home, and she wasn't sure if that should add to her happiness or take away from it. If he was off somewhere having fun, she was happy for him. But if he was back at that damn trailer, or off somewhere else feeling miserable and alone . . . well, she'd be sure to check in with him, let him know she was there for him, and that was about all she could think of.

She looked at her phone on the way into the house and that was what popped the happiness balloon. An e-mail from the company, reminding her of her next scheduled medical appointment.

Because that was her life. Because she had made commitments in that world, and because she made money there and knew where she belonged there. Whatever she was doing in Lake Sullivan, with her job or with Cal, it wasn't real. It was temporary, a distraction for her while she recovered enough to get back to her real world.

A good distraction, she told herself as she opened the front door and let herself in to the empty house. If she'd managed to forget about the rest of it for a while, that was good. Everything was going according to plan.

She just needed to remember that there *was* a plan. Something larger and more important than small-town community centers and handsome, charming distractions. She was the women's MMA champion, and she needed to remember that.

She typed in a quick reply to the reminder e-mail, confirming that she'd be there for the appointment. And when she went to bed, she tried not to think about Cal, or the center, or anything else that wasn't related to her getting healthy, getting fit, and getting back in the ring. She tried. But it took her a long, long time to fall asleep.

❧ Twelve ❧

CAL ARRIVED TO work the next morning to find Michael and his father waiting in his office. Somehow it was them being in his office that he found most annoying. They were clearly making a point, showing that it was their building and they had a right to visit any part of it they wanted. They might as well have peed in the corners of the room.

Cal was tempted to turn around and just start walking, but instead he smiled brightly at them. "Hey, guys! It's good to see you! What's up?"

His father looked taken aback, but Michael just rolled his eyes at Cal's fake charm. "You were seen in the parking lot at the community center last night. An inappropriate public display."

"Pull the stick out of your ass, Michael. It was a kiss." An amazing kiss, but its quality didn't make it any less appropriate.

"We've made it clear that we have concerns about the relationship," his father sputtered.

"And I've made it clear that I'm not looking for your approval." Cal shrugged his jacket off and kept talking as he hung it up. "I talked to an employment lawyer. He said that my employment is at will, so in general you can fire me if you want to. He said we could try for a wrongful dismissal lawsuit based on my right to privacy or something, but he said it'd be messy and not a guaranteed success." He strolled behind his desk and sat down. "But I don't think I'd sue you. So, you know, if this is a big enough deal for you, go ahead and fire me. If it isn't, I think you should stop wasting everyone's time with the threats and the bluster."

"We don't want to fire you!" His father sounded genuinely shocked. "Why do you keep rushing ahead to that? We just want you to remember who you are, and your obligations to your family!"

"By only dating family-approved women?" Cal shook his head. "No. I'm not interested in that."

"And you'd just walk away from the company?" Michael said. He sounded skeptical. "All because of a woman?"

"No. I'd walk away from the company, but not because of Zara. I'd do it because I won't live this way, with the two of you thinking you can run my life. I'm willing to follow your lead in business, but my private life is private." And while he was at it, he might as well keep going. "And that applies to any pressure you try to apply on a family level as well. If you can't support my decisions, fair enough. But I'm not going to listen to either one of you slamming either one of the Hales. So if I'm around, and you can't say something nice, say nothing at all."

"Or else what?" Michael scoffed. Another big brother who didn't realize his younger sibling had grown up.

"Or I won't be around." It was liberating to remember that he had options. "I can spend time with Mom without either of you, if I have to. And Michael, I can get a job somewhere else without any trouble. You understand that, right? I'm not like you; I haven't turned myself into a Montgomery Holdings specialist. My education, my skills—they're transferable. I'm working here because I'm loyal to the family, not because I have no other choice."

And that was the problem, Cal realized. The flash of clarity was somehow too bright, almost painful. For his father, at least, that was the problem. It wasn't about Zara, not really. Well, it was, but not because he didn't approve of her. It was because he feared her. He realized how tenuous his hold on Cal was, and saw her as a real threat to it. If Cal would just connect with a local woman, he'd have one more tie to the Lake Sullivan community, one more bond chaining him to the company and the family. But someone like Zara? Someone who'd left Lake Sullivan and thrived? She got in the way of that.

"You want to make sure I stay here," he said to his father. "I get that. But do you see that you're making it *less* likely that I'll stay?"

"Oh, don't flatter yourself," Michael said, sneering.

Cal turned to him and frowned. "Yeah. You wouldn't mind if I left. But if I do stay, you want to make sure I'm under your control. Doing as I'm told, not challenging you for your place in the company. So you're using this as an opportunity to throw your weight around when you know you've got Dad to back you up." He shook his head. "But it could backfire on you, just like it could backfire on Dad. Because you can't fire me, not without Dad's agreement, and he won't agree because his whole goal is to keep me in town and keep me working for the company. And if you can't fire me, but you can make me really resent working under you?" He saw Michael's expression change into something hard to look at, but made himself continue. "That's when I might start looking for ways to bump you out of your place in the company, so I could take over and not have you bugging me all the time."

He leaned back, suddenly tired of it all. "So that's where we're at, I think. Is there anything you guys wanted to add, or disagree with? If not, I've got work to do." He paused for just long enough to pretend he was giving them a chance to speak. "All right, then. As far as I'm concerned, the subject is closed. If you mention Zara or Zane Hale to me again, please speak with respect."

And that seemed to be that. Michael left the office looking like he'd swallowed a bug, but that was fairly close to his normal expression. Cal's father stayed behind for long enough to give him a cryptic, thoughtful look, but that was all.

Cal leaned back in his chair. He felt good. Light, and untroubled. He was looking forward to the future, leaving the past behind. And he definitely hoped that Zara Hale was part of his future. It was nice to have that out in the open.

"IT'S a stitch and bitch," Ashley said as if the words made sense. "You have to bring something to work on. Do you knit or anything?"

Zara stared at her. "You didn't mention knitting. And you absolutely didn't mention a *stitch and bitch*. You just said we should 'do something.' I was thinking . . . drinks maybe?"

"I didn't know about it until Mrs. Ryerson invited me this afternoon." She leaned in, her eyes bright with excitement, and whispered, "This is a total honor! There are women in this town who've been waiting for *years* to be invited to Mrs. Ryerson's stitch and bitch, and you and I are invited within weeks of moving to town. Yay!"

Zara was still staring. "But . . . why? I mean, what? We're supposed to knit? What is this about?"

Ashley leaned back a little, laughing triumphantly. "I have no idea! I've never been to one! But they do them here, I guess, and I live here now so I'm going to do them, and I got invited to a good one! And when I told Mrs. Ryerson why I couldn't make it, she was really excited to invite you, too. So we're going."

"To *knit*?"

"You could do some mending, if you have any?"

Zara shook her head slowly. Of course she didn't have mending. "You can just go without me," she said. "I'm a bit tired anyway. I was thinking about bailing tonight."

"No you weren't. And you're not bailing now, either. Just . . . I don't know, rip something, and put it in a bag, you can mend it and drink wine and bitch about stuff. Or whatever the hell it is we're doing. Or you can share my knitting, if you want. I have yarn, and Mrs. Ryerson said she has needles I can borrow."

"Do you know how to knit?"

"Of course not! I didn't know how to fish, either, but now I'm—well, I don't mean to brag, but I'm entering a derby this winter."

"Anyone can enter a derby." Zara might not have had the happiest childhood in Lake Sullivan, but she'd managed to soak up a few basic facts about the place.

But Ashley didn't seem concerned. "And anyone can knit, too. So let's go!"

Zara let it happen. She'd been caught off guard, she supposed. Softened by her time in Lake Sullivan. Tricked into a strange friendship with this ridiculous woman who was so excited about something called a stitch and bitch. If she was ever kidnapped by aliens, she'd probably end up going to their weird social rituals, too, just because she'd be too confused to object.

Ashley drove, which fit well into Zara's sense of abandoning herself to fate, and they made their way out of town to one of the houses by the lake. This one wasn't as palatial as some, but it was nice. Too nice. "Are you sure about this?" Zara asked. Maybe Ashley would just laugh and say the whole thing had been a prank, and they could go somewhere and have a couple beers and relax.

But Ashley had already reached into the backseat and retrieved a cloth grocery bag and a bottle of wine. "We're doing it," she said firmly.

So Zara let herself be led up the gravel driveway to the wide front porch. There was warm golden light shining out of the windows, and the night air was cool; Zara wanted inside, even though she wasn't sure what she was going to find there.

"Stitch and bitch," she muttered to herself, and then the door opened and Mrs. Ryerson smiled sweetly at them.

"I'm so glad you made it," she said. "Come on in; you can hang your coats there. We're in the back room."

They followed her back to find six other women of all ages sitting in easy chairs and on two long sofas, each of them with some sort of craft in their hands. They weren't all knitting. One was cutting pieces of fabric into squares, another had an easel set up and seemed to be painting something, and another . . .

Zara frowned at her. "Mrs. Grey?"

The woman smiled. "Hello, sweetie. It's good to see you."

The woman had taught Zara in second grade, and Zara had a sudden flash of memory, this woman giving her a sandwich—not once, but nearly every day. Zara had gone to her for lunch, even after she wasn't in her class anymore. And Mrs. Grey had provided, without ever making Zara feel bad about it. "It's good to see you, too," she said, and she meant it. But this was no place to go too deep into her memories, not with all these ladies watching her. "What are you working on?" she asked, crossing the room to examine Mrs. Grey's work.

"I'm crocheting lace."

Zara crouched down and stared at the delicate web spread over the woman's knee. Tiny filaments, thin even for thread, knotted together into an intricate, beautiful pattern. "What's it for?"

"I'm hoping it will be my granddaughter's wedding veil."

Zara squinted at the teacher. "You have a granddaughter?" She seemed too young.

And Mrs. Grey shook her head. "Not yet. But I have three children. And lace takes a long time to make, especially when I only work on it a couple times a month."

"So you might be putting all this time into it and it might never even get used?"

Mrs. Grey smiled slyly, then reached for her glass of wine. "I'll tell you a secret," she said in a stage whisper, and only then did Zara realize that the attention of the whole room was on them. "At a good stitch and bitch, the 'stitch' part is of secondary importance."

Zara leaned back a little. "So you guys are bitching about stuff?"

Mrs. Ryerson was beside them then, holding out a glass of wine for Zara. "It's not usually bitching," she said. "Just girl talk. I tried to get them to change the name to 'create and relate,' but it didn't take hold. But we banish the men for the evening and get caught up, and we have our needlework to make us feel productive." She smiled, then, and said, "I'm planning to show Ashley how to knit. Would you like me to show you, too?"

"Is knitting . . ." Zara looked down at the pattern on Mrs. Grey's knee. "Can you knit lace?"

"You can," Mrs. Ryerson said, "but I don't think there's anyone in our group who knows how to do it. If you're interested in working toward lace, you'd probably be best off learning to crochet."

"I can help you with that," Mrs. Grey said, setting her lace aside and burrowing through her bag before pulling out a much larger version of the needle she'd been using, along with a ball of mid-brown yarn. "Best to start big and work your way down."

"I don't want to interrupt your lace," Zara protested.

Mrs. Grey's eyes danced. "That's okay. I wasn't planning on doing much work after you two got here anyway. It'll be hard to keep close count of my stitches when I'm hearing about you and Calvin Montgomery!"

Zara stared at her, then at the circle of expectant faces. "What?" she managed, her mouth dry.

"Is it a secret?" Mrs. Grey asked. "I mean, you were making out in the community center parking lot, as I understand it. That's not exactly subtle."

"It's not a secret," Zara managed. "It's just—there's nothing—I mean, he's a friend of my brother's. . . ."

The woman with the easel shook her head. "Pointless to deny it, honey. You forgot you were in Lake Sullivan, right? Everybody knows everybody, and with a public declaration like that? Privacy is *gone*."

It wasn't so much that Zara had thought they were alone the night before in the parking lot. It was more that she hadn't thought at all. Hadn't wondered who might see them, hadn't been concerned about how it all might look. She'd been completely unaware of her surroundings, oblivious to anything other than Cal's strong arms and gentle smile.

"No," she said, mostly to herself, but willing to let anyone hear. "It was . . . it's not a thing! I live in New York! I'm just visiting here, just—" She made herself stop. This was a funny little bit of gossip for everyone else; she was the only one making it into a big deal. She forced herself to laugh. "Wow. Okay, yeah," she admitted to the painter. "I forgot I was back in Lake Sullivan. Good reminder, lesson learned." She took a deep swallow of her wine, and it shut her up, at least for the moment.

The other women mercifully changed the subject, and Mrs. Grey whispered, "Sorry. I didn't think it would be a touchy subject."

Zara forced another laugh. "No, it's fine. I'm just wound a little tight about that sort of stuff. Not good at, you know, at being casual about things. It's not a big deal." Not a big deal with Cal, and not a big deal that people knew about Cal. Not that there was anything to know.

"Do you want it to be a big deal?" Mrs. Grey asked gently.

"No! I mean, it really can't be. I'm going home." She'd already decided not to mention the occasional dizzy spells at her physical; she couldn't be sure they were related to her concussion, but the doctors would be stupid about it. She was going back to fighting, and once she was back in that world, there wouldn't be room for Cal. She couldn't afford the distraction.

Ashley was beside her now. Had been for a while maybe, but Zara's panic had made her vision tunnel a bit. "There are ways to make long-distance work," Ashley said. "It's a challenge, but not impossible."

Mrs. Grey raised an eyebrow. "Have you and Josh spent more than two nights in a row apart since you got together?" She shook her head in amusement and told Zara, "Josh is family, so I know what he's up to. Believe me when I tell you that, for those two, the 'long-distance' part is the travel they're doing together, jetting from Vermont to wherever she's shooting."

"It's not the distance, really," Zara said. Not the physical distance, at least.

"So what is it?" Ashley asked. She pulled a couple occasional chairs over to nestle in on either side of Mrs. Grey; apparently Ashley had abandoned her knitting lessons, at least temporarily.

Zara sighed, and looked at Mrs. Grey. "Josh is one thing. But Cal Montgomery? I do not have a good history with that family. No way. I'm not looking to spend time with any of them."

"Except Cal," Ashley prompted.

"I don't know, maybe not even him. The more we talk about this, the less I like the sound of it."

They were silent for a while, and then Mrs. Grey held the hook out to Zara. "You control the yarn with one hand, the hook with the other." She ran the yarn around as it should be and took a few moments to show Zara the basic stitches. Mrs. Ryerson wandered over with what were apparently knitting needles and busied herself with Ashley, and everything was peaceful for a while. Zara focused on what she was doing, trying to make the yarn behave, and listened with half an ear to the conversation going on around her, updates on families and careers, triumphs and frustrations.

When the next pause came in the conversation, Mrs. Grey caught Zara's eye and said, "What's your bad history like? With the Montgomerys?"

Zara had known the conversation hadn't shifted for good. And there was something about the crocheting, the simple rhythm of it, the feel of the yarn sliding through her fingers . . . something soothing. It made her feel safe, and ready to talk. "It's nothing serious, really. But Zane—my brother— and Cal have always been friends, so I was always a bit . . . a bit aware of the family, I guess. I mean, like it would be possible not to be, around here. You guys know that. In the summer there are lots of rich people, but in the winter? The Montgomerys run this town. And I was a pretty bratty kid. So when I got in trouble, a lot of the time it seemed to involve them."

"I don't get it," Ashley said. "What kind of trouble?"

Zara sighed. Was this stuff funny or sad? She wasn't sure. "Well, I was stubborn. And stupid. So one year on the night before Halloween some friends and I egged their cars. We couldn't reach the house from the street and we were too chicken to get closer, so we stuck to the cars. And they made a really big deal out of it. The Montgomerys could have just, you know, hosed the cars off and carried on, but they called the cops, and if it was anyone else, the cops would have just told them to get over it, but it was the Montgomerys so of course there was a big investigation. And they questioned a bunch of kids at school, and one of the kids I was with blamed it all on me." He'd told her later that he'd given her name because he knew she didn't have the sort of parents who would get her in trouble. He'd been worried that if he didn't tell the police something, his parents would take away his new cell phone. But she didn't think she'd share that part of the story. "And I wouldn't give up any other names, so it all got blamed on me. So I had to apologize to all the Montgomerys, even the boys." She'd forgotten about that, forgotten the smug look on Michael's face and the sympathetic mortification on Cal's as she'd stood in the foyer of their opulent home and repeated the rote words supplied by the police officer. She hadn't wanted to do it at all, but Zane had insisted that she make the problem go away before anyone looked at the family too closely and asked them just where their father was that week. "And I had to wash their cars, and do a bunch of chores in their yard. Raking leaves or whatever."

"That sucks," Ashley said gently. "But I'm not really seeing the part where you were stubborn."

"Well, that part came later," Zara admitted. "After the first time, I got a bit better at knowing who to work with, if I was going to do pranks." She'd learned to find other rough kids with nothing to lose; she'd learned that kids with money were weak and couldn't be trusted. "So they never caught me again."

"But you egged them again?"

"Hell, yeah. Almost weekly. One of the guys I was hanging around with had chickens, and he'd steal eggs before his mom collected them. We'd hit the Montgomerys' cars, wherever they parked around town, or the house—we got better at sneaking up on it through the woods—and when Michael was running in a cross-country race one time, we put on masks and jumped out from behind trees and pelted him."

"Wait a second." Mrs. Grey squinted at her. "I remember that! But he was in high school when that happened. And he's got to be six or seven years older than you? How old were you when all this was going on?"

"I don't know, ten or eleven?" Zara thought back. "Fifth grade. How old is that?"

"I was picturing you as a teenage hoodlum," Ashley said. "But you were just a little girl!"

Zara wasn't sure she liked where this was going. She was okay with being seen as a crazy, stupid kid, but Ashley sounded like maybe she was going to start asking where Zara's parents had been and why she'd been given so much freedom. "I was pretty angry when I was younger," she said quickly. "Really stupid. Wild. I didn't realize—" She stopped. It had been a long time since she'd thought about any of this. "I didn't think of them as people, I guess. I was just mad that they had all this stuff that I wanted, and that they seemed so happy, and they could just run around town and do whatever they wanted and everyone just smiled at them, and no matter what I did, people thought I was bad."

"A bit of a vicious circle?" Mrs. Grey suggested. "They thought you were bad so you did bad things so they thought you were bad."

"Right," Zara agreed.

"So what happened?" Ashley asked. "How did it end?"

"Zane caught me." Zara could still remember the strong hand clamping around her thin wrist as she'd had her arm pulled back, ready to the throw the egg. "Cal had told him I was doing it, but I denied it. So Zane followed me from home and tracked me through the forest and caught me."

"And did what?" Ashley's eyes were wide.

"I think it must have been the first time I'd ever lied to him," Zara said. "I'd told him I wasn't doing it, and then he caught me in the act, and he was *hurt*. And mad, too. He cracked the egg over my head and made me walk home all covered in yolk and told me I'd better not ever do it again. That was the him-being-mad part. But I might have ignored that, if that had been all there was. It was the him-being-hurt part that made me stop." She frowned. What the hell was she doing, telling something like that to these people? They were practically strangers, and she was yipping away like they were family. Time to get story time wrapped up. "So that was it for the eggs. But, you know, it kind of set a tone. There may have been a few other incidents over the years."

"And Cal was still friends with Zane through all this?"

"Yeah. Cal thought I was a brat, but he didn't take it too seriously." Another point Zara hadn't really remembered.

"I'd always wondered what the full story was on all that," one of the knitters said. Then she smiled. "Good for you! There've been a few times I wouldn't have minded throwing a few eggs at Winston Montgomery through the years!"

"And Michael's just as bad," another woman agreed. Then she looked craftily in Zara's direction. "Calvin has always been pleasant, though. And so handsome!"

There was some chatter then, about Cal's physical charms and the personalities of various Montgomerys, and Zara listened to it all but didn't seem required to speak anymore. She felt her shoulders gradually relaxing down from around her ears. This was okay. She'd done a little bitching, she was doing a little stitching. It was all working out.

Mrs. Ryerson came by to refill her glass of wine and laid a gentle hand on Zara's shoulder. "I'm so glad you came tonight," she said quietly. "And I'm glad you're back in Lake Sullivan. Even if it is just for a little while."

And sitting there in the warm room with the laughing women? At least for right then, Zara was glad she was back, too.

❧ *Thirteen* ❧

CAL WAS TRYING to play it cool, and not doing a very good job. He knew he needed to be low-key. If he went too big, too much too fast, Zara would bolt. He shouldn't borrow a yacht and take her for a moonlight cruise while caterers provided dinner and a violinist serenaded them. That would be a mistake. He'd heard the stories about Ashley's nonsense when she and Josh were starting up, and he knew he shouldn't repeat any of her blunders. But he should still do something special surely. Something that would stand out and show Zara he was serious.

He settled on reservations for dinner in St. Albans. He was pretty sure Zara would be happy to get out of town. But when he called her in the afternoon to work out details, he could feel the hesitation even over the phone line.

"I thought we could go for dinner," he suggested.

"Uh . . . actually, I have to work until seven. And then I

was thinking I should work out. You know, start getting back in shape."

He felt a flare of impatience and tamped it down hard. Yeah, she was trying to back out of it, but that was her right. If she'd changed her mind, she'd changed her mind. But that didn't mean he couldn't try to change it back again. "What kind of workout were you planning?"

She sounded like he'd caught her off guard. "Uh, cardio, I think?"

"Running?"

"Yeah, I guess."

"I can go with you, then. Show you some of the trails. There's some new ones, down by the lake. They wouldn't have been around when you lived here."

"I go pretty hard," she said. "This wouldn't be, like, a chance for much chatting."

But once they were done, once he'd worn off a bit more of her shell, maybe she'd let him take her somewhere else, somewhere they *could* talk. "That's okay. I like running. I don't need to be entertained."

A pause, and then she said, "Yeah. Okay. I was planning to leave from the community center around seven. It'll be dark by then—are the trails lit?"

"Not the ones I was thinking of, no. But I can find an alternate route if the moon isn't bright."

"You don't have to."

"I know I don't have to. But is it okay with you if I do? I don't want to pressure you into anything, but . . . it's just running. Pretty safe, I think."

"Yeah, pretty safe," she agreed, and it sounded like she was loosening up a little. "Okay. Yeah. That sounds good."

So he called the restaurant and cancelled the reservations,

made sure he had food and wine in his fridge, and tried to keep his mind on work until just before seven. Then he went home, changed into his running clothes, and jogged the few blocks to the community center.

Zara was at the front doors waiting for him, shuffling restlessly in her grey and black running gear. He wanted to greet her with a kiss, but her body language made it pretty clear that wouldn't be welcome. Damn it. Two steps forward, one step back. But even if he couldn't touch her, it was still good to see her.

"Ready to go?" he asked.

She nodded, and they set off. "Do you do a lot of cardio work?" It wasn't the best setting for conversation, but Cal was at least going to try. "For fighting, I mean? Is cardio important?"

"Some trainers push it, others don't," she replied. "I do a lot of sprint-based work, resistance bands, that sort of thing, more than running. Explosive power, anaerobic stuff." She shrugged. "But I like running. I do it for myself."

"Have you been running all along? Since you got here, I mean?"

"No." They were at the end of the block, about to cross Main Street and head over toward the school yard, before she added, "I was taking it easy. Because of my head. But I'm back on track now."

God, he wanted to talk about her head. Wanted to interrogate her, understand just how serious the concussions had been, what the prognosis was for the future. He wanted to know if she'd been scared, or if she still was. But her armor was up, almost full strength. If he pushed now, he wouldn't find ways to get past the barriers; he'd just push her away. And that wasn't what he wanted. Not at all.

"There's a full moon," she said. "The new trails by the water—would they get the light, or are they shaded?"

"Not much shade. Want to head down there?"

She nodded, and at the next corner they turned in that direction. The town wasn't big. One strip of commercial development down Main Street, and an extra strip one block down by the water. The places by the shore were more touristy: a small marina and boat charter place, a few gift and novelty shops, an artists' co-op, a specialty candy store. During the off-season they either closed up entirely or were only open a couple days a week, but they were busy during the summer when the cottagers and tourists came through. The front windows were dark now, showing Cal two reflected runners as they passed by.

"What do you do?" Zara asked, and the question was so out of the blue that Cal turned to stare at her. "I mean, with your time. I know you have a job, and you exercise, and then . . . what? You've got friends in town?"

"Yeah, sure. I know there's not a lot of stuff to do here, compared to the city. One bar, one restaurant. No movies unless we drive out of town. But there's good outdoor recreation—I sure didn't spend much time kayaking or rock climbing when I was in New York, and I felt like every breath I took when I was running was dragging pollution into my lungs."

"Nah. The pollution makes you stronger! It's like training at altitude—if you get used to the bad air, when you get good air, you're super-powered."

"Is that your own theory, or is it backed up by some sort of expert?"

"I *am* an expert," she protested, but he could hear the laughter in her voice. "I'm a professional athlete, remember?"

A pause, and then she added, "I was in talks to do a fitness video. But that kind of got put on hold. Still, I'm a definite expert. Working out in dirty air is good."

"Maybe we can stop somewhere and pick up some cigarette butts and strap them to your nose somehow. Would that be useful?"

"That would be great. Keep your eyes open."

She was relaxing now. Whatever had gotten her tense seemed to be wearing off. So Cal wasn't all that surprised when she sped up and darted in front of him, stretching her legs on the gravel path, pushing for more speed.

He matched her. With any other woman he'd dated, he would have been confident that he'd win any physical contest and maybe been wondering how much to pace himself in order not to make her mad about her defeat. With Zara, he figured he'd be lucky if he could keep up, and he loved it.

They flew down the pathway. A man walking a little dog appeared after they went around a bend, and the dog darted out into the path, trying to catch Zara as she ran past. She didn't break stride, just stretched and vaulted over the creature. Cal followed suit. His lungs were starting to burn, but he felt alive.

He pushed himself just a little harder, finding a spot by Zara's side, and they ran in tandem for a hundred yards or so. Then he tried to take the lead, and she refused to give it up. He pushed harder, and she matched him. They were in a full-out sprint now, Cal's longer legs enough to let him match Zara's power but not enough to actually beat her. They ran on, gasping for air, pushing, driving. . . .

And then Zara was gone. One stride she'd been right beside him, the next she seemed to stumble, and then he couldn't see her at all. He brought himself to a stop as quickly as he could and turned to see her standing in the middle of the trail, bent over, hands braced on her knees.

For a moment he felt victorious. Then she rolled to the side, barely catching herself with her hand and a knee, and his stomach dropped. This was something more than just being winded.

He didn't think about moving, but somehow he was just there, crouching beside her, supporting her as she shifted onto her butt, sitting in the dirt with her head between her knees. She was gasping for breath, but not as hard as he was. This was something else. He remembered her dizziness in the locker room when she'd heard about Zane's arrest. Damn it.

"Your head? Shit, Zara, are you okay? Dizzy?"

She lifted a hand, telling him she was okay, or telling him to shut up. Possibly both. He did his best to comply, feeling completely useless.

After a few agonizing moments, she said, "I'm okay. I just . . . I don't know. But I'm fine." She lifted her head, slow and cautious. "Just something weird. No big deal."

"Post-concussion syndrome," he said. He didn't care if it was a touchy subject, he was still going to mention it. "It's a real thing. Concussions are serious, and you're still recov—" He broke off as she rolled away from him, struggling to her knees with the clear intention of standing up.

"Hang on!" He reached for her, then drew his hand back. "I'll be quiet, okay? I'll sit here quietly. Just take it easy, don't push so hard."

It couldn't be easy for her to hear those words or follow that advice, he realized. She'd escaped her background and made herself a success by pushing hard, by being tough and charging through obstacles. Now she'd run into something she couldn't just bash her way through, and it was throwing her off.

She reluctantly resettled on the ground next to him, and he had the feeling it was her dizziness rather than his words that had prompted her.

They were both still breathing hard. He remembered the glorious freedom he'd felt, the joy in being alive and healthy and letting his body move the way it was meant to, and the memory twisted into something ugly and selfish when he realized that it was his competitiveness that had pushed Zara into overexerting herself. She'd suggested they go for a run. A quiet, easy jog, not a mad sprint. "I'm sorry," he said quietly.

She raised her head and stared at him through eyes that suddenly seemed a little too focused and intent. "What the hell for?"

"For pushing. Making you race."

"Oh my God, do you really think you have that kind of power over me?" She snorted. "I make my own decisions, Calvin!"

"Cal," he said quickly.

There was a moment when he thought she was going to make one of her own decisions right then and there, and it might involve her struggling up and trying to stagger away. But finally, her shoulders lowered a little and she quietly said, "Cal."

They sat there for a while, not talking until she slowly leaned forward, got her feet underneath herself, and rose. There were twigs stuck to her butt, but Cal managed to resist the urge to brush them off. Instead, he climbed to his feet and stood next to her, ready to catch her if she fell.

"I've got a doctor's appointment tomorrow," she said, her voice low and level. "They'll check me out. So I don't really need to hear anything more about this from you. Understood?"

"Will you tell me what the doctors say tomorrow?"

"If I feel like it."

"You don't give an inch, do you?"

"Give? Like, charity? You need me to give you things?"

Her voice was edgy, but teasing rather than vicious. She was obviously feeling better.

"Hell, yeah. I could use a little charity around you."

She looked at him, assessing. "Nah, I don't think you need it." Then she nodded down the path. "Does this come out by the old church?"

He tried to catch up with the topic change. "They tore that church down years ago."

"Really? That's too bad. I liked that church."

"They weren't still having services there when you lived here, were they?"

"No, I didn't, like, *go* to the church. But the windows in the back were broken, so we used to climb in sometimes and hang out."

What a different childhood she'd had from his. What had he been doing while she was breaking into abandoned churches? Golf lessons? Ski trips?

She started walking down the path toward the church site. He jogged a few steps to catch up. "I think it's probably closer to go back the way we came. Or we could cut through the woods there, and you could sit by the road until I brought the car around. Would you feel okay doing that? It's a safe town, and maybe you could stay in the trees?"

She turned and stared at him. "Really? You think I'm going to hide in the trees? In Lake Sullivan? At, what, seven thirty at night? Jesus, Cal."

Okay, good point. But what was she doing . . . was she starting to *jog*? "Hey! Where are you going?"

"Down to the church. Then we can circle back and go home along the road. Right?"

"You want to keep running? You almost passed out!"

She'd broken into a slow jog now. "No, I don't think so. I was just a bit dizzy. It's gone."

"You don't think so? Well, then, let's add memory loss to your list of symptoms! You were on the ground!"

"I sat down!" She was running faster now. Trying to get away from this conversation? Was he making things worse?

Probably. So he stopped talking, and ran along just behind her, hoping to drag her down to a lower speed. Possibly a walk. Best-case scenario, maybe she'd let him carry her.

But his wishes did him no good. She kept jogging, and he ran on, his heart in his throat.

"What are you doing back there?" she asked as they rounded the corner at the churchyard. "Oh my God, are you waiting for me to fall, and then planning on catching me?"

"Maybe."

"You are so annoying!"

"Yeah, I'm the annoying one here."

She stopped running and turned to face him, her hands on her hips, her jaw jutted out in challenge or warning.

He spent a moment wishing he could take back his words, then decided that he didn't want to take them back. And if he wasn't going to retract them, he might as well enhance them. "You snap at me whenever I express natural human concern. You pull me in and then push me away. You do things that are stupid and maybe even dangerous and just expect me to be okay with them. I understand that these are your decisions to make, but I think it's pretty damn selfish of you to make them without even taking a *second* to consider how they might affect people who care about you!"

"People who care about me? Like *who*?"

It stopped him for a moment. What must it be like to go through life thinking you were completely alone? And how sad was it that Zara was thinking like that even though she *wasn't* alone? "Your roommate. Bonita? I talked to her a bit when you were avoiding me, and she seemed pretty concerned about you. Zane loves you—" He raised his hands and nodded quickly in a sort of combined acknowledgment and dismissal. "He's going through his own shit and has no idea how to relate to you as an adult, but he loves you. You're not going to stand here and tell me he doesn't, are you?"

She wouldn't meet his gaze right away, but finally looked at him and shrugged reluctantly. "No, I won't tell you that."

"Okay. And I think Ashley likes you pretty well, from what I've seen. I'm sure there are others that I just don't know about. And, Zara, there's me. I'm the one you're ignoring right now, right? You clearly don't care how I feel, watching you run yourself ragged."

"Do I look ragged to you?"

"No, you look gorgeous to me. But it's possible that I'm a bit biased. Because of the 'caring about you' thing."

She stared at him and he could see the struggle playing behind her eyes. It would be so much easier for her to stay remote and untouched and safe. So hard for her to accept even this slight intimacy. She frowned and said, "So, what, do we make out now? Is that the plan?"

He snorted. "No way. I don't make out with annoying people." He turned and started walking along the street. And he let himself grin, since she couldn't see his face, when he heard her walking along behind him.

"You made out with me the other night! In the parking lot!"

"You weren't being annoying then."

"Oh. So it's not so much that you don't make out with annoying people. It's that you don't make out with people when they're *being* annoying." She was dancing around to the side of him now, trying to catch his eye.

"Do you think you're going to seduce me with nitpicking? Really?"

"Seduce you! Oh my God, as if that's what I'm doing!"

"Well, what're you doing, then? You're the one who keeps talking about making out."

"Oh, Cal, Cal," she said, her voice high-pitched enough to make it clear she was joking. "I feel so faint. I think I might swoon. Please, Cal, save me! Catch me!"

Well, she might just be joking, but that didn't mean he couldn't do it. He turned, leaned, wrapped one arm around her back and caught her under the knees with his other, and lifted her lightly off the ground. One of her hands instinctively wrapped around his neck while the other hovered indecisively in the air. They stared at each other and then slowly, carefully, she brought her free hand to his jaw and guided his mouth toward hers.

The angle wasn't right, but Cal took what he could get. And when she squirmed a little, trying to improve things, he let her slide gently to the ground, balancing her as she went, and not breaking the kiss for even a moment.

He pulled her unresisting body in against his, deepened the kiss, and lost track of everything but her warm skin, the faint, healthy smell of her sweat, her soft lips, and then, oh, God, the tiny, breathy sound she made when their lips parted for a moment.

He didn't notice the headlights until he felt her body stiffen and pull away from him. He let her go, watched the car pass, and then they stood there, both of them catching their breath.

Zara recovered first. "See? You did want to make out." Her smile was a dare, her eyebrows a challenge, but there was a softness in her smile that made it all okay.

"I guess so," he agreed. "You know me better than I know myself."

"Seems like." She started walking then, back toward

town, and when he caught up with her, she said, "This was a crappy workout. You and your obsession with public kissing got in the way of my exercise."

"Can I point out that both times that we've kissed in public, you started it?"

"I started it? What are you, six years old?"

She was stubborn. Competitive. Completely annoying. He reached for her hand and she let him take it and lace their fingers together. She was all that and more, and he wanted as much of her as she would give him.

EVERYTHING felt out of control, and Zara didn't like it. Well, she *mostly* didn't like it. She'd worked hard to put herself in a place where she could make her own decisions, and she liked to make them based on what was rational, and what was most likely to keep her in that place of independence. Getting involved with Cal Montgomery definitely wasn't going to help keep her life calm and controlled. But somehow, she couldn't bring herself to let go of his hand.

Would it be so bad? If she let him in a little, trusted him . . . well, she already did trust him, she supposed. He'd been around forever, in the background. The mess with Zane had been . . . it had been a mess. But probably not Cal's fault. And he'd been so good with Zane ever since, so kind and generous with his time. And damn, he could kiss.

"Have you had dinner?" he asked as they approached the parking lot.

The lie was on her lips before she'd even thought about it, put there by years of training in self-protection. She should tell him she'd eaten. She should get away from him, stop letting herself be stupid, go home and have a sandwich and a shower, and then go to bed. It was the smart thing to do. But the same rebellious instinct that had controlled her hand and kept it entwined with his now took over her mouth. It caught the lie and told the truth instead. "No, not yet."

"We're probably a bit sweaty to go anywhere public. But if you want, I can cook for us. I just live a couple blocks away."

Her stomach lurched nervously, but the sensation wasn't completely unpleasant. Going to his apartment. Being alone with him somewhere private. She knew what that meant.

And her protective instinct kicked back into gear and told her she should absolutely go. This relationship should get physical as soon as possible. They needed to quit talking so much and just get themselves into bed; sex would take care of whatever this weird tension was between them, this strange awareness Zara was developing for Cal. She just needed to sleep with him and get him out of her system. "Sure," she said. "Your place. Sounds good."

So they walked on, heading back toward the lake, and Zara eventually realized they weren't going to an apartment building. Which made sense. When she was imagining Cal's home, she was seeing him in a Manhattan high-rise, sleek and modern with floor-to-ceiling windows and abstract art on the walls. But there was nothing like that in Lake Sullivan. Apartments in small towns tended to be for poor people, and that didn't fit Cal at all.

Still, she was a little surprised when they turned into the driveway of a little stone cottage. It had one of the town's bronze heritage plaques on the wall, designating it as *The Fisher Home*; Cal saw her looking at the sign and shrugged. "I like to think of it as The Montgomery Home, but I guess the town council disagrees."

"They can't *make* you have that there, can they?"

He shook his head. "No. But it doesn't actually bother me, and it's pretty important to the heritage crew." He looked over his shoulder with mock caution, then turned back to her and whispered, "My mom."

Zara wondered what it would be like to have parents pressuring her to support their hobbies. Probably kind of nice, really.

She followed Cal through the front **door into** a house that looked nothing like its exterior. There were hardly any walls, just beams left behind as needed for support, and the living room, dining room, and kitchen were distinguished more by different types of furniture than by any actual barriers. She was pretty sure the furniture and fixtures and whatever were all high quality and expensive, and maybe the lighting was specially designed to give the place a warm, cozy glow, so really it was all artifice. But it worked. The cottage felt like a home, and Zara couldn't really imagine Cal living in that Manhattan high-rise anymore.

There was a small room to the left of the front door that Zara peeked into, and Cal said, "My office. It's boring. But the bathroom's around the other side of it. Upstairs is just my bedroom and bathroom and a little guest . . . probably guest closet would be the best description." He headed for the kitchen. "Do you want something to drink? Wine, or beer, or juice, or milk? I think that's about it."

"Sure, a beer. Thanks." She wasn't technically back in training yet, after all.

He pulled two out of the fridge, opened them both, and handed one to her. Then he grinned like a schoolboy. "I feel weird. I like having you here, but I think I'm thrown off because I'm all sweaty. So then I think maybe I should go shower, but that seems a bit impolite for me to get myself clean and not offer the same to you. And I have two showers, you could totally use one, but then are you just going to get back into your workout clothes, or do I loan you something of mine, which, you know, wouldn't fit, and maybe it's a bit early to be sharing clothes." He took a swig of his beer. "So that's where I am. You?"

"I'm thinking we should both shower, in one shower, and then not worry too much about clothes for a while."

He blinked hard. "Well, that's an idea with some merit, for sure."

"Some merit?" She fought past the insecurity and tried to channel her inner vixen. She added what she hoped was a sultry purr to her voice as she asked, "That's the best you can do?"

He huffed out a breath. "I just—you didn't even want to come out with me tonight. Right? This run was an excuse so we wouldn't have to have dinner together? So you're pretty clearly having doubts about things. Going back and forth. And I want to be sure you don't end up regretting anything."

"You think I'd regret sleeping with you? That sounds like you've got a bit of an inferiority complex."

But he refused to take the bait. "You know what I mean. I don't want to take advantage of you at a weak moment."

Zara had heard about enough of this. "Give me a break. You're trying so hard to be respectful and a good little gentleman that you're treating me like a child! You're stuck back at, like, second-wave feminism, thinking that any sex is taking advantage of a woman!"

"Second-wave feminism? Where are you pulling that from?" He sounded genuinely confused, and she wasn't sure whether to be irritated because he was getting off topic or because he seemed surprised she even knew the term.

"I'm literate, you know! I might not have gone to your fancy schools, but I can read! Did it never occur to you that a woman working in a male-dominated world might try to figure things out, and might do a bit of reading to get ideas?"

"So you're into feminist theory?" He still didn't sound

angry. He wasn't fighting with her, he was just genuinely interested.

"Maybe!" she spat back.

He nodded, and took a swig of his beer. "Any chance we could talk about that? I could cook some dinner—something manly, like steaks, so we wouldn't be challenging any gender paradigms—and you could explain the different waves to me. I've heard the basics, but I'm hardly an expert. It sounds interesting."

It was a trap. She knew it, and she had to get out of it. "So you're ignoring what I said I wanted. No sex, because you say so."

"Well, yeah. I'm not sure what kind of feminism you want to talk about, but 'no means no' is still going to be a part of it, right?" He was almost teasing now, but she could tell he was being cautious, not sure how far he could push her.

And she wasn't sure, either. "But the *reason* you're saying no is paternalistic! I'm an adult. I make my own decisions."

"And I make mine," he said firmly. "You don't like the way I phrased it? How about this: *I* don't want to be some-body's regret. *I* don't like the idea of you or anyone else waking up and thinking she made a mistake. That would be bad for *me*. So I'm not protecting you from your deci-sions. I'm protecting *me* from them."

She stared at him. What could she say to that? And what did she want to say? She frowned at him, and he nodded, an acknowledgment of her frustration that somehow didn't seem like he was making fun of it. He made her feel like they were in this together. She had no idea what "this" was, but it seemed to involve both of them.

And maybe she was okay with that. "Steak and what?" she asked. Then she added, "And no. If I'm not showering, neither are you. We can stink together."

"Okay," he agreed easily. Then he turned toward the fridge. "Steak and garlic potatoes? Then we'll both really stink. I can grill them outside. And maybe a Greek salad? Sound good?"

"Sounds great," Zara had to agree. She perched on a stool and drank her beer and watched Cal cooking, and tried to ignore how good it felt. How nice it would be to be able to relax into this sort of domesticity. She needed to resist. Her life was elsewhere. But for that night, at least, she let herself pretend it wasn't.

❧ *Fourteen* ❧

"I'M TAKING A class from your lady friend." Cal's mother had swept into his office only a moment earlier, offered a perfunctory greeting, taken a seat, and then produced that statement.

Cal squinted at her. "With . . . Zara? What kind of class?"

"Mixed Martial Arts." His mother pronounced the words as if each was from a partially known foreign language. "It's quite interesting."

"You're taking an MMA class?" And Zara hadn't bothered to mention that to him? "Why?"

"Why do you think?"

"Because you've always had a secret interest in it?" he said with hope but not much true optimism.

"No. Although I'm finding it less objectionable than I'd feared."

"You're doing it to spy on Zara?"

"I don't think I'd use the word 'spy.' But, yes, I did think it was a good opportunity to learn a bit more about her. To see her in her natural habitat, as it were."

"She's not an exotic animal. Her habitat is the same as everyone else's."

"So if she's not rare and exotic, what is it that you find so intriguing about her?"

"Pure carnal lust," Cal lied.

His mother'd had work done on her face over the years, but the lift of her eyebrow made it clear she hadn't bothered with Botox. "I don't think so. Not that she isn't a very attractive young woman. But there's more to it, isn't there?"

"Why are we having this conversation?"

She smiled. "Because your father and your brother are becoming tedious in their objections, and I want this nonsense to stop. If your interest in the young woman is temporary, it will be easiest for me to convince them of that and tell them to let it go. But if your interest is more long-term, I'll need to take a firmer hand with them and override their objections." Her calm expression made it clear that she had no doubt of her ability to succeed via either path, and he knew better than to challenge her. "So which is it? Temporary infatuation best ignored, or longer-term interest that should be recognized?"

"If it's up to me, longer-term interest," he said firmly. "But I can't guarantee that she feels the same way."

"Is that right?" His mother's smile was genuine, but still somehow fierce. "Good. It's about time you dated someone who made you work a little."

"She's making me work a lot."

"That'll be good exercise for you. After all, it's the trying that makes you strong."

He was pretty sure she was referring to something beyond their current conversation, but didn't bother to try to follow the thread. "Okay, well, I'll keep working at it."

"Excellent. And I'll work on Michael and your father." She rose gracefully and smiled at him. "I think I've got the easier task." Then she swept out, and Cal leaned back in his chair to process it all.

He wanted to call Zara. Wanted to set something up, make a plan, do *something* to cast another tiny thread between them, fastening them together, however loosely.

He checked his watch. After a bit of badgering the night before, she'd admitted that her doctor's appointment was in the early afternoon, in the city, but he hadn't been able to get an exact time from her. Still, he knew she'd be on her way down there now. So he shouldn't call, shouldn't distract her while she was driving. It wasn't like she didn't have enough on her mind.

He called Zane instead. Zara had insisted on setting her brother up with a cell phone and he was getting better about carrying it with him, but Cal was still a bit surprised when Zane picked up. He'd been prepared to leave a message, rather than actually have the conversation right then and there.

"What's up?" Zane asked.

"Uh, not much. You at work?"

"No, I'm working afternoons and evenings."

After the kids were out of school. Cal knew that. "So I guess you don't want to get a beer tonight?"

"We can if you want. I'm off work at nine."

Well, Cal had kind of been hoping to be with Zara by that time, but really, this was more important. Well, not more important, but it had to be done. "Yeah, okay."

"You planning to sit me down and tell me about you and Zara?" Zane asked.

Cal froze for a moment, then said, "Uh . . . yeah, actually. You already know? She told you?" That didn't seem likely somehow.

"Zara? Hell, no. But about ten other people have. You guys aren't exactly sneaking around."

"I didn't know you knew ten other people."

"I grew up here. I know people. And when they think they can get some gossip out of me, all of a sudden they all remember that they know me, too."

"Sorry," Cal said. "You should have heard about it from me or Zara."

"So it's a thing? Like, it's something serious?"

Cal snorted. "No idea. I'd like it to be, I think. But Zara's not exactly predictable, or tractable—I have no idea if she's going to let it happen."

Zane was quiet for long enough that Cal was about to pull his phone away from his ear to be sure the call was still connected. Then quietly, Zane said, "I think it could be good. For both of you. You know, if it got more serious. I'd be okay with it."

"Yeah?"

"Yeah. But you know, at the same time, standard big brother warnings apply, okay? You need to treat her right, and if you hurt her, I break your legs. That sort of thing."

"Both legs?"

"Maybe your arms, too."

"Okay. Good to have the clarity. But trust me, man. Zara is not the one you need to worry about getting hurt in this thing."

"Don't be so sure about that. She's not as tough as she acts."

"Yeah." Cal knew that about her. He loved that about her. But it was good to be reminded of it all the same. "Okay. Yes. I hurt her, you hurt me. Got it."

"And see what you can do to keep her from hurting herself, too."

"Damn, Zane. That one's a lot tougher."

"Important stuff always is."

"Since when are you so philosophical?"

"I've had a bit of time to do some thinking about things," Zane replied dryly.

After they hung up, Cal sat for a while, looking out the window at the lake and thinking about Zara. It wasn't what he'd planned when he'd manipulated her into coming back to Lake Sullivan, but he sure wasn't disappointed that it was happening.

Yeah, he was hooked. He just had no idea whether Zara was going to reel him in or cut the line and let him swim off, bleeding and dazed.

❧ *Fifteen* ❧

ZARA DIDN'T RETURN Cal's phone calls that night. She supposed she was being cowardly, but then she talked herself into it being a mark of independence. She wasn't at his beck and call, dropping everything to answer his questions at his convenience. Yeah, it was a lot easier to think like that than to examine why she didn't want to talk to him.

The next morning, she met Ashley for breakfast at the town's only café, which was also its only bakery. They found seats at one of the small outside tables. The air was cool, but the sun was warm and they were out of the wind. "They cleared me to start training again," Zara said. It felt strange to announce it, as if it hadn't been official until just then.

"That's fantastic!" Ashley made a bit of a face. "For you. Too bad for me, 'cause I'll miss you, but congratulations, really!"

"You won't miss me," Zara said. She'd thought about it, had spoken to Terry the day before, and it was all figured out. "Not right away, at least. I haven't talked to the center yet, but I think they'll be okay with me dropping down to part time. I could still do the classes—the stuff that I'm kind of good at—and that would give me enough time to train."

"And you can train here, in Lake Sullivan?"

"When they put me on a card—set a fight date—I'll need to kick it into gear a little, and probably go back to the city. I'll need to spar and grapple with people who can really test me, you know? But while I'm just working on strength and endurance? I can do that here. I talked to my trainer and he says he can come up one day a week, so if I go down one day a week, that'll be enough for him to keep an eye on what I'm doing. I mean, it's not like I'm trying anything new. I know the drill."

"Excellent. You'll be around for the next stitch and bitch." Ashley took a nibble of her egg white omelet, then said, "And this is all because of your passion for teaching MMA to children and housewives? Nothing to do with any tall, blond, and handsome men in the area?"

Zara shook her head. "No. Nothing to do with Cal." She meant it. Cal was . . . a complication. A distraction. He was an argument for her getting the hell out of Lake Sullivan, not for staying there.

But she'd made a commitment to Zane, and to the community center. There were the technical requirements of Zane's parole, that he live with her, but there was something more nebulous as well. They'd been kept apart for too long, and somehow, even though they were living together now, there was still distance between them, and she wanted to sort that out. And the classes at the community center?

"I'm just getting my ladies' class whipped into shape. I don't want to leave until Mrs. Ryerson kicks Mrs. Montgomery in the chest. And until Anna and Melanie will spar

with someone besides each other—they are *not* a good
matchup. And I want to see you get a really solid armlock
on somebody—you're not committing to it yet, but once you
do, it'll be great."

"I'm going to kick ass," Ashley agreed. "So you and Cal
are on? Off? I was thinking about inviting the two of you
out for dinner sometime, but would that be too couple-y?"

Zara scrunched up her face. "I have no idea. Yeah, it feels
too couple-y. I mean, we're temporary, at best. No point in
getting too comfortable with it."

Yeah, she'd be moving on, getting back to normal; there
was barely even going to be a delay in her usual fight schedule. She couldn't explain why she felt a bit deflated about
all of it, so she chose to ignore the sensation.

So when Ashley headed into the café for more napkins,
Zara pulled out her phone. She owed Cal a call . . . or maybe
she could go back to her old tricks. Not e-mail, this time,
but texting. Excellent. She typed:

Hi. Dr was fine. Everything's good. Thx for calling.

She sent the message and then kept the phone on the table
for the rest of the meal, trying to keep her mind on the
conversation with Ashley, waiting for him to text back. But
he didn't. Damn it. She sat there at the end of the meal,
staring at the phone, willing it to make a noise. But it sat
completely silent.

Ashley gave her a strange look. "What are you doing?"

"Practicing my psychic powers."

"Oh. Is that part of your training?"

Zara stopped staring at the phone and looked at Ashley
instead. "You've known me for a while now. I know we're
not, like, old friends, but you've got the basic idea, right?"

"I guess."

"Would you say I'm completely psycho, or just partly?"

"Uh . . . partly? Or maybe not at all. What are you talking about?"

"I think I have the emotional maturity of a preteen boy."

"Is this about Cal?"

Zara sighed. Damn, she was pathetic. Practically begging Ashley to ask her about it, just so she could say . . . what exactly? "These things seem simpler for other people. Like, they relate to each other as normal human adults, not whatever the hell I'm acting like."

"Preteen boy, I thought you said."

"I'm not sure that's right, though. I think it may be a bit unfair to the preteen boys out there."

Ashley looked at her watch, then settled back into her chair. "I've got five more minutes. Give it to me quick."

Zara knew it was weak, but she wanted a little . . . something. Not sympathy. Understanding? Maybe that. "I like him," she admitted, and it felt good to say the words out loud.

"No kidding. You've been making out with him all over town."

"No, not just . . . he's not just hot. I *like* him."

"Okay?"

"So that's it, I think. I like him. It's freaking me out. That's all."

"Well, why is it freaking you out?" Ashley sounded amused, but as though she could quickly tip over into being impatient if Zara didn't start making a bit more sense.

"I don't know. Isn't that scary? When you like somebody? I mean, obviously it won't work out. I'm not going to, like, marry Calvin Montgomery and get old with him. I mean, Zara Hale and Calvin Montgomery? No. That's not real, not in this universe. So it's going to end, right? And what if it's not me who ends it? What if it's him? What if he dumps me? He'd be nice about it, I'm sure, but that would just kind of make it worse, you know? Because I wouldn't even be able to hate him."

Ashley shook her head. "Yeah, okay. Maybe not a preteen boy, but not quite a functioning adult, either."

"But I'm right, aren't I? I mean, all that stuff's true, isn't it?"

"Well, I think theoretically you *could* marry him and get old together. That's not impossible, and certainly it's not because you and Cal aren't 'real' together. But sure, it's probably not going to happen. We don't get married to most people we date. So you probably will break up, and it probably will suck. But too bad. That's just the way life is. You have to live, right?"

"I don't like taking chances. Not at all. I don't think it's a good idea."

Ashley frowned thoughtfully. "You don't like taking chances? Your whole life—your career, at least—that must have involved taking chances."

"No. Not really. I mean, I minimize the risk. I work my ass off to make sure I'm strong and ready for every bout. I watch tape on my opponents and analyze how to beat them. I guess there's a chance of me losing every time I fight, but it's a small chance. I'm really good and I'm really prepared."

"And everything else, like coming here—you weren't taking a chance?"

"No, I was minimizing risk. I wanted to make sure Zane would be okay, so I came back here to keep an eye on him. That's all."

"So essentially, you're a great big chicken. You want something and you're afraid to go after it because it might hurt." Ashley shook her head. "I don't know what to tell you. Suck it up? I mean, there's not much else to say, really. Love is scary, but—"

"Slow down! Nobody's talking about love here."

"Okay, fine. 'Like' is scary. Is that better? More in keeping with your preteen feelings?"

"It *is* scary," Zara said slowly. "I don't like it."

"Great, that's easy!" Ashley stood up. "Cal seems like a good guy, so you should probably tell him to his face, but whatever, that won't kill you. Just say you're not into it, and you're done."

Zara groaned. "But then I don't get what I want!"

"What do you want? A risk-free relationship? The ability to care about someone without the chance of getting hurt? Honey, you can't get what you want because what you want doesn't exist."

"'Honey'?" Zara asked, glad of the distraction.

"I thought I'd try it out. Did I sound sassy?"

"You sounded weird. I don't think 'honey' works for you."

"Well. Disappointing. I tried something, but it didn't work. What a shame. But somehow, I will continue with my life." Ashley beamed beatifically, then nodded toward her watch. "I've got to go. I'm meeting with the contractors for the new house. The house I'm building with the guy I love, who I ended up with because I was brave enough to take chances. Stupid chances, in my case, but still, it all worked out. Sometimes things do all work out."

"Yeah," Zara said flatly. She supposed they did, for some people. But her pity-party guest was leaving, so she needed to snap out of it. "Good luck with the contractors."

"Good luck to you, too. Honey." And with that, Ashley was gone.

Zara sat and stared at her phone, which still wasn't making any sounds. She couldn't have what she wanted because it didn't exist. Fair enough. But what was she going to do instead?

She had no idea. She stood abruptly and headed for the community center. She'd talk to them about going part time, work out, and then she was supposed to be helping with a preschool gymnastics class. Until they found a replacement for her, she'd better stick to her old schedule. And maybe if she stayed busy enough, she'd be able to stop thinking about Cal Montgomery.

Not likely. But it was her best bet, at least temporarily.

CAL got the text just as he was packing up to leave the office for the weekend. He saw it was from Zara and braced himself for another brush-off like the one he'd received that morning. Instead he read:

> Do u want to do something tonight?

A moment later, while he was still recovering from his surprise, his phone beeped again.

> You've probably got plans already. Don't worry about it.

Damn it, she'd changed her mind in the space of five seconds. That had to be some sort of record. But at least she'd made an effort. After that dismissive morning text, he'd told himself he needed to give up on her, or at least back way the hell off and give her a lot of space. Apparently that technique had worked fairly well, and more quickly than he'd expected.

No plans, he texted. It was more or less true. He'd been going to meet up with some guys at Woody's, but they wouldn't miss him. Want me to cook you dinner?

Do u mind? Should I cook?

CAN you cook?

Not really.

I'll cook. I have to get groceries. Be at my place any time after six.

OK.

He left for the grocery store, wondering whether she was actually going to show up, and how many times she'd have changed her mind in the interim. Even with the doubts, though, he felt good. Excited. Things were happening. He was tying another thread between them.

Maggie, the middle-aged daughter of the grocery store owners, was behind the till when he checked out, and she ran a professional eye over the items he unloaded onto the conveyer belt. "Hot date?" she asked.

He looked down at the items. It wasn't like he was buying condoms or something.

She laughed. "Five different kinds of cheese? I didn't even know we sold five different kinds of cheese, not if you aren't counting slices or Cheez Whiz. And dark chocolate and strawberries? Damn. It's a cliché, sure, but a good one. Who's the lucky girl?"

Cal shook his head. "Sometimes a guy just likes to treat himself right."

"Yeah, okay." She looked over Cal's head toward whoever was behind him in line and said, "Hey, Nancy. A single guy buys five kinds of cheese, dark chocolate, and strawberries. You think he's eating all that himself?"

Cal turned to see Nancy Ferguson, the pastor at the United Church, behind him in line. She looked at the items on the conveyer belt, then smiled at him. "Zara Hale? I heard you two were spending time together. Tell her hello for me, will you?"

Thank God he hadn't bought condoms. But now that he was busted, he might as well commit fully. He stepped around the register and defiantly grabbed the biggest, showiest bouquet from the collection of cut flowers by the exit door. He handed them to Maggie to have the barcode scanned and watched as her lips twitched gleefully. "Really? Zara Hale?" she whispered as she handed the flowers back to him.

"They're for me," he replied, but he didn't bother pretending she'd believe him.

On the way out to the parking lot, his flowers got a wolf whistle from Andy Richards and an appreciative smile from two girls who looked young enough to be in high school, and as he unloaded the car at home, his neighbor stopped dog walking long enough to ask what the special occasion was. Cal just nodded his way through it all, answering as noncommittally as possible, and resisted the urge to flop back against his front door in relief once he was on the inside. He was safe. At least until Zara arrived.

He smiled at the thought, then wondered if the way he felt after the town's invasive interest in his life was how Zara felt after he asked her questions she thought were too personal. He'd have to be cool about the doctor's appointment and not grill her for details. Easier said than done, but at least he'd try.

The doorbell rang a minute or two after he'd slid his five-cheese chicken penne into the oven. Too early for the house to smell really good, but at least he'd finished most of the work.

He strode to the front door and opened it to find Zara

Hale wearing a dress. It was still fairly sporty, a simple black thing with a scoop neck, long sleeves, and a skirt short enough to show off her legs, but it was a dress. And she was wearing heels with it. Not super high, but not running shoes.

Don't react, his sense of self-preservation screamed at him. *Play it cool, don't comment until she mentions it.* "Hey, come on in," he said. So far, so good. "You look great." That was neutral enough, wasn't it?

"I feel like an idiot," she confessed. Except a true confession probably wouldn't make it sound quite so much like she was blaming him for her state.

"What? Why?"

"For getting dressed up! I always feel like such a fake when I wear a dress!"

"I've seen you wearing dresses before—like, for media stuff and interviews. . . ."

"Yeah, and media stuff and interviews make me feel like a fake!"

"Oh. Well, I can loan you some sweatpants and a T-shirt if you want. But I really hope you don't—I think you look great."

She frowned thoughtfully at him and he cooperated by taking off his apron to show he was still wearing his dress shirt from work and had left his tie on, although he'd loosened it and shed his jacket. "You look good," she admitted. "I'd feel like a slob if I was wearing sweats."

"Well, I can get changed, too, if you really want."

She looked at him thoughtfully, then reached out and wrapped his silk tie around her fist. She tugged him closer, leaned up, and her lips were soft but strong. She claimed his mouth, controlled the kiss, and made it instantly hot and wet and deep.

When she stepped back, he staggered toward her, searching

for more on instinct alone. She stopped him with the fingers of one hand, the tips braced hard against his chest. "I like the tie," she declared. "So I'll keep the dress."

"Perfect," he said when he had recovered enough to speak. Then he pulled himself a little more together and said, "Something to drink? Wine? Beer?"

"I'm in training," she said. "Just water is good. Or juice or something, if you have it. No alcohol."

"Orange juice?"

"Okay."

"You're in training?" he asked as he busied himself with finding a glass and pouring the juice. She'd opened the door, so he could step in, couldn't he? "So the medical went well?"

"It went great," she said, and he didn't have to look in her direction to know that she'd squared her shoulders and was looking at him with her chin thrust out pugnaciously.

The medical went well. That was all he needed to know, and clearly all she wanted to tell him. But he couldn't help pushing for a little more. "What'd the doctor say about the dizziness?"

"He wasn't worried about it."

"Because he didn't hear about it?"

"Thanks for the juice," she said, and walked into the dining area to look out through the picture window toward the lake. "You're up higher than I thought. Is there a path down the cliff?"

"Yeah. No lawn or any yard to look after up here, but there's a good level spot at the bottom. There's a deck down there, and a little boathouse."

"Nice." She turned back toward him and he let himself enjoy watching her move. She was compact, balanced, and there was a graceful confidence to everything she did. Everything physical that she did. Emotionally or mentally?

She still had power, he was pretty sure, but much less of an idea of how to use it.

He picked the flowers up off the counter and said, "Oh. In case you feel silly wearing the dress, let me feel a bit silly by giving you flowers. Totally retro, right?"

She was hesitant as she took the bouquet. "Flowers? Really?"

"I saw them and thought of you."

She was quiet for a moment, then said, "Thank you." She looked up from her flowers and blinked hard. "Nobody's ever given me flowers before."

"Probably because you're not living in the fifties."

"No. That's not why." She smelled the bouquet then held it out at arm's length and turned the flowers around so she could admire them from all sides. By the end of her inspection, she was beaming. It shouldn't have made Cal want to cry.

He needed to get a grip on himself. Safe topic? "So what does it mean to be 'in training'?" he asked. "What are you training for?"

She shrugged, still looking at the flowers. "Another bout, eventually, but they haven't got me on a card yet. They're meeting on Monday to figure out the details for the next round. It'll be a title fight, so they need to find someone who deserves a shot at it."

"But there'll be another physical before then? I mean . . ." He'd done his reading. He knew concussions didn't necessarily show up on MRIs or CT scans, knew that doctors relied heavily on patients self-reporting their symptoms. If Zara wasn't going to report things . . . Damn it. He needed to let it go, at least for right then. "Yeah. So. Uh, have you talked to Zane lately?"

He'd caught her off guard; he wasn't sure if it was the topic change or the topic he'd chosen. "What do you mean?" she asked cautiously. "I saw him this morning, but he didn't say much."

"Didn't mention my name?"

"No." She wasn't looking at the flowers anymore. "Why would he have?"

"Well . . . he heard about you and me. I mean, not that there is a 'you and me,' like, in a big way. But he heard what everyone else is hearing, I guess."

She was quiet for a moment, looking out at the lake. Then she said, "And? Was he mad?"

"No." Cal tried to remember the actual words Zane had used. "There were some basic threats obviously. But nothing big. Overall, he seemed okay with it."

She nodded slowly, then gave him a smile that was clearly forced. "It shouldn't matter, right? I mean, he's my brother. That's all. It's not some big . . ."

She trailed off and he was around the counter before he knew it. Once he was close, he wasn't sure how much touching was allowed, so he reached out and found her shoulder with his fingertips, like a nerdy seventh grader at his first dance. "He's family. Trust me, I know about family. The push and pull, the desire to be close at the same time you want space and freedom . . . I get it. I do."

She stood frozen for a moment, and then, even with just the light contact of his fingertips, he felt her relax. "He was okay with it," she said. "And everything else will just take care of itself."

"Or we'll take care of it," he said, managing to keep himself from tacking on the "together." "It'll be fine."

They moved to more neutral topics then, and it all went smoothly. They talked about themselves, told stories about friends and adventures, laughed about movies, and argued about books. They ate dinner, and Cal put the chocolate and some cream in a double boiler, and as he stirred, Zara peered around his shoulder, intrigued.

"I should start cooking more," she declared. "It doesn't really look that hard."

"Well, I'm making it look easy because of my expertise."

"You're stirring it. I could stir."

"Yeah, okay, you could melt chocolate. But did you know you should use a double boiler?"

"There's recipes, right? Wouldn't the recipe say to use a double boiler? I could read, and use, and stir. No problem."

"Okay, then, you make us dinner next time."

"Uh, no. I think we've established a tradition here, and in this uncertain world, tradition is really important. We shouldn't go breaking it without a really good reason."

He twisted around, brought his free hand to her neck, stretched his fingers out so he was touching from her shoulder right up past her ear, and kissed her. Nothing too crazy, just gentle and affectionate. Zara, of course, leaned in and intensified it a little, and it was hard to complain about that. He fumbled behind him for a washed strawberry, turned enough so he could see the chocolate and dip the berry, then lifted the treat slowly to Zara's lips.

She let him feed her, her lips soft as they wrapped around the berry. "The ladies at the grocery store said this was a cliché," he told her, his voice husky.

"Tradition," she corrected, almost whispering. "Very, very important."

"In this uncertain world."

"Exactly." She kissed him, not as deep this time, and he could taste the sweet, bitter, and tart on her lips. "Give me another."

"What about me? Aren't you going to give me one?"

"No." She kissed him again. "They're all for me."

He reached for another berry, dipped it, brought it toward her, and then popped it in his own mouth.

Her jaw dropped in mock outrage. "What kind of host are you? I thought Montgomerys were supposed to be classy!"

"No, we're not. Not at all." He dipped the next berry so thoroughly it was almost completely coated, then lifted it to his mouth and held it in his teeth, offering it to her.

"Okay, the ladies in the store were right—this *is* a cliché." But she stretched up anyway, found the berry, and bit it in two, their lips just brushing. Then they both chewed slowly, their gazes locked on each other.

Zara brought her hands to his waist and tugged at his shirt until it came untucked. "You're not going to pull your blushing virgin routine again tonight, are you?" she asked.

"I think my self-control in that area is pretty well used up." The way his body was reacting, his self-control in *all* areas seemed to have been used up.

"Thank God." She slid her hands under his shirt, her fingers cool against his abs. Then she grinned, happy and impish. "Another berry, please."

He found the berry, dipped it, and fed it to her. Two bites, nothing exaggerated or theatrical about her appreciation, and then she kissed him again and took a step backward. "Do you need to turn the heat off on that?" She waited until he did it, then said, "See? I'm great at cooking."

"You're a master chef."

She was still smiling as she kissed him, a real kiss this time, long and deep, and their bodies molded together as closely as the berries and chocolate had.

Damn it, Cal wanted this too much. And he wanted it too many different ways. He wanted hard and fast and rough, and he wanted slow and smooth and sweet. He wanted to take charge and make Zara follow him, in this one area, this one time. And he wanted to sit back and see what she would do, let her make the decisions and bring him pleasure. He wanted to kiss her lips, but he also wanted to drag his mouth lower, to discover her whole body. Too many wants, and if he didn't get control of things, he wasn't going to last long enough to satisfy half of them.

So when she started tugging at his belt, he caught her hands and held them in his. "You first," he murmured. And he reminded himself to make sure that was true for everything.

She seemed surprised when he pulled away, but didn't argue when he took her hand and led her toward the stairs, then up to the bedroom.

He flipped the switch for the bedside lamps but not the overhead light, and she looked around the room with interest. "Big bed," she finally said. Then she grinned. "Compensating for something?"

He shook his head. "I honestly never knew someone could be such a total brat and so incredibly sexy at the same time." He tugged at his tie, and nodded at her feet. "Shoes off," he ordered.

And she stepped out of them, easy as pie, no rebellion or even back talk. "Really?" he asked. "You're not going to argue?"

"No." She stood still, her hands at her sides, relaxed and waiting. "I think you can be in charge. For a while."

God, he liked the sound of that. He kicked off his own shoes, pulled his tie over his head and dropped it on the floor, then stepped toward her, gripped her hips, and walked her backward until she ran into the wall. She looked good up against a wall, waiting for him.

Whatever reticence or hesitations he'd had were gone now. Maybe she'd regret this, maybe he would, but that was too damn bad. It was too late to worry about that. He let his body cover hers, kissed her hard, slid a hand around her back, and pulled her forward while his other hand tangled in her hair and dragged her head back. Her body arched out toward him, sinuous and sweet. He kissed down her neck, pulled away long enough to tug at her dress and lift it over her head, and then had to take a moment to stand back and appreciate the view.

She wasn't as deliberately angular as some women he'd been with. Not skinny. Her ribs were only a faint line, but he could see her abs clearly, and muscles everywhere else, too. A thin layer of fat, enough to show she was a performance athlete, not a model or a bodybuilder. Her body was designed for use, and she'd worked hard to fine-tune it.

"I could just go get one of my posters, if all you want to do is look," she suggested dryly.

"I want to do a hell of a lot more than look." His voice sounded rough to his own ears, his desire overpowering his cultivation. "Besides, your posters don't begin to do you justice."

"I've got about one more second of confidence here, and then I'm going to get really self-conscious."

Well, he didn't want that. So he stepped back to her, kissed her deep, and let his hands run over her newly exposed skin. So warm, so smooth, and beneath it all, so strong.

He shrugged out of his shirt and let it fall to the floor, then reached behind her to find the clasp of her bra. He wanted skin on skin. And when he got it, he wanted more. "You're perfect," he murmured as he kissed his way to one warm, pale breast.

"And I can cook." Then his lips found their target and she gasped, arching her back without him asking for it this time, and she stopped talking.

The softness of her breast was almost surprising, compared to how hard her body was everywhere else, and Cal let himself be almost hypnotized by the contrast. He explored her with his hands and his mouth, stood back up to kiss her, and finally, exquisitely, let himself grind into her, his hardness straining through two layers of fabric, seeking her warmth.

But it wasn't time for that, not yet. He tugged her panties down as he fell to his knees and let himself taste and explore. She gasped again as his tongue worked; she squirmed, pressed against him and opened to him. He felt like he was being given a gift. An honor. And he worked to earn it.

He licked and nipped and sucked, let himself connect to her body and know what she was feeling. He brought her close to her climax and then backed away, brought her close again, and then felt her fingers tighten in his hair, a warning of what would happen if he teased her much more.

And he was teasing himself almost as much. So he let himself go, let *her* go, sliding his fingers inside her and adding his thumb to the rhythm of his mouth. She came quickly, her whole body shaking and arching into him, and she pulled his hair anyway, even though he'd done what she wanted. He didn't mind the pain, though, not when it came with the pleasure of knowing that he'd done this. He'd made Zara Hale lose control of her body, and she'd let him do it.

She fell back against the wall and he kissed his way up her stomach, between her breasts, savoring her relaxation.

"That was almost as good as the strawberries," she murmured when he reached her mouth.

He kissed her, then wrapped his hands under her ass and lifted her up, her body snuggling into his as he carried her to the bed. "Don't tell me you're going to sleep," he said, and she looked up innocently.

"Did you have something else in mind?"

"Maybe a little something, yeah."

"'Little,' huh? So the bed *is* a compensation." She looked at him for a long moment, then sat up and laid her hands on his belt buckle. "Remember what I said about you being in charge, but only for a while?"

"Yeah."

"Time's up," she said. And she moved incredibly quickly, hooking her legs around him, shifting, pulling . . . He had no idea what she did, but it ended with him flat on his back on the bed, Zara straddling him with a satisfied look on her face. "My turn now," she said.

And Cal had no problem with that whatsoever.

❧ *Sixteen* ❧

ZARA'S BODY WAS stretching and moving before her brain was completely awake, and there was a moment of almost frightening disorientation when her hand came into contact with something cold and metallic by her head. She jerked her eyes open and blinked in the dim light. A cast-iron head-board. She was in bed. Not her bed. Whose bed? How . . .

It came back to her. She looked around, but Cal wasn't there. There was a large window at the far end of the room, and the sky through it was showing the first signs of dawn. And Zara was waking up in a strange bed, alone. Not ideal.

She sat up and groped around for her clothes. She'd been stupid to wear the dress; it made her walk of shame that much more obvious. And it had probably made her look desperate the night before. What the hell had she been thinking?

Where was her other shoe? She'd carry them downstairs and put them on at the door, she decided, so their clicking wouldn't foil her escape.

She had her dress on and was crouched over, reaching under the bed to search for her shoe, when she heard steps on the stairs behind her. Play it cute or cool? How would she handle this?

But when she turned and saw the look of honest confusion on Cal's face, she found she didn't want to "play" it any way at all. "Why are you up?" he asked.

"Why are *you* up? What were you doing?"

"I went downstairs to use the bathroom—I thought it would be less likely to disturb you. I guess it didn't work." He was wearing his boxer briefs and nothing else, his hair was adorably tousled, and he looked like he needed to be wrapped in a cozy blanket and snuggled back to sleep.

But that wasn't Zara's role. "I was just going to head home," she said, trying to sound efficient. "If I get a couple hours sleep in my own bed, it's not like I spent the night technically. Right?"

"Why would it be bad if you spent the night?" He looked completely puzzled by everything she was saying and doing. He approached her cautiously and said, "I can make us breakfast. Now, I guess, but I was thinking maybe a bit later? We could sleep some more?"

Damn, a big part of her wanted nothing more than to crawl back into bed with him. But it would be too much. Too intimate. It had been one thing the night before when they'd had sex as an excuse, but now? "I'm okay. I have food at home."

He looked at her for too long, until it seemed like he was looking through her. Then he said, "Zara Hale, get your ass back in bed and go to sleep."

She blinked. It was an order, so she should rebel, of course. Who did he think he was to be bossing her around like that? But somehow she didn't feel the need. It was an order on the surface, but underneath, it was an opening. It gave her an excuse. She was going back to bed because he wanted her to, not because *she* wanted to. It wasn't her weakness that made her want to cuddle, it was his.

She set down her one shoe, looked at it, and said, "Your house ate one of my shoes. You owe me a shoe."

"Okay. Go to sleep now, and I'll give you a shoe later."

"You'd better," she grumbled. She kept her dress on, but she slipped back under the covers and turned on her side, her back toward Cal's side of the bed. She felt the mattress shift as he lay down next to her and she braced herself. Would he be wrapping his arm around her, pulling her in for a full spoon? And if he did, would she be able to stand it or would it be too much, too fast?

But he didn't do it. She felt the ghost of a touch of pressure along her back and realized that he was lying on his side, too, his back to her. They were bookends facing away from each but still touching, however gently. It was perfect. It was exactly as much as she could handle. And with that slight contact, she was able to let herself drift off to sleep.

When she woke up the next time, there was daylight streaming in through the windows, and when she rolled over, the other side of the bed was empty again. Damn, Cal was pretty good at sneaking around without waking her up.

She stumbled to his bathroom and cleaned up a little, brushing her teeth with his toothpaste and her finger, then took a deep breath to call up her courage and headed for the stairs. When she got to the top of them, she saw her shoes, both of them, lined up in the middle of the tread where she couldn't miss them. It was enough to make her relax a little, and she hooked her fingers into their heels and headed down the stairs.

Cal was wearing sweat pants and a T-shirt, sitting on one of the stools at the counter, reading the paper. He saw her and stood up, smiling. "Morning. You want coffee?"

"Sure." She wanted more than that, she was pretty sure, but she couldn't say exactly what. She wanted to touch him. Not for sex necessarily, although that would certainly be fine, but just for . . . just to say good morning. A hug, a quick kiss, some gesture of affection. Damn, that was it. She wanted him, but that part was easy. It was the liking him that she didn't really know how to handle.

And she was too chicken to experiment, so she just trailed after him over to the coffeemaker and let him pour her a mugful.

She set her shoes on the floor and added milk and sugar to her cup, aware of him watching her a little too closely. "What? Am I doing it wrong? Is this not the proper way to drink coffee?"

"Calm down, Grumpy."

"Well, what are you doing?"

"I'm watching how much stuff you put in, so I can make it for you next time."

Next time. He might just mean if she had another cup of coffee that morning. It wasn't a marriage proposal or anything. No need for her to get too happy *or* too scared about any of it. She took a sip of her coffee and made herself turn to look at him. "Thank you for the shoe."

"You realize that it's not a new shoe, right? I just found your old one."

"If that's how you want to play it."

And when he smiled at her that way, it somehow made it clear just how stupid her paranoia was. This was Cal. It was okay if she wanted to touch him.

So she set her mug on the counter, and he leaned forward just as she stretched up, and their kiss was sweet and affectionate and exactly what she'd wanted.

When he pulled away, he licked his lip gently and said, "Breakfast? Does being in training mean you have to eat something special?"

"At this stage? Just healthy stuff—whole grains, unsaturated fats, lean protein. I'll worry about making weight later on."

"So no bacon?"

"Damn. I love bacon. Maybe a little bit?"

"And toast, and eggs? And fruit?"

"Sounds good. Should I do something?"

"You can sit. Drink your coffee. I like you watching me."

So she sat. He fried a few slices of bacon and poached eggs and cut up fruit and she felt like she was being taken care of. Sure, there were other people who cooked for her sometimes, but most of them were paid for the service, or were making a meal for a group. This? Just Cal, and just her. She liked it.

And when they were done eating and she felt another burst of anxiety and thought it might be time to escape, he asked her to help him with the dishes, and of course she couldn't say no to such a reasonable request. The warm water was soothing, and Cal's arm brushed against hers as they worked. She felt herself relaxing again, and when she had washed the last dish and dried off, she turned to Cal and tucked a few fingers from each hand just inside the waistband of his sweatpants. Then she looked up at him with her eyebrows raised, waiting for the verdict.

His smile was the only answer she needed, but she was happy to take his kiss as supporting evidence. "Upstairs," he murmured.

"Not here?"

"Condoms are upstairs. I could go get them, but I'm afraid I'll be gone for five seconds, come back, and you'll have gotten spooked and taken off."

She hadn't known she was quite that transparent. "Upstairs, then." She took his hand and led him back to the bedroom, stopping halfway to get rid of his T-shirt.

It was a bit different this time. The night before, they'd figured out the basics, but now they were fine-tuning the details. When Zara had kissed Cal's neck last night, he'd tilted his head away and his breathing had quickened in appreciation. This morning, she let herself map out the exact spots that got the best reaction, from the soft skin just behind his ear to the hollow above his collarbone. She played with nipping and licking and sucking and kissing, finding her rewards in his quick gasps and one long, low moan of pleasure. She abandoned his neck with reluctance and consoled herself with his chest, strong muscles beneath a light, natural expanse of hair. And as she worked her way lower, she felt his body responding, all of his muscles tensing as she worked her way down over his hard belly to the waist of his sweats. And then she worked her way back up.

"Zara," he growled, clearly not too impressed with the change in direction. She kissed his mouth, and after a moment's persuasion, he looped an arm around her waist, pulled her over so she was half straddling, half lying on him, and kissed her back properly. "You're a tease," he murmured.

"If you don't like it, you can leave anytime." She moved her mouth back to his neck and his arm tightened around her head.

"This is my house," he managed, though his voice was tight. "You think I should leave my own house?"

"Only if you don't like what I'm doing." And with that she slid down, tugged his pants and underwear out of the way, and took him in her mouth.

"I like what you're doing!" he gasped. "I'm staying."

She hummed her contentment and kept going. She liked what she was doing, too. And at least for a while, she was staying.

"I should go home at some point," Zara said. It was midafternoon, she was in his bed and in his arms, and Cal didn't want her to go anywhere. Possibly ever.

"If you wait a little longer, your clothes will make sense again. You'll have skipped the day entirely and it'll be back to the right time for wearing a black dress."

"A black dress is an anytime dress. That's what I've been told. It's why I bought the damn thing."

"Well, then, you should just wait a little longer because I don't want you to leave yet." He was getting pretty good at cataloging her reactions, and he told himself that she'd tensed up much less after he said that then after he'd said similarly cozy things earlier in the day. Small victory, but he'd take it. Especially since he was pretty sure she relaxed more quickly, too.

"I should work out," she said softly.

"We've had a pretty good workout, haven't we?"

"No. We've had fun. Workouts aren't fun, they're terrible. They're hard, and they hurt, and they make you want to puke."

"Damn, your workouts are a lot tougher than mine."

"Yeah, well, your workouts aren't your job."

"Do you like your job?"

"I like getting paid."

"That's all, though? If there was no money, you wouldn't do it?"

"I don't know. I'd probably still do parts of it. But no way would I train so hard. And I wouldn't do all the promo stuff, that's for sure. They might be sending a camera crew up here to film footage about what a great person I am, giving back to the community and all that shit. It's going to be brutal."

"Because you think it's not true?"

"Because I know it's not true. I'm here for Zane, not for the damn community. I mean, as soon as he's stable, I'm gone. It's fake to pretend otherwise."

She'd be gone. He knew that. It wasn't something she'd been hiding. But it still wasn't what he wanted to think about right then. So it was his turn to tense up, and she wasn't as ready for that reaction as he'd been so he managed to get right away, shifting his legs around and sitting up on the side of the bed before she'd even realized he was moving.

"Are we pretending I'm going to live here forever?" she asked. Her tone was carefully neutral.

He sighed and flopped back on the bed. "I guess not, no."

"Can we just not think about it?" She ran her hands over his shoulders. "You know, 'live in the now' or whatever?"

"Just so you have an excuse to not tell me anything about your head?"

"The only excuse I need is that it's none of your business." She was frowning, but as he watched her, she looked away, swore softly, and then looked back without the frown. "You're going to keep pushing on that?"

"I don't mean to push, but, yeah, I'm going to keep *caring* about that. I want to know you're okay, and that you're taking care of yourself."

She rolled her eyes, then shrugged. "You're right. I didn't tell the doctor about the dizziness. Because I didn't need to. There's a lot of bureaucracy and really strict rules about it all. But I know my body, and it's fine. I did the baseline tests—they give us a test once a year when we're healthy, and then after we get hit in the head, they do it again and look at the results to be sure they haven't changed—and it was fine. No signs of trouble. So it's all okay."

"Except for the dizziness."

"Yeah," she said reluctantly. "So, you know, I'll keep an eye on that. I've been really careless with my eating and my exercise. So being a bit dizzy a few times could totally be related to any of that."

"Or it could be a sign of something hidden in your brain."

For a moment he thought she was going to brush him off, but she didn't. Instead she said, "Yeah. It could be. So like I said, I'll keep an eye on things. I'll take better care of myself and get back in touch with how I'm feeling and I'll see how it goes. Okay?" She tilted her head and looked at him. "Okay?" she asked more insistently, and she reached out and playfully poked him in the ribs. "Is that good enough for Captain Worrypants?"

"It's *Colonel* Worrypants," he corrected. He caught her hand before she could poke him again. "You'll tell me the truth? I'll try not to bug you about it, but that'll be a lot easier for me to do if I know you aren't hiding things. Okay?"

Her nod was grudging, but he was pretty sure she meant it. He added, "And if it is bad news—like, if it's the worst news and you can't fight again?" He held his hands up quickly to fend off her outraged glare. "Just absolute worst-case scenario. That's all." She relaxed enough that he was pretty sure she was listening as he added, "Even if it came to that, it wouldn't be the end of the world. I mean, you have other skills, other ways to be useful. Ways to earn money, even. Maybe not as much, but enough. Right?"

"What are you talking about?" She gave him a sidelong look. "I'm not doing porn!"

"What? Jesus, no, not porn!" He wasn't sure whether to be alarmed or amused, and settled for putting the idea out of his head, at least temporarily. "No. But the stuff you're doing at the community center? You just got thrown into that, with no training, and you're doing okay. You could figure out what parts of it you like most and get trained for those parts. Like, teaching kids, or the women's class or whatever. Organizing clinics for people. You could do any of that. I mean, you're going to have to do something after you retire from MMA, right? You're not going to keep fighting until you're sixty-five. So if whatever that something is comes a little sooner, that's not a tragedy. Really."

She didn't look at him. She was quiet for a moment, then shook her head vigorously, as if clearing it of unwanted thoughts. "Well, I'm fine, so it's nothing I need to worry about right now. But okay. I'll skip working out today. But tomorrow, I am on it. No goofing off."

"Okay," he agreed, and tugged her down into the tangled sheets. "Tomorrow. But for the rest of today, you're here. Right?"

"If you insist," she agreed, and she wrapped her arms around him and made them both forget about everything that wasn't right there in the bed with them.

❧ *Seventeen* ❧

IT WAS FRIGHTENING how easily everything seemed to fall together. Zara managed to pry herself out of Cal's bed by Sunday morning, and he had some family event that night, so after she worked out, she went home and called Bonita and killed time. But when Cal called her around nine and said his dinner was over and he was lonely, she was out the door in a flash, carrying a prepacked overnight bag with clothes to wear to work the next day. And it all went on from there.

She didn't let herself think about the future, of course. But living in the moment was enough to keep her more than busy. Her routine was simple: work and training during the day, Cal in the evenings. She trained hard, and learned to anticipate her dizzy spells and take a break before they took over. She was pretty sure they were getting less frequent, too. Everything was good.

She was surprised to find herself actually looking forward to her women's MMA class. All the students from the first day had come back for the second, and then again for the third. She skipped ahead past a lot of the technique she really should have been teaching them and suited them up in sparring gear as often as possible. They did everything at about one-third strength, but even so, the first time Mrs. Ryerson punched Mrs. Montgomery in the gut, Zara was braced for outrage.

It didn't come. Instead, Mrs. Montgomery stood a little taller and said, "That wasn't as bad as I imagined. Do you mind doing it a few more times so I can really get used to it?" Mrs. Ryerson had been happy to oblige.

The other women were paired off with partners Zara judged to be roughly the same size and strength, which meant they were separated from the friends most of them had come with. It was interesting to see how insecure that made them initially, and then how quickly they got over it after trading a few punches.

There was more talking and joking than in any MMA gym Zara had ever stepped foot in, and some days she thought the women's abs were getting a better workout from laughing than from the formal exercises, but that was okay, too.

She went home at the end of each day with stories to tell Cal, and he responded just right. One afternoon they were downtown and walked past Lake Sullivan's version of a department store, one big room with everything from cookware to clothes, and she pulled him inside and over to the craft section.

"Pick a color," she ordered, gesturing to the bins full of yarn.

He looked at the display, then at her. "For what?"

"I'm going to make you a scarf."

"Really? Is that going to be in the same way that you 'make dinner' by putting take-out food into serving dishes?"

"No! I'm going to crochet it, for real! I already know how,

more or less. But for most crocheting you have to, like, count, and pay attention. But Mrs. Grey says that I can make plain rectangles by just doing stitches until I get to the end of the row and then turning around and doing stitches back in the opposite direction. And a scarf, really, is just a long rectangle. So I'm going to make you one. You need to choose a color. I was thinking about doing one for Zane in that greeny-grey color, so don't choose that one."

"You're going to make me a scarf?" He looked . . . damn it, he looked touched. Zara had *wanted* that, she realized. She'd wanted to make some sort of gesture, give him some sort of hint about how she was feeling. But now that it was actually happening, it made her squirm.

"Maybe," she said quickly. "I might not do it at all. I promise nothing."

"Okay," he said gently, as if he sensed her internal conflict. "Just hypothetically, if I was going to get a scarf, I'd probably want one that was . . . I don't know, maybe blue? Like that blue there."

Zara squeezed the balls of yarn as if she knew what she was doing and was testing to be sure they'd be suitable. "Okay. I'm going to buy some blue yarn, but not for any specific reason. Afghans are rectangular, too, and so are placemats. There are a lot of rectangular things I could make with this yarn."

"Book cozies," Cal suggested.

"Do books get cold?"

"Not cold, really, but lonesome. It's a psychological comfort for them."

"Okay," Zara agreed. "It's possible I'll start making book cozies. Scarves are a long shot."

"I'll just hope, then," he said. His smile was gentle, and sweet, and it was more or less impossible to keep herself from kissing it.

He kissed her back, then nudged her away a little. "Get your fetish under control," he whispered. "There's a woman over by the garden department giving us the evil eye."

She kissed him again. "She's just jealous. She heard us talking about scarves, and she wants one."

"She can get in line. Make mine first."

"I can neither confirm nor deny that I'm making one at all." She found four balls of blue yarn, then grabbed a fifth and sixth for good measure. She really had no idea how much yarn was in a scarf.

She let herself lean into Cal's strong chest, just for a second. It wasn't a snuggle, she told herself. Just a moment of warmth. That was all. But it felt good, so good it was scary.

So she made herself push away, and headed down the aisle toward the checkout desk. On the way, the woman from the garden department passed by and gave them another dirty look, and they both giggled like guilty children. It was perfect. But it was temporary, she reminded herself. That was what she needed to remember.

CAL loved hearing his phone buzz and looking down to see that Zara was trying to get hold of him. It didn't happen that often, but whenever it did, he gave himself a moment to enjoy it before picking up. He stepped out of the boring meeting and said, "Hang on," into the phone. He made it to his office and then added, "What are you wearing?"

"Sweaty gym clothes. You?"

"Describe the sweatiness, please."

"No, I don't think so. But is there any chance you could give me a hand with something?"

Cal felt like his whole body had been electrified. Zara was asking him for a favor? He hoped it was something big.

Like labors of Hercules big. He wanted to slay monsters for her, or steal something from a god. He was a bit less enthusiastic about cleaning a really big stable, but if that was what she asked, he'd do it. Absolutely. "What do you need?"

"Well, 'need' is a little strong."

Of course it was. "How may I serve?" he amended.

"That's better. Yeah, I like that."

"Your wish is my command."

"Nice. Okay. I'm actually just looking for some muscle."

"And you thought of me? I'm incredibly flattered." He actually was.

"Don't get carried away. But I've got stitch and bitch tonight, and Margie Dawkins is bringing a quilting frame. I don't know what the hell that is, but I guess they're . . . maybe not heavy, but bulky? I don't know. Anyway, Margie's got tendonitis and Ashley can't come tonight, the quitter, and everyone else is kinda old, and there's stairs involved. So can you come with me to stitch and bitch, help me carry something heavy or bulky or something, and then go away so the ladies can bitch in peace?"

"Yes. I can do that."

"You caught the 'go away' part, right? Because Mrs. Ryerson will probably invite you in, but you're not allowed to accept. I don't want to be the idiot who brought her boyfriend to stitch and bitch."

"Your what?" he asked quickly. Too quickly. Too desperately. But he wanted to hear it again.

Of course, Zara wouldn't cooperate. "Huh? I don't want to be an idiot, I said."

He didn't think he wanted to let this go. "I got that part. And then after that, you said something about bringing your—what was it? Was it 'boyfriend'? Was that the word you used?"

"Seems unlikely."

"I know what I heard, Zara Hale. I know my girlfriend's voice pretty well, and I can recognize it when she—"

"I could work on your scarf tonight," Zara interrupted. "But only if I'm in a good mood. If I'm feeling crabby, I'll probably just make a bunch of potholders. Or those weird dishrag things. That's what I'll work on if I don't feel like making someone a scarf."

He smiled at the phone. If she'd been there, he would have kissed her, and she would have pretended to squirm away, but not gone far. "What time do I need to be there?"

"Seven o'clock sharp. You know where the Ryersons live?"

"I do."

"Okay. Thanks." She hung up without saying good-bye.

He should have gone back to the meeting, but instead he stood in his office, staring out the big windows, and let himself enjoy it. Zara had called him her boyfriend. She'd done it once, and she'd probably do it again. It was an occasion. A momentous occasion.

He was going to get her more flowers. Possibly he'd fill the house with them. She'd asked a favor, and she'd called him her boyfriend. Everything was going well.

❧ Eighteen ❧

THAT FRIDAY, A gang of them went to The Pier for the season's closing. Cal and Zara and Josh and Ashley, Josh's cousin Kevin, and Zane. It was a good mix. Another couple made it okay for Cal and Zara to be a little bit cozy, but the single folks kept it from being too unbearably cute. It wasn't a double date, just a group of people who all got along. Some of whom were having trouble keeping their hands off each other.

Zara tried to distract herself from Cal by watching Zane. He was sitting next to Josh and they seemed to be getting along well. They'd been in school together, a grade or two apart, and had enough to talk about just focusing on the good ol' days. It was a big night and there was a steady stream of visitors to the table, waltzing through to say hi and check in. Zane seemed okay with that, too. Sometimes people asked him about the future, and he was calm and collected. He didn't have firm plans maybe, but he seemed generally optimistic about things.

Cal brought his lips close to Zara's ear and said, "If you lean any farther in that direction, you're going to fall out of your chair."

She jerked back guiltily, and based on how quickly he got out of her way, it seemed like he'd expected the reaction. "Why can't he talk to me like that?" she hissed. "Just chatting about his plans or whatever. Why is it so hard?"

Cal shrugged. "Maybe you just care too much. It's hard to be casual about something when the other person is too intense. And it'd be pretty scary for him to stop being casual at this stage, when he's still probably pretty unsure about a lot of things." His lips quirked in a way that always made her want to kiss him, partly because he was adorable and partly because the smirk seemed to precede him making fun of her, and a kiss seemed like a good way to silence him before he spoke. But she kept her distance and Cal said, "Sound at all familiar? Someone being worried about committing to things because of a lack of control?"

"I can't imagine what you're talking about," she said, an eyebrow raised in challenge. He just quirked his lips again, and this time she gave in to the urge and kissed him. Quick and light, barely more than a peck, but when she glanced back toward Zane and he looked away too quickly, making it clear that he'd seen the kiss, her cheeks flamed anyway.

She'd hardly even been thinking about boys in terms of sex when Zane had gone away, and it was hard to get used to . . . well, hard to get used to a lot of things. Hard to get used to having him in her life at all, or at least for more than an awkward hour every other week. But definitely weird to have him seeing her with a guy, especially when that guy was his best friend. She wished she wasn't in training so she could drink. But her discipline held and she took a sip of her juice.

Cal tugged her back a little closer to him, and when she resisted, he leaned toward her. "He's fine with it," he said firmly. "You're the only one feeling weird."

"Great. So I'm feeling weird, *and* I'm the only one feeling that way. I'm all alone. Did it ever occur to you that it might be a bit easier if I wasn't flying solo on this?"

"If it makes you feel any better, you're starting to freak me out a little."

"Yes. Much better. Thank you."

"How much weirder would you feel if I asked to stay at your place tonight?"

She swivelled her face toward him and knew her eyes were wide. "My place? With Zane there?"

"Not in the room with us, I hope. But two stories away in the basement? Yeah. You have to drive him home anyway, right? You're the designated driver? So I could tag along with you when you drop him off and then you could drive us back to my place. Or I could just stay out there overnight. With you."

"And my brother."

"I think he's probably noticed that you haven't been spending many nights at home lately."

"Maybe not. Maybe he just thinks I'm really quiet."

"And really careless about where you leave your car."

"Yeah, maybe that, too."

"Or maybe he knows you're an adult and doesn't have a problem with you spending the night with your boyfriend."

She froze. She'd slipped up and said it once, and now it was just a thing they said?

Cal felt her reaction and snorted, half amusement, but half frustration. "Fine. I don't think he has a problem with you spending the night with some guy. Some random guy, nobody important. But if it's a problem, don't worry about it."

Zara stared at her fingers as they wrapped around her glass of juice. The glass felt so solid, but it would shatter if she pressed too hard, or banged it against the counter. It would break if she didn't take some care with it.

She took a deep breath and turned so she was facing Cal head on. "Do you want to stay at my place tonight? I have to drive Zane home anyway, so it'd be convenient if you came along."

He looked at her for a long moment. His eyes were warm and affectionate, and she wanted to remember his expression. Then he said, "I don't know. Do you have scratchy sheets? I really prefer sheets with a high thread count. And I like my own pillow."

"Such a pain in the ass," she muttered, but she let him wrap his arm around her and pull her in tight against his chest. It wasn't that hard to stay in the moment, she'd found, not when the moments were as sweet as this one.

That was when her phone rang. She leaned away from Cal and burrowed around in her pockets for her phone.

As soon as she saw the call display, she knew. She'd been stupid, letting herself settle into life here in Lake Sullivan. Her real life was elsewhere, and it was calling her now. Calling her back home.

She stood up and took a few steps away from the table before she made herself answer. Andre's voice was familiar, but too loud and forceful. "Zara! Great news! We've got a fight lined up for you, a great fight. Great competitor. It's going to be fantastic, but you need to get back to the city and start training right away. Zara?" A pause while Zara tried to find her voice. "Zara? You there?"

"I'm here," she finally croaked.

"Fight's in Vegas on December eighteenth," Andre crowed into the phone. "The challenger is Anna Cade."

"Anna Cade? She's not in my weight class, is she?"

"She's losing the weight, coming down to bantam."

"Why?"

"To fight you. You're the golden girl, you're the star. She wants some of that glory, so she's coming to get it. If she can get the weight off and stay strong, it'll be a hell of a fight."

Zara felt dazed. She'd sunken into her cozy Lake Sullivan life, where her biggest challenge was finding someone to help her move an old lady's quilting frame, which had barely turned out to be heavy at all. She'd gotten soft, and for her real life she needed to be hard.

A bout with Anna Cade *would* be a hell of a fight, and she liked the challenge of it. But something still felt wrong. "December eighteenth? That's six weeks from now. Why so soon? That's not enough time to train properly. What the hell happened to me being a valuable investment and needing to make sure my brain was in good shape?"

"You passed the physical, Zara." Andre sounded confused, and maybe a little hurt. "You said you wanted to get back in the ring as soon as possible. I worked hard to get you what you said you wanted."

She had said that. It was what she wanted. But she really hadn't thought she'd get it. "Six weeks," she said. "Can we put it off another month or so?"

"They've had a few cancellations and they need to fill the spots. And have you been following the news? There've been a lot of injuries lately, so there isn't a deep pool to draw from. They need a headliner for this card. You're fit, right? You've been in training? So you'll be fine. And I already said you'd do it."

Because she had said that was what she wanted. "What if I'm not ready? I mean, I can get my conditioning worked out in six weeks, if I really go at it, but what about my head?"

"You passed the physical. You told the doctor your head was fine. Is there something I need to know about?"

"No! No, it's fine. But this will be . . . is it enough time since my last fight?"

"It's almost four months. That's about right, or even a little long."

It was about right. They tried to have three or four fights a year, which meant three or four months between each one. This was business as usual, and she was only disoriented because Andre had told her it would be a longer gap this time. If he'd changed his mind on that, it was a good thing. She had nothing to complain about. "I'm just having a bit of trouble catching up," she admitted.

"Well, fair enough, but kick yourself into gear as soon as you can. You need to get fit. So give Bonita a call and let her know you're coming home, and I'll see you on—"

"No, wait. I can't come home. I need to stay here. I can train here, right?"

"What? What the hell are you talking about? How are you going to train up there? Seriously train? All your people are down here."

"Well, they can come up. They're used to travelling; they know the drill. We'll say it's a real training camp."

"That's insane. They have other fighters they're working with, you know. Why the hell would all of them move to the middle of nowhere instead of one of you moving back home?"

"Because I've made commitments here. I'm supposed to be living with my brother. It's a term of his parole. And I've got a class I'm teaching at the community center—"

"Jesus, Zara, what the hell happened to you? Where's your focus? Your drive? Are you going to tell me that you've got tea parties you need to go to, or you've found a place you like to get your nails done and you don't want to leave? All that crap up there is just filler. You know that. Your life is down here, and it's time for you to get back to it."

"My brother is not *filler*." Zara let her voice be cold. Andre doubted her focus? Well, she was about to laser-beam his ass, and he could see how well she could focus then.

He was silent for a moment, long enough for her to imagine him taking a couple deep breaths and collecting himself. When he spoke again, his voice was more level. "Of course he isn't. That's important, and we'll find a way to make it work. But the rest of it is—"

"The classes are important, too."

"No, Zara. Training is a full-time job, and it's one that needs to be done down here. You want to keep teaching classes up there? How are you going to make that work?"

She had no idea. Helping Zane. Teaching the classes. And Cal, whether she'd mentioned him to Andre or not. These were the reasons she didn't want to leave Lake Sullivan.

These were the things stealing her focus and making her weak. "I'll sort things out and get back to you," she told Andre, and she ended the call.

She stood quietly for a moment, then realized that everyone at the table had stopped talking and was watching her. Waiting. Maybe they'd overheard parts of the conversation, or maybe her body language had given her away. She made herself smile. "They got me on a card, for mid-December. I'm fighting Anna Cade—she's coming down a weight class."

"That's great," Ashley said cautiously.

"Yeah." Zara forced the smile just a little wider. "It's really exciting. I'm looking forward to it!"

"When are you leaving?" Cal asked. His voice was level, but tight. She hadn't managed to really look at him yet.

"I don't know," she admitted. "Soon, I guess. I need to sort a few things out."

"I can talk to my parole officer tomorrow," Zane said quickly. "I think he'll be okay with me staying alone."

Yeah, Zane wasn't going to be sorry to get rid of her.

"And there's only one more class scheduled for our MMA," Ashley said. "We were just going to spar anyway, right? So, I mean, it'd be great if you could be there, but we can make it work without you. The center can just grab a random person to make sure we're safe or whatever. It'll be fine."

Another person clearly not too upset about seeing her go. "Yeah, good," Zara said. "Thanks. That's all good."

Everything was good. Everything was getting back to normal, and that was what she wanted. She forced another smile and tried to think about Anna Cade. A strong opponent. A worthwhile fight. It was great! Exciting!

She sipped her juice and tried to pretend she was just stunned from too much happiness.

"MORE flowers?" Maggie at the grocery store asked.

Cal nodded. "You bet. They make me feel pretty." He leaned in a little closer and whispered, "You should try scattering the petals over the top of a nice bubble bath. I love it!"

"Uh-huh." She inspected the rest of his purchases with equal intensity but less comment, and he headed out of the store, bouquet in hand.

His enthusiasm waned a little when he arrived home and found Zara sitting on his front porch steps, her expression somber. But he forced himself to put on a brave face and pulled the flowers and grocery bags out of the back of the car.

"You okay?" he asked as he walked up the path to the door.

"Yeah," she said. "Perfectly fine. Fit to fight. No worries."

"And yet I'm worried. Get the door for me, will you?"

"Keys?"

"It shouldn't be locked."

"Seriously?" She turned the knob and pushed the door open with a disgusted snort. "I was getting cold out here. I could have been inside?"

"Sorry." He carried his groceries to the kitchen, set them on the counter, and said, "Has anyone snuck in between times, or can I be the third person to give you flowers, as well as the first and second?"

"The old ones aren't even dead yet. Not all of them."

"Are you refusing my flowers?"

It was not a good sign that he still found her eye rolls completely adorable. "No, of course not." She reached for them and smiled. "They're beautiful. Thank you."

"You're welcome." He pulled juice out of his grocery bag and poured her a glass, then pulled a beer out of the fridge for himself. "So." He handed her the glass of juice and nodded toward the sofas. "You're leaving." They hadn't really talked about it the night before. It hadn't seemed like there was much to say. But he didn't think he could just let this go, not without . . . without *something* more.

"Yeah," she said quietly. "I'm leaving. With the fight scheduled, I need to get back in shape, and I can't do that here."

Cal wasn't sure what part of that he wanted to talk about first. Well, he was damned sure he wanted to yell at her about her head and how she should probably never get back in the ring and sure as hell shouldn't be doing it so soon. But she didn't want to hear that from him. Better to wait until he was a bit calmer and could figure out a way to sneak up on the topic. So in the meantime he said, "If it helps, with the parole thing, I can stay with Zane, or he can come stay here. If that does any good."

She blinked hard again before saying, "Yeah, thanks. I'm hoping he can just live on his own, but if they don't like that, or if Zane doesn't like that, I appreciate the offer."

"So what else can I do? How can I help?"

She looked down at her flowers, poking at one of the blossoms before saying, "I'm moving back to the city. You caught that part, right? I mean . . . thank you. For being so generous and everything. But I'm *leaving*, Cal. Do you get that?"

"You mean you're dumping me."

"Not dumping. But I'm not going to live here anymore. So . . ."

So that was it. He was no longer convenient, so he was out.

He had no right to act surprised. She'd never made a secret of her plans, and he'd been the one chasing her, right from the start. "Yeah, okay," he said, but apparently that wasn't quite enough for her.

"What do you want me to say?" Zara demanded. "Am I supposed to quit fighting and come live here forever?"

"Is that an option? Because, hell yeah, that would be great. I could see more of you and you could avoid brain damage—sounds like a win-win."

"Enough with the brain damage!"

"Why? Because you're pretending it's not a possibility?" He wasn't going to hold back, not if this was his last chance to talk to her about it. "Damn it, Zara, you know it could happen! I mean, anytime you get in the ring with a trained fighter who's allowed to hit you in the head, it's a possibility, but in this case? When you're not recovered from—no, don't make that face, *you're not recovered* from your last concussion. I can't believe you're taking the chance. And mid-December? What is that, five weeks? That's not enough time to get fit, is it? So you'll be even more vulnerable! Jesus, Zara!"

"It's six weeks."

"Oh, okay, then. No problem." He tried to take some of the bitterness out of his voice when he said, "What if you just said no? You could tell them you need more time to be sure your head's okay."

"I already told them it was fine. They gave me a clean bill of health."

"So tell them things have changed."

She stared at him. He couldn't read her expression, but he didn't think she was angry. Confused maybe, certainly some brand of upset, but not really angry. He softened his tone. "What would happen if you didn't fight?"

"They could take the title away. If I refuse to fight without a good reason, they could take it away."

He nodded. He didn't give a good goddamn about the title, but she did. "So we can either persuade them that you do have a good reason to refuse, or . . ." He shrugged. "If you get better and want to fight again, you can win the title back. Right? And if the concussion stuff keeps on being a problem—I know you don't want to hear it, Zare, but you'd have to retire anyway. So either way, where's the harm in turning down this fight?"

"You don't know how it works. You make one poster for them and you think you're an expert? It's not as easy as you make it sound."

"What, now you're only doing things that are easy? Sorry, I didn't realize."

"Shut up," she grumbled. She looked back down at the

flowers and said, "Can we just not think about it? For tonight, at least, can we just be *here*?"

He stared at her for a moment. Forget everything else? Tempting, but possible? "We can try," he said. And they did. They made dinner, and ate it together, and then they made love, slow and gentle. Cal didn't want to admit it, but it felt like they were saying good-bye.

❧ Nineteen ❧

ZARA'S FINGERS WERE tight around the steering wheel. It had been so easy physically to load up her belongings and drive out of Lake Sullivan, and so nearly impossible emotionally.

It wasn't just leaving Cal that was hard. They'd left things open that morning; she was just going to spend a few days in the city and see how training felt, and maybe she'd try to talk to Terry, the head of the organization, if she could think of anything to say. Cal had offered to call him on her behalf and she'd shut him down, of course. She had a manager, and if there was something Andre couldn't do, then she'd do it herself. She didn't need her boyfriend—

She caught herself. *Boyfriend.* That word again. Was that what Cal was? If he ever had been, was he still? The bags of clothes on the seat behind her sure made it seem like she was leaving Lake Sullivan for good, but . . . but what?

Zane's probation officer had said it was okay for Zane to

live alone as long as he kept going to work regularly and Zara checked in on him. And Zane had said he was fine by himself, although Zara wasn't feeling totally comfortable with that claim. Again, though, Cal had stepped in and said he'd make sure Zane was okay.

It was kind of hard to leave the guy behind when he was still involved in her brother's life. Kind of hard to leave him behind even without that.

She couldn't get over the feeling that she should be pulling a U-turn and heading back to Lake Sullivan. But somehow her discipline held and she made it to the city. Her apartment was in Queens, only a few blocks from the gym where she did most of her training, and she stopped there only long enough to empty the car. It wasn't the best neighborhood and leaving anything inside a vehicle was an invitation for someone to break in and take it. But as soon as that was done, she headed for the gym.

That was what she needed. A good workout, some training with her old crew, and she'd get back into real life with no trouble.

She pushed the heavy door open and slipped inside, then stood there for a moment, just watching. Everything seemed so normal. She'd taken breaks before, of course, and she knew the gym kept functioning even without her presence. But it was still strange to see it happening right before her eyes.

Bonita was the first to notice her, glancing over as she took one of her thirty-second rests from the kettlebell training circuit. "Damn," she called over the grunts and conversations of the men around them. "I was getting used to having the apartment to myself!"

"Too bad for you," Zara replied. "I'm back."

Bonita jogged over for a quick, sweaty hug, then jerked her head toward the mats. "I've got to keep going," she said.

Zara nodded. There were others to greet now, trainers and coaches and other fighters, and they were a good distraction. She set up some training and sparring times, arranged for fight tapes to be e-mailed to her so she could start watching Anna Cade's technique, and then heard someone from over her shoulder say, "Or you could just wait 'til she shows up and watch her live."

Zara turned to look at whoever it was. Some young guy she didn't know. "What are you talking about?"

His smile told her he'd gotten the reaction he was hoping for. "You didn't know she started training here? Your manager's the one who set it up."

She stared at him. "Andre? Why the hell—" She stopped talking. She needed to play this right, and that meant not showing weakness or confusion to whoever this clown was. "Yeah, okay," she said, and turned away from him.

Damon Malicki, the head coach, had watched the exchange. "Come talk to me," he said.

She'd been working with him for years. She trusted him, surely. If she didn't, she needed to go find a new gym fast. But she was pretty sure she did, so she followed him off to a slightly more private corner of the gym.

"Andre didn't mention that to you?"

"Is he *managing* her? He set up a fight for me with someone else he's managing?"

"Not officially," Damon said. "As I understand it, he's trying to sign her but he hasn't done it. Not yet."

"But you're training her." It wasn't unheard of for opponents to come from the same gym, but it wasn't anything Zara had ever experienced before. Bonita was still working her way up the rankings, not ready for a title shot yet, and the only other women at the gym were even lower ranked than Bonita.

"I am."

"So how are you supposed to, like, give me strategies? Are you going to be telling her how to beat me up?"

"I'll do my best for both of you," he said. Then he paused as if thinking over his next words. "Andre didn't tell you about this? I'm sorry, I would have given you a call when I took her on—not to ask permission, just to give you a heads-up. But I assumed he'd already done that."

"No." Again, it wasn't unheard of for managers to have fighters face off against each other. The MMA world just wasn't that big, and any manager who was trying to make a living needed to have quite a few fighters under contract. But Andre not telling Zara about his plans? There was something wrong. Seriously wrong.

She wanted to call Cal. How weak she'd become, and so quickly! She'd only really known him, as an adult, for a couple months. Only been . . . whatever they were . . . for even less time. And already she wanted to go crawling to him for help. Damn it. She needed to get tough again.

And she was going to start that process by talking to Andre. Without Cal's help.

"I just want to keep her safe," Cal said. He and Zane were at Woody's, as usual, and Cal was pretty sure he'd had too much to drink. Not sloppy drunk yet, but certainly saying things he shouldn't. "She won't let me take care of her, of course. But that just makes me want it even more. Because she's so strong, but she shouldn't have to be."

Zane seemed amused. "There's nothing wrong with being strong. It's not what you have to be, it's what you *get* to be."

"Okay. Yeah, okay, good point. But she shouldn't have to use her strength so often. That's what I mean."

"Use it or lose it," Zane said with a shrug.

"Really? You think that's true?"

Zane seemed to think it over. "Maybe not. There's people who can surprise you. They never seem to stand up to anything until one day all of sudden they do." Another shrug. "And the other direction, too. I mean, I thought I was a pretty tough kid, but after a while it wore me down. It wasn't making me stronger anymore, it was just . . . killing me."

"You have no idea how much I wish I'd been more helpful with that." Cal slammed his beer down on the table. "And now I don't want to make the same mistake with Zara. I listened to you when you said you didn't need help, and you were lying, you bastard! So now what if Zara's lying? What if she does need help, and I'm sitting around here with you instead of doing something?"

"What would you do exactly?"

"I have a long list of possible activities."

"Do any of them make any actual sense?"

"A couple of them might."

"Give me the top two."

Well, that was a little more structure than Cal had been expecting. The top two. Huh. "Well, I think me getting my ass to the city is probably part of both of them. I really don't think I can do a lot from up here."

"Okay. And then, once you're down there . . ."

"I could talk to Terry. Try to figure out some business reason why it would be better for her to fight later, and convince him of that."

"And then after Zara cuts your balls off for interfering, what's the next step?"

"Well, yeah, that's where the plan gets a little sketchy."

"That was your best idea? Or was it the first runner-up, and you're about to reveal the beauty queen idea now?"

"The other idea is just . . . hanging around. Being there.

Keeping an eye on her, watching if she's getting dizzy or anything, trying to talk to her. It's a lot less satisfying than the direct intervention."

"But a lot more likely to leave you with your balls attached."

"An important point."

Zane sighed. "This is serious? The concussion thing, it's a real risk? She said the doctors told her she was okay."

"She lied to the doctors. They were basing their diagnosis on inaccurate information."

"Yeah. That's not good." Zane sipped his beer. "You'd really do that? I mean, could you do that? You've got a career up here, you know. Might be kind of hard to do it from a distance. And look, Cal, it's not your job to rescue the Hales. You're just a guy, not our guardian angel. You didn't let me down ten years ago. Not before it went bad, and not after, either. You did the right thing. I appreciate it. But you're not actually responsible for looking after us forever."

"I want to help you both. Because I care about you both."

"You and Zara weren't together all that long. It was intense, I guess, but still, not a lot of time. And she just left town yesterday. You don't think you should maybe just settle down a little and adjust to the new situation? You're really going to drop everything and move to the city for her? Just like that?"

Cal knew that everything Zane was saying made sense. But he also knew how he felt, and what he was prepared to do. "Yeah," he said. "I think so. Well, I won't drop everything. I'll set some of it down carefully, and I'll bring some of it along with me. It's the slow season at work, and there's nothing super pressing going on. So really it's just the moving that's a problem. But, yeah, I'll move to the city for her. At least, I'm going to try to. Who knows if she'll let me?"

"Okay," Zane said after a moment. "That's a bit crazy, but okay."

"I'll go back and forth, probably, for work. We can get together when I'm in town, and keep in touch with texts and e-mails and stuff."

Zane snorted. "Zara would kick your ass if you skipped out to be with her and I went off the rails back here all on my own. Is that what you're worried about?"

"I'm just worried that you'll miss me. I am very good company. All others will pale in comparison to me."

"I'm pretty sure I'll live through it."

"You're being brave. I appreciate that."

"I actually wouldn't mind a slightly longer leash," Zane admitted. "When you and Zara hooked up, it was great—I could just live, without having her worried little face staring at me all the time."

"She cares about you."

"I never said she didn't. But it was a bit claustrophobic, and it was good when she got distracted."

"She's not much good at subtlety, is she?"

Zane snorted into his beer. "No," he said, making it clear that he was understating the case.

Cal smiled into his own drink. It felt good to have a decision made. Even if it was a strange decision, a wild jump into an unknown future, at least he was going to be doing something, not just sitting around and fretting.

He thought about how to approach Zara and his enthusiasm faded a little. It wasn't like she'd invited him, or even hinted that she'd like him to come.

She didn't own the city; he could find a short-term rental somewhere, or stay in a hotel even, and that was really none of her business. And then if he was in town anyway, they might as well spend some time together. . . .

Yeah, that was weak. But it was the best he had, so he'd better just hope Zara was in a charitable mood when he arrived.

* * *

"IT'S bullshit, Andre." The bastard had put her off for almost two days, saying he was out of town and couldn't make a meeting and wasn't this really something they should discuss face-to-face, and now that he was finally back, he was telling her it wasn't an issue. "If it was no big deal, why didn't you mention it?"

"Zara, we don't normally discuss my business. We discuss your business. That's my role."

They were in a corner of the gym, somewhere quiet enough for a conversation but still not exactly private. So Zara tried to keep her voice down. "You didn't think it was my business to know who coaches my next opponent? You didn't think maybe I should know that she's thinking about dumping her management and is being recruited by half the guys in the business? Bullshit."

"So you've said. And I'm not sure what I can say to change your mind. So let's let it go for now and move forward. Your training is going well?"

"Should I give you the canned answer I give to the press? The one that I want my opponent to hear? Or do I tell you the truth?"

"Is the truth something problematic? Are things not going well?"

"Things are going great! It's a short camp, but I'm lucky that I really held on to my conditioning, even during a break, so I'm really just fine-tuning at this point. And I'm really looking forward to the fight—Anna Cade is a great young fighter with a lot of potential and it's inspiring to see her dropping a weight class to make the matchup happen!"

"That's your canned answer, I assume." Andre did not sound amused.

"It's the only answer I've got, as long as you're trying to recruit someone I'm scheduled to fight."

He stared at her and there was something in his expression that reminded her that he'd come from the streets, just like she had. He might have a better smooth polish, but that didn't mean he wasn't rough underneath. "You might want to think twice before asking me to choose between you and Anna Cade. She's just as good looking as you are, she hits like a damn sledgehammer, and she *likes* doing promotion. She loves the modeling, and does a good job at it. That girl is the future, Zara, and if you're not careful, you're going to be the past."

It stung, but she didn't let him see her wince. She knew too well how vulnerable her career was without hearing him remind her of it. She made her voice cool and level as she said, "Okay. I don't think you actually have a lot to do for me in the next few weeks, do you? My sponsors are all lined up and the fight time is set and I'm not going to be looking at any new deals right before a fight. So let's take a break. You focus on the future. I'll focus on training myself to knock the future's damn head off in the ring."

He nodded ruefully. "There's that old fire! Now, if you could just channel that drive, and use it to give you energy outside of the ring—"

But Zara didn't need to hear the rest of whatever he had to say. She pushed to her feet and headed back to her training. Like most of the fighters, she worked out twice a day, and she and Damon had figured out a coaching schedule that would keep her and Anna apart for most of the time. And this was Zara's time. She worked out, pushing hard, and maybe there was a little dizziness a few times but she was able to get past it. Whatever the issue with her head was, it was getting better. Nothing to worry about.

She walked back to the apartment with Bonita, bitching

on the way, and Bonita was more sympathetic than usual. "He's a sleazy bastard. No loyalty at all. If I'd known he hadn't told you, I would have called and let you know, but damn! Who'd have thought he wouldn't have told you?"

"Yeah," Zara agreed glumly. Andre was sleazy. That part was annoying, but not a huge surprise. The troubling aspect of it all was that he thought Anna was better than her. Maybe just at the promo side of things, but if he really was trying to sign Anna, he'd want her to win her fights. He wouldn't have let the company set up this card if he hadn't thought Anna would be able to take Zara down. Wouldn't have been so willing to piss Zara off if he thought she would be the winner. A lot of the money in women's MMA came from sponsorships, sure, and a lot of that was based on crowd reaction and looks. But crowd reaction came from good fighting. From winning. It was all connected, and apparently Andre thought Anna was better than Zara at all of it.

Was he right? Was she washed up? Not just because of her concussion, but because of her attitude?

She didn't want to think so. She wasn't quite as hungry anymore maybe, but she was just as tough. Hell, maybe she was tougher. When she'd been starting out, she'd let Andre push her around more, been more willing to do his stupid promo stunts. Now she was strong enough to say "no" more often. And he was going to dump her for it.

"Ooh, hot man alert," Bonita said as they approached the apartment. "Maybe he's a little clean cut for you, but I like the preppy type."

Zara followed Bonita's gaze and found Cal, leaning against the hood of his car, watching them approach. Her breath caught. Cal. He was here. He'd . . . She caught herself. She couldn't leap to conclusions. She didn't know he'd followed her. Not for sure. Maybe he'd just . . . just . . . no, damn it! He'd followed her. He'd come for her.

He watched them approach and she could feel his trepidation. He wasn't sure how she was going to react.

"Nobody's dead or anything?" she asked as she stopped in front of him.

He swallowed. "Everybody's fine. I just missed you."

She was vaguely aware of Bonita standing behind them, but didn't let it slow her down. She stretched up and wrapped her arms around Cal's neck, and he grinned and lifted her a little, and then there they were, making out in public *again*. And everything was absolutely perfect.

❧ *Twenty* ❧

IT WAS KIND of scary how well things went after that. Cal found a short-term rental apartment about ten minutes from Zara's place, and when Zara was at the gym, he'd be at his apartment, catching up on work. She'd call him when her workout was over and they'd meet up somewhere and spend the middle of the day together. Long lunches, walks around the city, lazy hours in bed, making love and napping and waking up to do it all again. It was paradise.

Or damn near. Sure, there were things they couldn't talk about. Zara's head was the main thing they avoided. No questions from him and, after the time he offered her an aspirin as she massaged her temples, no signs from her. And they didn't talk about the upcoming fight. Or about how long Cal would stay in the city. Cal told himself they were both just focusing on enjoying the moment. No worries about the past or the future.

Cal was in love. He knew it, and didn't even try to fight it.

Most days they stayed close to home so they wouldn't miss Zara's gym time, but she took one day off a week and they were more adventurous then. They decided to do all the tourist stuff that they'd been too cool to explore as permanent residents of the city, and it felt like they were on vacation together. No, it felt like they were on their honeymoon.

They took the subway into Manhattan and walked through Central Park, bundled up in warm sweaters, scuffling their feet through the fallen leaves. Whenever Zara got excited about something, she'd skip ahead and turn around to walk backward so they could have better eye contact, and his heart sang at her enthusiasm and her boundless grace and energy.

They visited the Museum of Modern Art, and Zara tried hard to hide her yawns, faking polite interest in whatever works Cal stopped in front of. After an hour or so, he gave her a lengthy treatise on the imagery of the red fire alarm against the stark grey brick of the wall, the way it invited viewers to examine the role of danger and excitement in their mundane lives. He suggested that she should reflect on how the work might speak to her, and how she might be the red fire alarm that people living grey lives in Lake Sullivan could admire. When she finally realized it wasn't a work of art at all, just a regular fire alarm on an otherwise empty wall, she punched him in the shoulder, but not hard enough to leave a bruise.

At the Bronx Zoo they watched a baby gorilla climbing all over his mother, clearly showing off until the silverback wandered over and the baby suddenly got shy. Cal looked at Zara and wondered if she wanted to be a mom herself, with a little one crawling all over her. He wondered if they could be parents together. He wrapped his arms around her as they stood by the glass, watching the family within, and she lifted her hands and rested them on his. Was she thinking the same things he was, or was it just a cute scene to her? But asking her would have meant talking about the future, and he didn't think he could risk that. Well, it would have been too early to ask anyway, he told himself. They were still new, still figuring things out. The future would come in its own time.

He spent a lot of time at the gym, watching her. Admiring her. She was strong, sure, and fast and balanced and tough. But he was most impressed with her focus. When she watched the other fighters, looking for weaknesses, she watched with her whole body, her whole being. And when she practiced her technique, she moved with a fierce grace, a strange mix of unconscious ability and deliberate concentration. She'd warned him he'd be bored, but he never was. He was absolutely, completely content.

It wasn't always easy to find food that fit Zara's training diet, but Cal got used to that, and found himself searching for recipes online, trying to find ways to spice up the endless lean-protein, low-fat fare. He was on his laptop at Zara's while Zara was in the shower when Bonita snuck up behind him and looked over his shoulder at the screen. "She doesn't like rye bread."

"Oh." He squinted at the elaborate sandwich on the screen. "Probably wouldn't be good with white or wheat."

"Probably not," Bonita agreed. She flopped onto the couch opposite him and he watched her warily.

Cal had been in the city for almost a month and had spent a fair bit of time in Bonita's presence, but couldn't really say he knew her. They'd both been friendly enough, but just casual greetings, no real conversations. Something told him that was about to change.

So he waited, and finally Bonita said, "She's not training hard enough." It was strange how something could be phrased so neutrally and still sound like an accusation.

"Are you sure? She's putting in a lot of hours."

"Not as many as Anna is."

"Maybe she's working harder while she's there. Being more intense."

"She's not. She takes breaks, more than she ever has."

Because of her head? Judging by the expression on Bonita's face, she thought there was a different explanation. "Maybe she just doesn't want to fight anymore," he tried.

"Well, that'd be great. Really, it'd be super. If she'd found something else she loved just as much? And if she was good at it? Hey, I'm not a hero—it'd be great for my career if she quit. One less person above me in the rankings. But there's one little problem with that plan." She waited, then snorted in disgust when he didn't supply her with whatever she was looking for. "She *hasn't* quit. She's scheduled for a fight in two and a half weeks, and she's not fit for it. That doesn't just mean she'll lose—it means she could get hurt."

Well, Bonita certainly knew how to get his attention. "Why are you telling me this?"

She frowned as if he was stupid. "I look at how she's trained for other fights, and how she's training for this one, and I try to figure out what's different between then and now. . . ." She raised an eyebrow in his direction.

"Maybe *she's* different," he said.

"Then she should get the hell out of the game." There was a firmness to Bonita's voice that was hard to deny. She knew what she was talking about; Cal didn't. There was no point in arguing with her.

"Is anyone else seeing this, or just you?"

"Not Andre, if that's who you're hoping will save you. Well, he probably sees it, but he's not going to do anything about it. He's too busy kissing up to Anna."

"What about her trainer? Her coach?"

"They're confused. In the past, she's been so motivated herself that they've had to spend half their energy trying to slow her down and keep her from peaking too early. Now it's like she's following their advice, so they can't really complain too much, you know?"

They heard the door to Zara's room open and Bonita settled back on the couch, trying to look casual. So whatever solution she had in mind for Zara's situation, she obviously wasn't planning on being part of an intervention, at least not then and there.

Cal leaned back and smiled as Zara slid a cool hand inside the collar of his shirt and along the tops of his shoulders. It would be so easy to be distracted by this, to trust Zara to look after herself and go back to their easy life of enjoying each other and falling in love. So easy, but maybe not right. "You want to go for a walk?" he asked, and she nodded easily.

"We should be outside as much as we can before it gets really cold."

So they bundled up and headed out, and walked hand in hand through streets that were becoming familiar, if not quite homelike.

"What was Bonita after you about?" Zara asked after they'd gone a few blocks. He braced himself, but she didn't pull away. She just shrugged and said, "Thin walls. I got the tone, but not the actual words."

Well, this was either going to be easier than he had any reason to expect, or she was lulling him into a false sense of complacency. He carefully said, "She's worried that you're not training as hard as you normally do. She thinks you might be unfit for the fight."

"So you're worried about my brain, and she's worried about my body."

It was an invitation. It had to be. Cal had no idea why, but it really seemed like Zara was willing to talk about this, at least a little. "Yeah," he admitted. "Something like that. Well, I guess now I'm worried about your brain *and* your body. And the way they could go together. Like, if you're overpowered and can't control the fight, it might be hard for you to protect your head the way you want to."

"My training is fine. I'm fit." She said it with such certainty.

But Bonita had been just as certain. Cal was torn. "Bonita said you weren't putting in as many hours as you used to. She said you were taking more breaks."

"I'm not, and I am."

"You're not putting in as many hours, and you are taking more breaks?" She nodded, he frowned. "But you're still fit. As fit as you usually would be?"

"I will be in two and a half weeks, yeah." She raised her chin, ready for a fight. But there was no heaviness to her, no jagged edge that might cut him if he dared to disagree. She'd fight him, but she didn't want to hurt him, because she trusted that he didn't want to hurt her. These past weeks— not talking about what she didn't want to talk about—had done that, he realized with a start. They'd built up enough trust that they could have this conversation now.

"Okay," he said. "I believe you. Your body will be fit."

She smiled at him, and then was gracious enough to explain herself. "I've been working on explosive strength, not long-term endurance. My strategy is to take her out hard, right away. A fight is, maximum, five five-minute sprints. There's no marathon, so there's no point training for one. I used to train for both, the sprint and the marathon, and that was fine. I was young and had too much damn energy anyways, so it wasn't bad for me to channel it into training. But I didn't need to. Most of my fights last less than a minute. That's how long this one will last, too."

"And if it doesn't? If it goes the full twenty-five?"

"I'll be ready," she said.

And he believed her. They walked in silence for another block, then turned into the little park by the subway station and kept walking.

Finally, Zara said, "You're not going to ask about the other? About my head?"

"Is anything new? Anything you want to tell me?"

"Yeah. There's something new."

He stopped walking and turned to look at her. Her chin was still up, but there was a trace of something different in her eyes. Not fear, exactly, but something close to it. "I made an appointment with a neurologist. One that's not associated with the company. Day after tomorrow. I want to just . . . I don't know. I want to have all available information. That's good, right? Just to know what's going on."

He didn't want to breathe in case he somehow broke the spell. But she was waiting for a response, so he said, "Yeah. I think that's good. That's important."

She nodded and turned to start walking again. He reclaimed her hand and asked, "Can I come with you?"

Another nod. "Yeah. Thanks."

And they walked on without saying any more, but with their hands gripped just a little tighter than before.

"SO what's the point of being here?" Zara demanded. She'd gone through all the tests, forced herself to answer all the questions honestly, even with Cal sitting there listening, and now this so-called expert was giving her nothing? "You don't *know* if it's safe? You don't know if my brain is still scrambled?"

"It's impossible to say," Dr. Thorne said. Zara had chosen her from the list of neurologists supplied by her GP because the name sounded fierce and strong, like someone who would understand Zara's fighting instinct. But she was beginning to wish she'd made another choice. Still, Dr. Thorne didn't seem like she was going to be pushed into making any declarations. "Nothing shows up on your MRI or CT scans, but that doesn't mean too much. Your symptoms are mild, and could be attributed to the stress of training. So maybe your brain has recovered, at least as much as it ever will. But maybe it hasn't."

The doctor leaned over her desk. "And even if it has recovered this time, there's still a lot we don't know about the long-term effects of concussions. There's reliable data showing a connection to symptoms that look a lot like Alzheimer's and Parkinson's, even thirty or more years after the injury. We know that every concussion adds to the likelihood of this outcome. We know that every concussion is harder to recover from than the one before, and is more likely to cause permanent brain damage. That could take the form of cognitive difficulties, moodiness, depression— *permanent* changes to the brain."

She leaned back now, and gave Zara a minute to absorb it all. Then she said, "If it were up to me, head protection would be mandatory for all boxing and MMA events. My understanding is that athletes wear this protection when they spar as part of their training and are still able to demonstrate their skills. But that's not something I can influence. What I can say is that with two concussions in the past year, you are at much higher risk of permanent brain injury than other athletes in the sport. I would strongly recommend that you not fight."

Zara had thought she was ready to hear this. She'd hoped

that the doctor would give her good news, something to calm Cal down and maybe soothe her own jitters, but she'd thought she was prepared to hear the bad if it came. She'd been wrong. "But you'd have recommended against me fighting if I'd come to you before I got any concussions, right? That whole wearing-headgear-when-fighting thing?"

The doctor sighed. "I would have, yes. I understand competitiveness, but I don't understand the need to risk serious injury."

Zara nodded her chin toward the photo on the wall behind the doctor's head, showing the woman on a racing bicycle, with a number strapped on her chest. "But it's okay for you to ride bikes? They never wipe out, never get sideswiped by cars?"

"I wear protective gear. I minimize the risk."

"But there still is a risk. If you wanted to get the health benefits, you could ride a stationary bike at home. But you want do something real, something that makes you feel alive. So you take the chance."

"I do," Dr. Thorne said slowly. "I take that chance, but I wouldn't take the chance you're thinking about taking. By my standards, it's too risky. Absolutely."

"But there's nothing clear. No big warning signs, no flashing lights." Zara glanced at Cal, then looked back at the doctor. "There's nothing I could show to the fight officials that would tell them I'm unfit to fight. You're just operating on general impressions and probabilities, not proof."

"I could write a note saying I advise against it," Dr. Thorne said. "I'd be pleased to do that. But, no, I can't actually show any proof of your individual condition."

Zara's nod felt a little jerky. "Okay. Thanks anyway."

"Should I write the letter?"

"Sure. I'll put it in my scrapbook."

"We can still use it," Cal said. He'd been quiet all day, holding her hand whenever it was possible but otherwise staying out of things, and she'd appreciated it.

So she didn't snap at him, just shrugged and said, "For what? They won't let me out of the fight, not without something that proves I'm unhealthy. They'll just say I'm scared of her."

"Let them say it! Who cares?"

"I care!" She shook her head. "I can't back down. They'll take my title away, and everyone will think I'm a quitter. Andre's already trying to switch from me to Anna, and I think the company might be thinking that way, too. They want her to be the new face of women's MMA. So I'm supposed to give up and just let her take my spot? No way."

He had his mouth open to respond, then looked at the doctor and bit his lip instead. The lecture wasn't cancelled, just postponed.

And it stayed that way for several days. Zara tried to go back to the way they'd been before, but the doctor's advice was always there, hanging between them. Every smile Cal gave her seemed forced, and when he kissed her, it felt like good-bye.

She put up with it for three days. Then she walked into his apartment after a day of training and saw a packed duffel bag by the door, and it seemed like the bottom had dropped out of her world. "Going somewhere?" she asked, trying to sound light.

He nodded. "I need to spend a couple days at home. There's a problem at the furniture plant—nothing huge, just some new equipment that isn't working right—and someone needs to take care of it."

"Oh." It would be easier, safer, to just let that go, but she couldn't. "And then you'll come back?"

It took him too long to answer. "I don't know," he finally said.

She made herself swallow through a throat suddenly gone

tight and dry. "Because you need to be there for work?" she said desperately.

He shook his head, but didn't say anything right away. Finally he spoke. "I don't want you to fight."

"I know." What else was there to say?

"I'm asking you not to."

She didn't really know what that meant. Well, she understood the words, but he'd spoken them like they had extra weight, extra meaning, something she wasn't quite getting. So she thought about it for a while. "Like . . . like what? What does that mean?"

"What does it mean that I'm asking you not to?" He sounded incredulous. Apparently everyone already knew this code in rich-kid-land.

"Are you calling in a favor? Like, I owe you one, and you want to collect?"

It was his turn to think for a while. "Not exactly. That would be a sort of transactional exchange, right? And I'm asking for a relationship-based—whatever. Favor."

"You don't know what it means to me," she said desperately. "You don't understand why it's important."

"You're right, I don't. I can't for the life of me figure out why you'd risk your life on this."

"Not my *life*."

"Maybe your life. Fighters have died before, you know. In the ring. Boxers, martial artists. It happens. But even if it's not your actual life, it could still be huge. Brain damage could change your whole personality. I like your personality. I like you the way you are. So you tell me, what's so important that it's worth risking that?"

Zara fought to put it into words. "Maybe you can't understand it. Because you were brought up as part of something— part of everything, really. The whole town knew who you were, and they were all so proud of every damn step you took. Me?" She didn't want to get too excited, didn't want to sound pathetic or like she was looking for pity. So she took a few deep breaths before saying in a calmer voice, "Nobody ever claimed me, or wanted to know me, and they sure as hell were never proud of me. Nobody. Not until I got good at MMA. Now I have people who want to do business with me. *Me*. Sure, yeah, they're using me, but at least I'm something worth using. You know? They pay attention to me. There's a whole bar in Lake Sullivan I don't want to go to because it would be too intense. Because they're interested in *me*." He was still listening, at least, so she gave it a little more. "And you want me to throw that respect away? Make myself look like a coward in front of people who care about guts more than they care about anything else? No. No way. I won't do it."

He was quiet then, staring at the packed bag as if it held the secrets of the universe. Then he whispered, "I love you."

It should have been a moment to savor, but her mind skittered right over the words to what she was sure lay beneath them. "So that means you can't be with me?" she demanded, trying to keep her voice from rising too high.

"I love you the way you are. I don't want you to get hurt, and I don't want you to change, because who you are right now is perfect, and I can't stand the thought of you getting hit in the head and walking out of that ring being somebody else. If you're even able to walk out at all."

She fought for breath, for calm. He was saying this to her *now*. Telling her he loved her. Using the words as a tool to control her, a part of her brain said. But another part told her that he was being honest, in response to her own honesty.

But she couldn't hear this, not two weeks before a huge fight, not when she was already fighting her own fear and doubts. "You love me as a fighter," she spat. "That poster? Half fighter, half whore? You came up with that because you have some sort of a . . . a fetish or something! You only know me as a fighter, and that's a huge part of who I am. So don't pretend I won't change. If I walk away from this bout, if I give up, that would change me. Absolutely. Being a fighter is who I am, and if I'm not that, then neither one of us knows who the hell I'll be."

He stared at her. "You really think you being a fighter is something that depends on you stepping into the ring?" He sounded amazed, almost scornful, but his voice softened as he said, "You were the toughest little kid I ever saw. You and Zane, staring down the world together, neither one of you giving a damn inch to anybody. You were a fighter when you broke that Albertson kid's nose for picking on some other kid, and you were, what, seven? He was a couple years older and you took him down. No fear. Just fight." He smiled at her now, sad but warm. "You were a fighter when you randomly declared egg war on my family. You kept that going for almost a damn year. I wouldn't have stopped you except my dad was threatening to call out the big guns, the cops and the child welfare people and whatever, and I knew you'd fight them, too, and they might hurt you. You were a fighter when you went up to visit Zane after he got in trouble, travelling all that way on your own as a sixteen-year-old. Hell, you fight with me all the time." He shook his head. His voice was low and intense as he added, "You're a warrior. It's in your blood, in your heart. It doesn't have a damn thing to do with martial arts. It's just you."

She didn't want to cry. Not about this, not about anything. And not in front of Cal. "I can't . . ." she started. But she'd already said that. "I have to . . ." But she'd said that, too.

"You *can* do anything. And if someone's telling you that you have to do something, that's who you should be fighting against!"

It was so easy for him. So clear, so simple. But it wasn't that way for her. "I have to fight," she said.

He wasn't looking at her anymore, just staring out the window toward the street below. Finally he whispered, "I'm not sure I can watch that."

"You don't have to watch it!"

"I'm not sure I can know about it. Or watch you train for it. I can't stop talking to you about it. I did my best. I gave you space and you let me in, and now . . . I don't know if I can stand to be in, not if being in means standing by when you insist on doing something we both know is stupid and dangerous."

She felt cold, even though the apartment was well-heated. "What are you saying?"

"I don't know exactly. I need some time to think about it." He shook his head. "Like I said, I need to go back for business. I'll use the time to think, I guess. You can—" He stopped short. "No, I guess not. You've already decided, so there's no point in you thinking about it anymore. You'll do what you want, and I'll just have to figure out if I can deal with it."

She wanted to rage at him. It would be so much easier to be angry. But she wasn't. "Is this . . . are you breaking up with me? Is that what's happening? If that's what you're doing, you should say the words, okay? You need to just spell it out. I'm not good at—"

"You're good at whatever you try to be good at!" The anger faded out of his voice quickly. "But yes. I think if we call it something else, if we say we're still together, just not in the same place, I think I'll still go crazy." He shook his head. "I think I'm going to go crazy regardless. But maybe not. Maybe less if we're . . ."

"Fine." She'd found a bit of anger now, enough to get her out of the apartment and maybe even partway home. "We're done. We're over. You can go running back to your safe little life, and I'll stay out here where things aren't so damn easy."

"Don't play it like that. You're the one keeping it from being easy. Your pride, your competitiveness. Nobody's making you fight, nobody but *you*."

"Yeah, sorry I didn't just give in and do what you thought was best. It must be really hard for you to feel so responsible for saving the Hales all the time. *Noblesse oblige*, that's what it's called, right? You're the great master, forced to make decisions for your underlings because we can't possibly take care of ourselves?"

"That argument would be a hell of a lot more compelling if you weren't about to do something that everybody thinks is totally stupid."

"Everybody? Maybe everybody in your little world. But not everybody in mine. In my world, we're expected to tough it out, not go running home to our mommies." He wasn't fighting anymore, she didn't think. But that killer instinct made her keep going. "Hey, you called the cops on Zane when he didn't follow your rules. What are you going to do to me? Got any new ways to ruin people's lives?"

It was too far. Way too far. She knew it as soon as she said it, but somehow she still wanted to say more. She wanted to burn everything to the ground so she could keep herself warm with the flames. She wanted to spew anger and hatred like lava, wanted to let it cool into the stone she needed to be for the next two weeks. And maybe longer, because she had a feeling she was going to need a lot more strength to get over Cal than she'd ever need to prep for a fight.

But she managed to control herself. "Thanks for the last couple months," she said as she pushed the apartment door open. "They were fun."

She headed for the door of the building then, refusing to look behind her, refusing to admit she was hoping to hear his voice calling out to her, stopping her. He didn't make a sound. Zara got all the way to the street before the tears came. That was her only victory for the day.

❧ Twenty-one ❧

CAL WAS PRETTY sure the man who'd supplied the faulty equipment for the furniture factory was about to cry, and even so it was hard to stop berating him.

"We're losing money every second that line isn't working," Cal said. "This close to Christmas, we're not going to lay off fifteen workers until you can get your shit together!" Michael had thought the layoff was only good business, but Michael was an asshole. "So you're costing me sales *and* I'm paying for fifteen men to sit around doing nothing, all because you couldn't write down a few numbers properly?"

"We sent an order confirmation—" the man began.

"Written in your own code! We bought from you because you're supposed to be experts in the field! Experts at making equipment, and supplying equipment. Instead, you've supplied crap!" Cal took a deep breath and tried to calm himself. It wasn't like he gave a damn about furniture manufacturing, after all. "So now you need to make it better. I don't want to hear any more excuses; I want this fixed. Do you understand?"

The man nodded.

"Well, then go get on it! I'm going to be here first thing tomorrow morning and I want to see your guys here installing the new equipment. Clear?"

"Yes, sir," the man said, and scurried away.

Cal watched him leave, feeling vaguely disgusted. With himself, not the poor salesman. Since when was bullying okay? Why did he think it was acceptable to treat people that way? Was it just because he was a Montgomery? Zara would say—

But he caught himself, almost in time. It didn't matter what Zara would say. Zara was gone. She'd rather get her brain slammed into jelly than live happily ever after with him.

So Cal needed to stop thinking about her and move on.

He wished there was someone else around who needed a good yelling-at, and when he realized just how hard he was looking for something to complain about, he left the factory and headed to the gym. Where, of course, he was reminded of Zara. Damn it.

He lifted weights anyway, working until every muscle in his body was shaking, and then he took off, running into the falling night. He and Zara had jogged together often and it wasn't easy to find new paths, routes that weren't haunted by her memory. He pushed on, though, working his exhausted body to the point of revolt. He was staggering a little by the time he slowed to a walk at the end of his street and started toward the house.

And then he stopped altogether when he saw the car in the driveway. Zane's Mustang. Well, Zara's Mustang, which Zane had been driving since he got out.

He forced his feet to start moving again.

Zane stepped out of the car and met him at the end of the driveway. "Welcome home. You look like shit and I heard you were having a temper tantrum at work. Want to get a beer?"

"If I start drinking, it might be a while before I stop."

Zane shrugged. "I can babysit you, if you want to let go."

"Even if my 'letting go' involves me saying some uncomplimentary things about your sister?"

"Would it?" Zane's gaze was intent, despite his casual words and body language. "Doesn't seem like you'd get all that upset about anything she did if you didn't care about her."

"Yeah, I care about her. Way too much." Cal looked toward the door of his house, then back to Zane. "Come inside. I'll have a shower while you order food. And then I'll get drunk. That should solve everything."

They were eating pizza and Cal was on his third glass of scotch when the doorbell rang.

There was a moment of stupid, wonderful hope when he heard the door open and somebody let themselves inside. Zara had come, he thought. She was going to—well, he wasn't sure what. Best case would be that she was going to drop out of the fight. But what if she'd just come to tell him to stop being a baby and get his ass back to the city because she wanted company while she trained? Would he go?

It turned out he didn't have to answer that question, because the voice that rang out from the entry hall, while familiar and female, was not Zara's. "Calvin?" his mother called. "Are you home?"

For a brief moment he was tempted to roll off the couch and scurry away, finding somewhere to hide. And from the look on Zane's face, he wasn't the only one considering that approach. But Zane's car was in the driveway, the lights were all on, the place reeked of pizza . . . too many clues. "Back here," he called, and he and Zane both pushed themselves to their feet.

The front hall was only a few steps long, and Cal's mother was in the main room before he was even standing up all the way. She cast an appraising eye at him, smiled politely at Zane, then said, "Drinking, are we?"

"*I* am," Cal replied. "And you can be, if you want."

She hesitated for a moment, then said, "Do you have any more of that Chilean Malbec?"

Cal nodded and headed for the kitchen. It wasn't completely unheard of for his mother to drop by unannounced, but usually her visits had a purpose. She'd arrive, drop something off or issue a carefully phrased directive, and be gone. Staying for a glass of wine was different, and he wasn't sure what it meant.

"Good to see you, Zane," he heard from behind him. "Is your sister still in the city?"

"As far as I know," Zane replied. He and Cal had poked around the problem with Zara a little, but they hadn't dived right in, so Zane was probably low on facts. But he was also being discreet; if Cal's mom heard about his relationship issues, she'd hear about them from Cal.

"She must be looking forward to the fight?" his mother asked.

"I guess so. Honestly, I haven't talked to her much lately."

Cal returned then, handed his mother her glass of wine, and took a deep breath. "Zara went to the doctor and was told that fighting was dangerous, but she's going to do it anyway. I told her I couldn't watch her do that, and she . . ." Well, there was the difficult part. But there was no point in pretending it wasn't true. "She didn't care enough about me to walk away from the fight. So we broke up."

The other two didn't speak as Cal drained his glass of scotch and refilled it. He sat down and took a sip, and finally his mother said, "Was that how you presented it to her? She had to make a choice? You gave her an ultimatum?"

"No!" At least, he didn't think so. "I just—told her. I said I couldn't watch her do it."

Zane was still quiet, but he was the one Cal's mother was looking at when she said, "Cal never knew his grandfather—my father. He died in Vietnam when I was little girl. A career sergeant." She glanced at Cal and added, "And every time he reenlisted, my mother threatened to leave him. She said he was putting his honor and his concern for his friends ahead of his love for her and his duty to the family."

"I'm not sure you can equate military service to MMA fighting," Zane said carefully.

"They're not the same. But they're not that different." Cal's mother seemed placidly confident as she sipped her wine. "My father didn't reenlist because he wanted to serve his country. He did it because it was all he knew."

"And because he wanted to look after his men," Cal broke in. "It's not the same at all!"

"Looking after his men was more important than looking after his family?" Another sip of wine, and his mother shrugged. "You're right. It's not the same. But for my mother? She supported him in the end. He risked his life, and she went along with it. And when he was killed, she felt guilty for not having done more to stop him. I know she did."

Cal stared at her. What was he supposed to be doing with this perspective?

His mother smiled gently, as if he'd asked the question out loud. "Would she have felt any better if she'd left him, and he'd gone over anyway and been killed without even the comfort of knowing he was loved? Or if the ultimatum had worked, and he'd stayed home, would he always have resented her for it? Would they have ended up apart anyway, because he wasn't able to forgive her for taking that choice away from him?"

"They might have broken up, but they'd both be alive," Cal retorted. He wasn't really sure what argument his mother was making, but he didn't think he liked it. "That's important, isn't it? I mean, sure, in a perfect world Zara would not fight *and* we'd be together. But the world isn't perfect. If I can only have one of those things, I want the one that makes her safe. I want her to not fight, even if it means she hates me."

"If she was for sure going to die, you'd be right," Zane said. He sounded too sober, and too sad. "But this? She's taking more of a risk than you want. That's all. It's not as black and white as you're making it out to be. So you have to ask yourself: How much of this is about loving her, and how much is about controlling her?"

Cal stared at his friend. "Is that how you see it? You haven't argued with her about this. You haven't really tried to get her to change her mind. Is that because you think she's making the right decision, or just because you don't want to control her?"

"It's not about being the right decision or the wrong decision. It's about it being *her* decision." Zane glanced at Cal's mother before adding, "I spent ten years not being allowed to make my own choices about much of anything. It's no way to live. So I wouldn't want to try to take Zara's choices away from her, no. But also . . . come on, Cal. It's Zara. She's . . . she's Zara. If she's made up her mind on this, you really think anyone's going to persuade her to change it?"

Cal *had* thought that, he realized. He was Calvin Montgomery, after all. He was good at things. He persuaded people, achieved goals, found solutions. And Zara was

just . . . Damn it. Had he really been thinking that way? Zara
was just a Hale, just a poor kid with a poor family who
should be enthusiastic about accepting his guidance and
wisdom.

He'd never thought it consciously, certainly. And he didn't
think he'd thought it unconsciously all that much. It was
pretty hard to spend any time with Zara and see her as
anything other than her own woman. But maybe there'd
been a tiny bit of snobbery inside him, just enough to make
him believe what he wanted to believe?

"I can't change her mind," he said slowly.

"And she couldn't change yours, or you wouldn't be
here," Zane responded.

"But I'm right!" Cal said.

"And so is Zara," his mother said calmly. "Right that it's
her choice. Her privilege to decide what risks she wants to
take."

Cal leaned over far enough to find the bottle of scotch
and slosh a bit more into his glass. He was right, and Zara
was right. So maybe their breakup was right, too. Even if it
felt totally wrong.

Or maybe there was still something he could do. Zara
wouldn't change her mind, not with the way things were.
But maybe he could do something to change the situation
around Zara, something that would make the choice different. Maybe he could still save her, even if he couldn't save
the relationship.

ZARA woke with stiff, sore muscles. It had been stupid to
overtrain this close to an event, but she'd had too much
energy, too much negativity, and she'd needed to wear it off.

It was either working out hard or getting drunk, and the second would have been much worse for her training.

Andre had been at the gym, watching her, and he'd come over as she'd been pulling off her sparring gear. "You're back," he'd said, sounding almost surprised. "You're ready for this fight."

She'd sneered at him. "I'm a professional. Of course I'm ready." And she hadn't been able to keep herself from adding, "I've been watching your girl. She's good, no doubt. But I'm better."

He hadn't argued, and she'd known he'd realized the truth. The fight would be a tough one, but Zara would win. As long as things didn't go wrong with her head.

But she couldn't think like that. She rolled out of bed and stumbled to the kitchen. She was adding bananas to her protein shake when her phone rang.

Cal! she thought, and the hopeful excitement blossomed in her chest. It turned to something bitter when she looked at the call display, and she tried to swallow it down before saying, "Hi, Terry."

"Zara. We need to talk."

"About what?" She didn't want to feel defensive, but there was something accusatory in his voice.

"About your head. About post-concussion syndrome and the risks associated with receiving another head injury when the previous one is not fully healed."

Her body was cold, and she dropped the banana so she could hold on to the counter for stability. "What are you talking about?" she almost whispered. "The doctors checked me out. They said I was fine. That was weeks ago, Terry. Your doctors said I was fine!"

"And what did *your* doctor say, Zara?"

"What are you . . . what are you talking about?" She tried to think it through. What did he know? And did it matter? "I saw a doctor, yeah." How did he know that, how did he know? "She said it was always dangerous to get hit in the head. Big deal. There was no proof. Nothing to get me a medical exemption." She didn't know if she'd have used it, if it had been offered, but it hadn't been offered, so that didn't matter.

"So why didn't you mention it to me?"

"Why would I? It wasn't important."

"I'm not sure I agree. We should talk. Do you want to come to the office, or should I come out there?"

She didn't want him in her home, didn't want any more turmoil or confusion in her personal space. "I'll come down there."

"I'm here all day. I can see you as soon as you get here."

He hung up the phone, and she stared at it. He knew she'd been to see the doctor. The only person who'd known about that was Cal. Cal and Terry were friends. And Cal wanted to keep her from fighting. Her hands were shaking, and her brain had stopped working properly. Instead of coherent thoughts, all she had were flashes of images. Cal running with her, their strides matching. Cal smiling at her when she came into a room, his gaze finding hers and holding it for that one extra moment of connection and intimacy. Cal in bed, watching her like she was a miracle he was privileged to be close to.

And Cal yelling at her, telling her it was stupid for her to fight.

He had betrayed her.

Her phone rang again and she managed to pull herself together at least enough to look at the call display. And when she saw the name there, every uncertainty drained out of her, replaced with a cold, hard rage. Her hand wasn't shaking anymore as she lifted the phone to her ear.

"You calling to gloat?" she spat into the mouthpiece. She didn't give him time to answer. "I trusted you, and you stabbed me in the back. Go to hell, Cal. I never want to see you again."

She ended the call and resisted the urge to throw the phone across the room. Cal had betrayed her, and Terry knew more than he should, but that didn't mean things were over. *Nothing* was over, not until she said it was.

She jolted to her feet. She'd go see Terry, she'd control the damage, she'd keep fighting. Nothing was over. She was still in it.

She'd always been good at tapping into her anger and using it to give her energy and determination. Calvin Montgomery thought he could beat her? He thought he was going to win by cheating?

Hell, no. She wasn't going to let that happen.

She needed to stay angry. If she slowed down and let herself think, let herself feel anything but rage, she was pretty sure she'd fall apart. The fight? She'd handle the fight. Cal, going behind her back? No, she couldn't think about that. Not if she was going to function.

IT took longer than it should have for Cal to put the phone down. When he did, he had to make himself look across the table at his mother and Zane, both of them looking about as blurry and confused as Cal felt. "I think I caught her at a bad time," he said. It was stupid to try to cover, since they'd been sitting close enough to have heard Zara's tone, if not the actual words she'd used. But if he didn't admit it had happened, maybe he wouldn't have to think about it. "We should try again later. Or, Zane, maybe you should be the one to talk to her about it."

Zane was watching Cal a little more closely than was comfortable. But finally he nodded and said, "Yeah, okay. I'll go get a couple hours of sleep, and then give her a call. I mean, this is a good plan. We've got good ideas here. We just need to get her to listen to them."

Which she apparently wasn't going to do if Cal was the one talking.

He walked his visitors to the door. They'd stayed all night, working with him, trying to figure out ways around Zara's concerns. Zane's commitment made sense, since it was his sister they were trying to save, but Cal's mom? She'd gone above and beyond.

He gave her a quick kiss on the temple as she headed out the door. "Drive safe, Mom. You're tired."

She shook her head. "I don't feel tired. That was . . . invigorating. It felt good to be part of something." A quick squeeze to his hand before she said, "We'll find a way to make it work, Calvin. Don't give up."

He stood in the doorway and watched them both drive away, then dragged himself back to the table. It had all made so much sense, as they'd worked it through. Zara knew fighting wasn't a good idea, but she just couldn't see a way around it. So they'd come up with that alternate path. They'd found a way for her to keep her pride, maybe even strengthen her reputation, without risking herself.

If Cal had just figured it out sooner, before he'd thrown the relationship away, maybe he could have had it all. Zara, safe *and* with him. If he'd spent more time thinking about finding ways to give her what she wanted instead of just convincing her to do what *he* wanted.

But he'd left, and she wasn't going to forget that. He looked down at the notes they'd taken the night before. It was still a good plan. But Zane would have to be the one to convince Zara to give it a try. Cal had messed up, and Zara wasn't interested in forgiving him. He was just going to have to find a way to accept that.

❧ *Twenty-two* ❧

ZARA FOUND WAYS to distract herself on the subway ride to Manhattan. She braced her back against the seat and pushed herself up so she was holding all her weight with her quads, and she made herself stay like that while her thighs started to burn and tremble. Physical pain was better than feeling anything else.

By the time she was downtown, she was sweaty and her breath was coming in jerky little gasps, and she knew people had started staring at her. She didn't care.

When the train reached her stop, she stood up, then stumbled and caught herself on one of the poles as her legs tried to give out. An older woman, heavy and tired looking, reached out and touched her shoulder gently. "Are you okay?" she asked, and that tiny bit of kindness was enough for Zara's eyes to fill.

"I will be," she said, and pushed her way out of the train.

A block to the company headquarters, a tense elevator

ride to the top floor, and then Zara was dealing with Terry's never-too-impressed assistant.

"He knows I'm coming. He said I could see him whenever." Zara couldn't face the idea of sitting there, waiting for Terry. She needed to get this over with and move on.

The assistant made a noncommittal noise and spoke into her headset, looking almost disappointed when she had to wave Zara through to the inner office.

The door opened before Zara could reach it, and Terry was there. He was a big man, lots of muscle with a bit of late-middle-aged fat on top of it. He squinted at her, then guided her inside and shut the door behind her. "It's not the end of the world," he said gently.

And she started sobbing. Her rage couldn't carry her in the face of kindness. Still, the tears were completely humiliating, a betrayal of every woman who'd had to be strong in a man's world. She was tough! She didn't do this! But somehow she just couldn't stop.

She turned away, buried her head in her hands, and tried to apologize. Terry didn't respond right away, but after a few moments she felt something cool and hard brush her hand, and looked over to see a tumbler of water. "Try to take a sip," Terry's voice rumbled by her ear.

Good. A goal. Something concrete, something to focus on. She took one breath that turned into a shuddering sob halfway through, then another that she managed to exhale with only a little quaver. A sip from the glass helped, the cool water soothing as it washed through her burning body.

"I'm an idiot," she mumbled. "I'm so sorry."

"You're not an idiot. And what are you sorry for? For crying? Don't worry about that. I have fighters in here crying all the time. The intensity you need in the ring doesn't just shut off when you're in the real world. You feel things. It's allowed."

She took another sip, not sure whether to believe him, but grateful for the words whether they were true or not. "I don't cry. Not in public."

"This isn't public. Don't worry about it." He let her take another sip, then said, "Now, if you were planning to say sorry for not telling me about a serious health concern? Yeah, that might deserve an apology."

Her head. That was what she was here about. Strange to realize how far it had been from her mind. "Oh. Yeah. I don't know, I just got a second opinion. The doctor couldn't find any proof that I couldn't fight, so there wasn't much point in telling you. Right?"

"There's a point in telling me you're not sure you're healthy," he said firmly.

"Why? The commission isn't going to give me a ban. And anything short of that is no use."

"Bullshit. Stop feeling sorry for yourself and do a gut check." She stared at him, but apparently he was done being gentle with her. "You want to be the victim here? 'Oh, boo hoo, I have to fight even though I don't want to'? Bullshit." He stepped away from her and started moving around the room as if his thoughts were too strong for his body to stay still. "If you don't think you're ready to fight, then don't fight. It's that damn simple. You can talk to me about keeping the title, and I can try to leave it with you for a while, but if you lose it? Big deal! You'll either win it back or you won't. Still not a big deal."

"That's easy for you to say—" she started, but she caught herself. This wasn't Cal she was talking to. Terry had pulled himself up from the streets just like she had; he knew why it was important. "People respect me because of the title." Surely he could understand that.

But he shook his head. "People respect you because

you're a hell of a fighter, you're tough, and at least most of the time, you're smart. The title? It's just a title. It's not *you*."

The same things Cal had said to her, more or less, but she hadn't been willing to hear them from him. She'd thought he couldn't understand.

Which she'd been right about, she reminded herself, and she tried to dig up some of that anger. He'd betrayed her. She had trusted him, more than anyone else, and he'd come to Terry and told him everything. She leaned her forehead against the cool glass of Terry's floor-to-ceiling windows and tried to find something solid she could hang on to and believe in.

"How bad is your head?" Terry asked, his voice gentle again. "What did the doctor say?"

She sighed, too tired to play the game. "You've already heard this. Cal probably has a better memory than I do. I mean, whatever he said, he'd have put it in the worst possible way, but the facts would be right."

"Cal? Calvin Montgomery?" Terry sounded genuinely confused. "What does he have to do with any of this?"

And there was the familiar, welcome anger. "Was that your deal?" she demanded. "You're not supposed to admit it came from him?"

"Zara, what are you talking about? It was Andre who mentioned this to me, not Cal Montgomery."

She spun around to stare at him. Andre. Not Cal. Andre. It made no sense, but if it was true . . . "No. I never told him about the doctor. Cal's the only one who knew."

"I can call Andre and ask for clarification if you want." Terry looked thoughtful. "He didn't seem to have details about the diagnosis. He just said I should know you'd seen a neurologist." A moment's thought and he added, "Does he handle your business expenses? Does your insurance paperwork go through him?"

The world was spinning, but this time it wasn't her head making her dizzy—it was her heart. "He takes care of all my bills," she said, her own words sounding far away. "My insurance . . . yes. It goes through his office."

"So that's how he knew," Terry said, as if Andre was the important part here. "But why did he tell me? He's your manager, but he's going behind your back? What's going on there?"

Zara wasn't sure she cared, but she tried to focus her mind on the issue, at least for a moment. "Anna Cade," she said. "He's trying to sign her—maybe he already has. He thinks she's the future and I'm the past. But we've been training together, sparring against the same partners." It all seemed so empty, but she kept talking anyway. "I'm going to kick her ass. She's good, but she's not as good as I am."

"He's an idiot," Terry said. "And I won't tolerate this sort of thing in my organization. I'm going to investigate this, Zara, and if that's what happened, if he breached your confidence like that? He won't be doing any more business with us, and I'll make sure everyone knows why."

It should have felt like a victory, she supposed, but it didn't. She stared out the window, trying to make sense of anything. "I made a mistake," she said. Obvious, but still not easy to say. "I blamed Cal for you finding out."

"I'm still a bit confused about that. How would Cal know about the doctor?"

Because he'd gone with her, and sat by her, and supported her. Because he'd cared enough to fight with her and try to change her mind. Because he'd been part of her life, until she'd pushed him away and ruined everything.

"I'm out of the fight," she said. The words didn't even hurt. "I'm probably healthy for it, but I'm not sure. I shouldn't take the chance. And . . ." She swallowed. "I have something more important I need to be fighting for."

He gave her a long look, then said, "You're sure? I can try to keep the title with you, but I can't guarantee it."

It would hurt to give that up, she had to admit. But not nearly as much as it would hurt to give up Cal. "Do what you have to do. I'm really sorry about the short notice. I should have figured this out a long time ago."

He shrugged. "I can make it work."

"I'm sure you can." Her cheeks were still stiff from dried tears, but she could barely even remember why she'd been crying anymore. She felt light, as if she could float out of the office and bounce gently down the stairs to street level. "I can make things work, too," she vowed.

A quick kiss to Terry's cheek and then she was gone, striding toward the elevator, phone out and dialing as she moved. She'd been wrong, but now she was going to make it right. That was the only thing that mattered.

❧ Twenty-three ❧

"I LEFT HER two messages," Zane said as he slid into the booth opposite Cal at Woody's. "Hopefully she calls back soon."

Cal nodded and finished his glass of scotch. He was trying to remove himself from the situation, trying not to think about Zara or the hole she'd left in his life. "This would be easier if you'd stop talking about her."

"Easier?" Zane looked genuinely confused. "Oh, you mean easier for you. The moping. You'd be able to drink yourself into oblivion with less effort if I stopped talking about her." He looked disgustedly at Cal's glass. "It's barely six o'clock and you're already that sappy? You need less scotch, more beer. You should be belching and scratching your belly, not whining. Come on, man! Let's have a little less self-pity, okay?" He raised his hand and made some sort of signal to their server, apparently ordering a drink.

Cal stared down at his glass. Everything was over with

Zara, and it was his fault. He'd been the one to walk away. Another woman might have given him a second chance, but Zara? No. She wasn't looking back. He'd loved her and she'd . . . she'd spent time with him as long as he was well behaved. And still he couldn't seem to make himself let go. "I'm so screwed," he mumbled.

"Patriots are playing tonight," Zane said. "The Dolphins, I think."

Cal squinted at him. "Football? We're going to talk about football?"

"Sure. Why not? I mean, if you want to talk about Zara—okay. Make sure you remember who you're talking to, but the general stuff? I can handle that. But is there really anything to say? You tried, and it didn't work out. That sucks. I'll talk to her about the plan for getting out of the fight, once she calls me back, and we'll see how that goes." He waited for a response, then said, "You heard anything about Brady's knee? Is he going to be playing tonight?"

"You think talking about sports injuries is a good way to keep me from thinking about Zara?"

"I knew it was bad as soon as I started saying it. I hoped maybe you weren't paying attention."

Cal snorted, then leaned back to let the server put a pitcher of beer and two glasses on the table between them. It wasn't like he'd have been able to forget about Zara anyway, not at Woody's with her face staring down at him from all the posters, not at home, where every inch of the place seemed to hold a memory of her, where his sheets still carried the hint of her scent.

"I'm going to drink too much to drive. I'm staying at your place, okay?" Zane asked, and when Cal didn't argue, Zane poured two glasses of beer, shoved one toward Cal, and raised his own. "Alcohol," he proclaimed. "If we keep trying, maybe one of these times it will actually make something better." Then he drained half his glass.

Cal did the same. As toasts went, it was honest, at least. "If I'd stayed—" he began, but then he stopped. If he'd stayed, what would have been different, really? Anything? Maybe, but he could never know. "Shit." He took a deep breath, laid his hands flat on the table and said, "I don't care about football. You want to play pool?"

"Yeah," Zane agreed, and they headed for the table.

They were just finishing their first game when Cal felt . . . something. Something that made him turn around and look toward the main doors. So he was among the first to see Zara come inside.

She looked strangely nervous, maybe because the place was essentially a shrine to her greatness, but her gaze slid right over the life-sized cardboard cutout that guarded the entrance, and scanned the crowd. He stood frozen until she saw him, and then still couldn't move as she worked her way through the crowd in his direction.

Zara. Zara was in Lake Sullivan, and she seemed to be there for him.

She looked beautiful. Tense and unhappy, tired and uncertain, but beautiful. She came and stood in front of him, and for a moment it was enough for him to just stare at her.

Then she said, "I thought you told Terry about the doctor."

It took a while for the words to make sense. "The neurologist? You thought I told Terry? Why?"

"Because he knew, and you were the only one who *could* have told him." She stopped, then miserably added, "That's what I thought."

"Wait. You thought he knew, or you thought I told him? I mean, what's going on? Does Terry know?" And if he did, what did that mean?

She took a deep breath, then said, "Can we get out of here? Can we go somewhere and talk?"

He almost roared his agreement, but then caught himself. It seemed like she was willing to listen to him now, but he couldn't be sure how long that would last. He didn't really know what was going on, so he couldn't judge how she'd react to much of anything. And he was pretty sure it was still important for her to hear the plan, the ideas he and his mother and Zane had come up with the night before. She needed to hear it from someone she'd be more likely to listen to.

"You should talk to Zane," he made himself say. Damn it, was he blowing his chance? But it was more important to be sure she was safe.

"Zane?" She frowned over at her brother, leaning on his cue stick by the pool table. "About what?"

"He can explain," Cal said. "I mean, if you have questions or whatever, give me a call. But you should talk to him first."

Another frown at Zane, but then she nodded. "Okay. I'll talk to him. Listen to him. Whatever. But, Cal . . . can I just say I'm sorry? To you, I mean, before I go talk to him. I made a mistake this morning, jumped to a stupid conclusion, and . . . I'm sorry."

It was almost enough. Enough to make him lose his discipline, stop doing what he thought was best for her and start doing what he thought was best for him. If she'd said one more thing, he'd have given in. He'd have tried to be with her, tried to talk to her himself.

And if he'd been unable to persuade her and she'd gone ahead and fought anyway, it would be because he'd gotten greedy and tried to take more than he could hold. "I need to go," he said quickly.

He threw a few bills on the table and headed for the door. Probably Zane was watching him leave. Probably most of the bar was, considering they were all locals and all knew either him or Zara or at least some version of their story. Yeah, probably every set of eyes in the place was on his back. But the only ones he felt were Zara's. And that imagined gaze stayed with him long after he left the bar and headed down the darkening street toward home.

"HE wants me to explain his plan to you," Zane said as he and Zara settled into the booth. "Our plan, kind of. Him and me and Mrs. Montgomery, believe it or not. But honestly, Zara, mostly his. He was really working at it, trying to use all his business sense and whatever, trying to find a way to make it so you'd be okay with not fighting."

She felt numb. Why were they still talking about this? She wasn't going to be fighting. She didn't care about that anymore, at least not right then. All she wanted to talk about was Cal. But Cal had wanted her to hear this, whatever it was, so she kept her mouth shut and listened.

"It's built around the idea of making you into even more of a celebrity," Zane said. "And Cal knew you wouldn't like that, but he thought you might go along with it, on certain terms. He wants you to go big, and be the spokesperson for head injuries in women's sports. There have been lots of male athletes who've spoken up about it, but no really famous women yet. So he wants to build this whole campaign—he has lists of people to talk to, and ways to spin it—and he figures that if you go that way, you'll be making it totally clear to everyone that you're not backing out of the fight because you're scared. You know?"

"I already backed out of the fight," she said numbly. Cal had been making plans to help salvage her pride? They'd fought, she'd told him she never wanted to see him again, and he was still worried about making her feel better? "I told Terry this morning. I drove up here to tell Cal. And to . . . to apologize."

Zane was watching her carefully. "Apologize for what exactly?"

"For not trusting him. Not listening to him."

"And how do you see things going from here?" Zane asked. She didn't answer right away, and he sighed. "Trust me, Zare, I'm really not looking for details on my baby sister and her boyfriend. It's just, he's pretty busted up right now, but he'll get over it. If you're planning to come back and get back together with him? I don't think you should do that. Not unless you really mean it. If you're still going to be doing your *I'm just killing time with this guy while I'm stuck in Lake Sullivan* thing? I don't think that's fair to him."

The words stung. No, more than a sting. They hurt. But not because they weren't deserved. She had treated the relationship like that, at least at the start. She'd held back, resisted, made Cal work too hard for every step of progress they made. "So what are you saying?" she almost whispered. "He won't take me back?"

Zane snorted. "No. He probably will. But what I'm saying is you should think it through. Because you're a good person, and you don't want to hurt other people, and if you get back together with him and then dump him the next time the MMA world comes calling? That's not fair to him. He deserves to be with someone who wants to be with him, you know?"

"I do," she said. She knew she meant it. "I want it more than anything."

Zane gave her a long look, then nodded slowly. "Okay. So while we're on it . . . there's one more thing he deserves. He deserves to know that. Because I don't think he does right now. I don't think he ever has."

It was hard to breathe for a moment. Her chest was too tight, and she didn't seem to know how to loosen it. Finally she drew a shuddering breath. She wasn't going to cry anymore, so she nodded hard, willing the tears to stay where they belonged. "Okay. Yeah. I need to fix that."

She pushed out of the booth, not sure where she was going, but feeling the need to move. "Give him this, okay?" she said, and pushed the grocery bag she'd brought with her across the table toward him. "I need to . . . I don't know. I need to get myself in order. And then I'll find him, and, yeah, I'll . . . I'll make it better. I will."

She was a few steps away from the table when she heard her brother call her name. Damn it, she wasn't sure how much more of his truth telling she could take. But she turned around and waited.

His face was softer now, and he smiled at her as he said, "You decided not to fight? For real?" She nodded, and he bobbed his head back at her. "That's a good call, Zare. That's smart. I'm proud of you."

Okay, the bar wasn't super well lit. Maybe he wouldn't be able to see the tears welling in her eyes. "Yeah?" she asked.

"Hell, yeah. Super proud. You're doing great, Zare."

"You, too." She swallowed hard, and waited until she was sure her voice would be more controlled. "I'm proud of you, too. Everyone at the community center loves you, and you're making friends, and . . . yeah. You're doing great, too."

He nodded slowly. "We're Hales. We might not do things the easy way, or the smart way. But we don't quit. Right?"

"Right," she said. Maybe it was a strange thing to be proud of, but she'd take it. "So I'm going to keep working at it. I screwed up, but I'm going to keep going."

"If you need me for anything, let me know."

"Yeah, okay." It was supposed to be casual, she knew. Zane was already pouring himself another beer, looking around the bar for someone to hang out with now that his grumpy best friend and weepy sister had abandoned him. She was supposed to just leave, and pretend none of it had ever happened.

But she was a Hale. Not too caught up in doing the smart thing. So she took three big steps back to the booth, leaned over, and gave him an awkward but sincere hug. "Thank you," she whispered.

He looked embarrassed as she pulled away. "Nothing to thank me for. It's up to you now. Go make it work."

She nodded. That was her mission. "Okay," she agreed, and she had to keep herself from running as she left the bar. She knew who she wanted to talk to, and she knew where to find them.

The lights were all on at Mrs. Ryerson's home, and from the cars in the driveway, Zara knew she'd been right. It was a stitch and bitch night, and the gang was all there. Mrs. Ryerson answered the door and gave her a quick hug before saying, "Don't even explain to me, because everyone else will want to know, too. Get your coat off and come on!"

Sure enough, as soon as she stepped into the back room, there was a chorus of greetings and inquiries. Zara took the glass of wine someone pressed into her hand and let herself relax into an empty spot on one of the long sofas. This felt right. She wanted to be with Cal, sure, but she wanted to be sure she did it properly, the way he deserved. She needed a chance to rehearse and plan what to say, because she couldn't stand the thought of hurting him any more. She needed to do this right, and these women could help her do that.

"I dropped out of the fight," she said. "I wasn't sure my concussion was healed enough, so I dropped out."

"That seems wise," Mrs. Ryerson said approvingly. That simple.

Zara shrugged. "I guess. But I made another big mistake." She sighed. "Is it okay if I talk about this? It might be kind of long. I don't want to, like, take over. . . ."

The women all laughed, and one of them whose name Zara couldn't remember said, "Honey, we've been listening to each other's troubles for twenty years now! A fresh story? You don't need our permission to give us something new to talk about!"

It felt wonderful to spill it all. The women were good listeners, making sympathetic noises at all the right places, frowning thoughtfully as they tried to understand what she'd been thinking, and then looking pensive as she wrapped up. "So I love him." Probably strange to admit it to them before telling Cal himself, but they needed to know the full situation if they were going to help her. "And I think he still loves me. I mean, it's only been a few days since he said it, so he probably still does." She hoped. "But I don't think that's enough. I mean, he shouldn't just love me, he should trust me, right? He should know I care about him, and won't hurt him again. I need to show him I'm serious, and committed."

The ladies were quiet for quite a while, and then it was Ashley who finally spoke. "I know this might not always be a good idea," she said. "But have you considered a grand gesture?"

⋅३ *Twenty-four* ६⋅

CAL WAITED BY the phone all that night, but Zara didn't call.

There was a knock on the door around eleven, and Cal was halfway down the hall before he even realized he'd started moving. But when the door opened, it was Zane standing there. "She didn't come by?" he asked, and Cal shook his head.

"She dropped out of the fight," Zane told him. "Before I even told her about your plan, she quit. She's not fighting."

The strongest emotion was relief, absolutely. Relief so strong he was almost dizzy with it. But rolling around underneath that was something else, something angry and frustrated. She'd dropped out of the fight before he'd seen her at the bar. So he could have talked to her then, could have tried to salvage something of their relationship. He'd walked away when he could have just stayed with her, and now? What the hell did he have now?

"She'll probably call you tomorrow," Zane said. "Probably. She said she wanted to get some things straightened out." He held something fuzzy and blue out in front of him. "She wanted me to give you this."

Cal reached for it and stretched it out. Clearly handmade and, judging by the irregular shape of it, not created by a master craftsperson. "She made me a scarf," he said softly.

"Kind of," Zane agreed with a doubtful look at the item.

Cal let his arms fall to his sides and slumped back against the wall. Was the scarf a good-bye present, or a positive omen? He had no idea.

"So what am I supposed to do now? Just sit here and wait for her?"

Zane nodded slowly. "Honestly? If you can? I think you should, yeah." He saw Cal's expression and added, "You can call her if you want. I don't think it'd be the end of the world or anything. But if you can hold off, give her a little space, and let her do this on her terms, I think it'd be a good thing."

It wasn't easy, but Cal followed Zane's advice. He forced himself to go to bed, managed to get a few hours of restless sleep, and made himself presentable before going to work the next morning. Once he got there, he stalked around the office and growled at anyone who spoke to him and shamed himself in general, and every time his phone rang, he looked at the call display with a horrible mix of anticipation and dread. But it was never Zara on the other end of the line.

He stayed at the office, pushing paper around on his desk and achieving nothing, until about five o'clock, and then he headed for the front doors. He'd run again, he supposed, maybe do more weights, to exhaust himself and hopefully shut off his traitorous brain.

But he was only in the hallway, not even to the front foyer, when he heard Zara's voice. "I just want to talk to him." Cal stopped walking, bracing himself to face her.

But then he heard Michael respond, "I'm sorry, he's not available."

"Do you really think you can just lock the door? Like I'm not going to ever run into him and talk to him? Or like I won't just call him on the phone?"

"Not ever? No, I sincerely doubt it will take him that long to realize what a mistake this all was. I think he knows it already, to be honest. I just don't want you to make a scene at our place of business. Why don't you call him and arrange for him to finalize the breakup somewhere else?"

"Michael." A new voice now, and it was enough to make Cal move out of the hallway and into the foyer, where he saw Michael looking defiantly at their mother while Zara watched the whole scene. "This is none of your business, Michael." Their mother's voice allowed no doubt. "Please don't interfere."

"This is absolutely my business," his brother retorted. "Look around you! This is, by definition, *my business*. And I don't want Cal's nonsense here."

And that was when Cal finally stepped forward, drawing surprised looks from the others. "It's not nonsense, Michael. But I don't really want Zara here, either—she shouldn't have to put up with your crap."

"It's fine," Zara said quickly. She smiled at Cal, tentative but real. "His crap isn't too impressive. It's easy to ignore."

Michael stepped away then, making a small noise of disgust as he went, and Zara turned back to Cal. "Can we talk?" she asked.

"Not in—" Michael started.

"Shut up, Michael." Their mother smiled beatifically at

all of them. "Cal, do you want to head out, or would you rather take Zara to your office?"

He nodded toward the door. "You ready to go?" he asked Zara, and she followed him outside. Which was a start, at least, but not an ending. But he had no idea what the next step was. "Where to?"

She looked undecided, then nodded toward the little park across the street. "Can we sit there?"

It was cold, with a dusting of snow already covering the ground, but Cal didn't object.

They sat on the wooden bench, and Cal waited. Zane had told him to let Zara do this her way.

And she seemed prepared to take charge, reaching inside the fabric bag he hadn't noticed she was carrying and pulling out a large manila envelope. Then she took a deep breath and said, "I'm sorry I didn't trust you. I should have. And I'm sorry if I've made it seem like I'm not into this. If that's what you thought, I'm sorry. Honestly, it was what I wanted to be true. But I screwed up. I thought I could spend time with you and keep it casual, but then I went and fell in love with you. I tried to pretend that wasn't true, but it was, and . . ." She frowned down at the envelope in her hands as if she'd lost her train of thought. "Yeah. That's what happened. I love you." Another pause, and then she shrugged. "Oops."

He stared at her. It was kind of hard to be angry about her reluctance to love him when he was feeling more or less the same way about her. Hard to be angry at all when he could still hear the echo of her *I love you* bouncing around in his heart. "So we're both screwed," he said.

She looked at him, a quick moment of brilliant eye contact before her gaze returned to the envelope. "Kind of, yeah. Except . . . okay, I get why it's not exactly what you'd have wanted. I mean, I don't fit your family's idea of—"

"No," he interrupted. "My family isn't a problem. You're right, their crap is unimpressive. And it seems like Mom's on my side, so really, that battle, small as it was, is completely over."

"Yeah, I guess that's fine. I mean, you've never really let them get in the way of this, have you?" She sighed. "You didn't let anything get in the way, except for me. And I get that I'm not a good bet. I flaked out on you. I let you down. You're afraid I'm going to do it again."

He let the words sink in for a while. "Well, yeah," he said.

She started tugging pages out of the envelope. "Okay, here's the thing. I'm doing this because of you, but I'm going to do it whether you want to be with me or not. Okay? I mean, it's not—what did you say? It's not transactional. It's not something I'm giving in exchange for what I want—I'm not sure you even want me to do it, to be honest. Possibly this whole thing is a bad idea. If it is, I blame Ashley."

"You lost me a while ago," Cal said. But already he was finding it hard to care. If he could have this? More of Zara's bewildering determination, her unexpected conversational leaps . . . if he could have more of this, even if it was temporary, he wanted it. He felt his shoulders lower with the realization.

She gave him a tentative smile. "If you like it, it was all my idea," she clarified. Then she flipped over the pile of papers and turned the top bundle so he could read the words. "I made an offer on a house. It's on the same street as yours, but down a bit. It's bigger. You might want to stay living where you are, and I totally get that—I love your little hobbit house. But I couldn't just invite myself to live there, and it's not really big enough, and I thought maybe I was sending kind of the wrong message if I kept living in a rental. Because I want to be here for good. That's what I'm committing to. You don't have to say anything in return, and if things don't work out between us . . ." She frowned. "Well, that would be very bad, and I can't say I'd stay here forever if that was the case, but you know, I'm doing what I can. I'm committing."

"You bought a house?" he managed.

"Yes. Well, I made an offer, and they accepted. There's lots more paperwork, and an inspection. I didn't have much time, so really I mostly bought a house. If this one falls through, I'll find another one." She peered at him anxiously, then pulled out another sheet of paper. "And it's important that I have a house because a dog wouldn't like my place in Queens."

"A dog?"

She flipped the page around to show him a grainy color printout of a nondescript brown mutt. "His name is Max, he's living in the shelter right now, but I can pick him up whenever I'm ready. He's . . . okay, he's a *bit* negotiable. I mean, if you hate dogs or something, I don't need to have a dog. But the new house has a fenced yard, and they say Max loves to run, so he could do that with us . . . or just me, if you don't want to, but hopefully us."

"You bought a house and a dog."

"It's like the Twelve Days of Christmas. But not quite twelve things. Still, there's a few more."

"What else?"

"I got my job back at the community center. Just part time, but that's okay." She took a deep breath. "Because I still plan to train. I agree that I shouldn't be fighting now, with my head not quite right, and I like your plan, the one Zane told me about. That'll keep me pretty busy, but it's something I can do from here mostly. And as soon as my head is better for sure, I'm going back. I'm going to kick Anna Cade's ass, and everyone else's, too. That's okay, right? I mean, I commit to you. To living here, and building a life with you, if you'll let me. But I need to do something. To be someone. I want to keep fighting."

"Are you asking me?" he asked.

She frowned. "I'm not asking permission. No. But I'm asking you to be okay with it. Does that make sense?"

"It does." He wouldn't want her to ask him for permission, he realized. It would be too out of character, and her character was what he loved. "I'll try to be okay with it. I promise."

"Okay," she said, and there was a little tremble in her voice as she exhaled. "That's a good start. Good."

He reached for her hand then, their cool fingers finding warmth as they pressed together. "You didn't have to do all this," he said.

"Because you would have given me another chance without it?"

"Yeah."

"I don't want you to give me a chance, like you know I'm going to mess up again. I don't want you to have doubts, or be sorry that you love me."

"I'm not," he said, and knew the words were true. "Even before all this, I don't think I was really sorry. But now? I feel much better about it."

She squinted at him as if trying to judge his sincerity. "There's a couple more things," she said.

"I don't think we need any more."

"Too bad. I've had the stitcher-bitchers running around like chickens with their heads cut off putting all this together. You're getting all of it." She flipped her pages and pulled out a picture of a man in a sweater with a bunch of unintelligible letters and numbers running down beside it. "I'm going to make you this sweater," she vowed. "And it's really hard, and I'm terrible at crocheting, so it's going to take me a long time. But I'm going to do it. Remember you said I could be good at anything I wanted to be good at?"

He nodded, and she said, "I'm going to get good at crocheting, and I'm going to get good at loving you."

"If you want, you can skip the first one and just focus on the second."

Her eyes were warm now, and he couldn't feel the winter weather at all. She leaned in and gave him a quick kiss. "No. I'm going to do both. And I might learn to cook. Like, for real. Maybe."

"I like doing the cooking."

"Okay, good, forget the cooking then!" Another kiss, and this time she didn't pull away as quickly. Instead, she snuggled in next to him and they both looked at their entwined fingers as she added, "I arranged for all my stuff to get shipped up here. And I fired Andre. And . . . oh, I almost forgot!"

She sat up so quickly her head almost caught him in the nose, and then she triumphantly waved a sheet of paper at him. "I entered the triathlon for next year's Splash. Kayak, mountain bike, and 'speed hiking'—that's just running, right? On a trail? I don't know, but I'm going to find out. You want to do it with me?"

"Next summer?" The girl who wouldn't plan more than a couple days ahead wanted him to enter a race with her the next summer? "Yeah. I want to."

"Excellent." She sighed, and she snuggled back into his arms. "We're going to kick ass."

"I think I'm going to make a change at work," he said. It was still new, nothing decided yet, but it felt right to talk to her about it. "I think you were right that I won't be satisfied being Michael's number two, not long-term. I might try to split the furniture business off and really make something of it. If that doesn't work, I might quit altogether and do something else."

He felt her nod against his chest. "Okay," she said. "Maybe I can help. I mean, there's not a really strong connection between furniture and MMA, but if you wanted an endorsement or something, I could do that. Or if you wanted to do something else entirely . . . I don't know. I probably wouldn't be too useful. But I could learn to cook a bit, so you wouldn't have to make meals while you're working really hard."

"We could just order takeout," he said.

She peered up at him then. "I could learn to cook if I wanted to," she said firmly. "It really can't be that hard. There's probably classes I could take. And if there aren't, then I could find a teacher and start the classes. Cooking is not impossible."

No, nothing was impossible. Not for Zara, not once she put her mind to it. "I just meant I didn't care about the cooking. If I had to choose between you spending your energy on that or your energy on something else, the something else might win."

"Really? What kind of 'something else' did you have in mind?" He could hear the laughter in her voice, but the beginning of a little heat, too. They should probably get the hell out of the park soon.

"Scarf manufacturing maybe. Or flower arranging, or dog training, or fishing or kayaking or whatever else you might want to do. I want you to have everything you want. Always."

"I already do," she murmured.

And public park or not, he couldn't let that pass without a serious kiss. She was ready for him, twisting around and reaching up to wrap her hands around his neck as their mouths connected. She was Zara, and she was with him. He was what she wanted. That was all he needed to know.

❧ Twenty-five ❧

"WE SHOULD JUST stay here tonight," Zara said. She was curled up on Cal's couch, warm and cozy. She didn't want to go anywhere.

"Wait, what? Stay here in my hobbit house?"

"Oh my God, I honestly didn't think you even noticed I'd said that. It wasn't meant as an insult. It's nice here. Like a house for fashionable hobbits."

"My house isn't for hobbits," Cal said. He came over from the kitchen, Max trotting along adoringly behind him. The dog had been with them for a week, staying at Cal's or the rental while Zara finalized the purchase of her new place, and he'd already figured out who was in charge of food. His loyalty had been clear from that moment on.

"There's nothing wrong with hobbits," Zara said, reaching a hand out to scratch Max's ears.

But Cal wasn't ready to move on. "Hobbits are small. My house is full sized."

"Hobbits are fictional. Maybe everything else in their imaginary world was huge, and they'd be normal size for our world."

"I don't think that's right. Also, my house isn't underground. I think hobbits live in burrows."

Zara gave an exaggerated sigh. "Hobbits don't live anywhere, they're not real. But fine. Hobbits shouldn't live here. I was just trying to say that it's a bit small, but in a cozy way. Homey."

"Oh. I think, for future reference, that you could just say 'cozy' or 'homey.' I don't think you need to bring hobbits into it."

She slid off the couch and stood in front of him, then laced her fingers together behind his neck. It was nice to just hang off him, trusting him to hold her up. "Is this us, in the future? Just hanging out, bickering about hobbits?"

"Maybe. I think I'd be okay if it was."

"Yeah," she said. "I'd be okay if it was, too."

"But not right now," he said quickly. "Because we have a commitment."

She made a face. "Hey, maybe we could go to Woody's instead! You've been wanting me to go to Woody's! Or maybe we could invite Zane over. Make sure he's okay. I've been a little worried—"

"No, you haven't. Zane's fine and you know it. And we're going to Woody's to watch Anna Cade's title fight. She's going to win it, obviously, and you're going to see the whole damn town not care. You're going to see them not change their mind about you. And when you're training to take her on and get the title back? You're going to have the whole town behind you, cheering you on, and that's going to make you even more powerful than you were before."

"You've got it all planned out, huh?"

"Absolutely. Submitted for your approval, of course, but

that's just a technicality. This is one more of my brilliant plans, and you'll agree to it because you're brilliant enough to see its value."

She laughed, but didn't argue. "So, no Woody's tonight. Could we stay here, and, like, push bamboo shoots under our fingernails? 'Cause in comparison to dinner with your family . . ."

"My mom stood up for you."

"Dinner with your *mom* would be fine."

"Well, let's go say hi to my mom, and maybe have a drink, and then since we're there anyway, we might as well have some dinner, right?" She looked at him doubtfully, and he smiled at her, sweet and easy. "You don't have to come," he said. "You can stay here in the hobbit hole, all snug and warm, and I'll go, make an appearance, and come back as fast as I can. They're my family—my problem."

Nicely played. Excellent, subtle guilt tripping. "No, I'll come." She leaned over and ruffled the long fur on Max's neck. "You'll miss us, right? But you'll guard the house?"

The dog didn't disagree, so the humans pulled on winter boots and jackets, and then Cal grabbed the black heels Zara had left by the stairs to be sure they came along. She raised her eyebrows and he shrugged. "They're hot," he said. "Dinner isn't going to be too much fun for me, either, you know. So at least if you're wearing heels, I can think about that and be a bit distracted."

"Sure is great that we're doing this," Zara groused. But she caught his hand as they walked out to the car, and he gave her a kiss before she slid into the passenger seat.

They drove quietly through the snow-covered streets, their headlights picking out familiar landmarks and then washing right over them, as if they didn't exist when the car wasn't pointed in their direction. As if the world was just there for Zara and Cal to look at. It would be nice to live in that sort of a bubble for a while, she decided. But probably not something that either of them would want long-term.

They pulled into the driveway and right up to the front door. It felt strange to be coming to the house as a guest, and Zara gripped Cal's hand a little more tightly than usual. The drive and the walkway had been carefully shoveled and salted, but a chilly wind blew in to remind them of the season. So they hurried for the front door, which Cal knocked on once, then pushed open.

"Hello," he called.

When there was no immediate answer, Zara turned to him, her eyes bright. "Maybe they forgot! We could just—"

"Stop that," he said. "Here's your shoes. I'll take your coat. Then we'll go find them."

Zara grudgingly complied and they walked back past the formal living room with its white-on-white color scheme. It was a relief to know they wouldn't be sitting in there, where Zara was almost guaranteed to spill something. They headed down a wide, wood-panelled hall, past several doors half open to rooms too dark to inspect, and then Cal said, "This was always my favorite room, when I lived here."

He pushed the door open and Zara saw the blazing fire, the billiard table with a game in progress, the bar, with drinks on it . . . but no people. Perfect.

"Come on in," Cal said, and Zara did, and then it happened.

"Surprise!" they all yelled, pouring out from behind furniture and the bar, and from around the corners. "Welcome back!"

Cal's family was there, even Michael, although he was looking sour about the whole thing. Of course. The others were more important anyway. Zane was there, and Josh and

Ashley, and most of the stitch and bitchers, and the women's MMA class. There were a few other people from the community center, and that was all. It wasn't a big crowd. But it was big enough. It was enough to remind her that she had a place here, and people who cared about her and were happy to have her back. That was the only thing that mattered.

Zane was the first to give Zara a hug and a kiss, and then there was a lineup of others waiting to greet her. She'd been celebrated before, after big wins, interviewed and admired and photographed. But she'd never felt this sort of genuine warmth, never felt that people were happy about who she was rather than what she'd done. She tried to soak it all in, and eventually made her way back over to Cal, dazed but happy.

"Nice to feel wanted?" he suggested.

"It feels nice to feel wanted by you," she said. "The rest of it? Yeah, it's nice, too. But I came back here for you, Cal. I'm staying here for you."

He moved fast, grabbing her and pulling her close, and they both ignored the surprise and amusement of the crowd. "For you," she repeated, and he kissed her.

"Thank you," he said.

"Thank *you*," she returned. She smiled at him, and he smiled back at her. Their fingers were entwined, their bodies close. It was all she could ever want. Everything else was details. She and Cal would handle them together.

KEEP READING FOR A PREVIEW OF
CATE CAMERON'S LAKE SULLIVAN NOVEL

Just a Summer Fling

AVAILABLE NOW FROM BERKLEY SENSATION!

JOSH WONDERED IF he would have had the self-control to say no if Jasmine McArthur hadn't been sitting over at her table watching them with such wicked interest. If it had just been him and Ashley. She'd been tipsy, maybe, but not really drunk. And, damn it, she was a beautiful woman. Long auburn hair, dancing green eyes, and a hell of a body. It was too bad that she was an actress, but everyone had faults.

And now, in the bar, she wasn't acting like a spoiled movie star. They were working through their alphabet of Vermont hazards. "M" had been easy, both of them saying "mosquitoes" at the same time and then moving on. "N," though?

"'Norwegians?'" Josh suggested. "There are a lot of them up here. But they're ex-Norwegians. They came generations ago. And I don't know if they're a hazard, exactly. Not all of them."

"I think Norwegians are a noble people. Not a hazard. And I already let you have 'Dutch' for 'D.' This list is serious business, Josh! It can't just be an excuse for you to slam different countries of origin."

Josh nodded. "Yeah, okay. That's fair. So . . . 'N.' Maybe 'neighbors'? Mine are okay, but only because they're distant. Most people up here like their space."

"I guess that's why you'd live here." She nodded as if pleased to have an answer to the question of why anyone would settle in such a godforsaken land. But then she smiled and he wondered if he was being a little oversensitive. She liked the lake, after all. "Okay, 'neighbors.' What's 'O'?"

But that was when Jasmine arrived. Josh smelled her familiar perfume before she'd even tucked her hand into the back of his jeans, that familiar claim of ownership that he hated so much. He reached behind him to pull her hand out, but he tried to do it subtly. Ashley couldn't see what was going on back there and he'd just as soon she not know about it.

"So, you two are getting along?" Jasmine asked. Her smile was sharp. "I was just going to call for the car. For myself. Josh, can I trust you to make sure Ashley gets home safely? Eventually?"

She'd taken her hand out from inside his jeans but now she had it resting on the curve of his ass, her fingers digging in a little where they wrapped underneath. How many people in the bar were seeing that? Seeing her treat him like a possession that she could paw at will, or give away to her friends if the whim struck her?

He stepped away from her entirely. She and her husband had a lot of friends, and most of those friends were Josh's clients. He really couldn't afford to alienate her, but he wasn't going to stand there and let her molest him, either. "I'm just about to head out myself," he said, working to keep his voice light and calm. "Ashley, maybe you want to go with Jasmine?"

She nodded slowly. "Yeah. Okay."

"Oh," Jasmine said. Her disappointment was a little too blatant to be real. The emotions Jasmine displayed for public consumption rarely had any relationship to her actual feelings; Josh had learned that the hard way. "But you two seemed to be getting along so well. Do you just need a little more time? I don't *have* to leave now. . . ."

"No," Josh said firmly. He didn't want to get dragged into whatever the hell this was. "Like I said, I'm about to go." He set his empty glass down on the bar and nodded. "Ashley, it was nice to meet you. Enjoy your stay in hazardous Vermont. Be safe."

She grinned at him. Damn, he liked her smile. And he liked how often she used it.

"I'll try. I'm a little worried that I haven't identified all of the risks yet. If I'm approached by something from 'A' to 'N,' I feel like I'll be prepared. But if something from 'O' on attacks . . ."

Jasmine laughed. "You two have a little game! How adorable!"

Josh was not a fan of being called "adorable," and from the expression on Ashley's face he could tell she felt the same. So he smiled just at Ashley as he said, "We are pretty fucking cute."

"Might as well accept it," she replied, and her shoulder shrug was a lot more relaxed than it would have been a moment earlier. Somehow, in that quick second, they'd become a team. The two of them united against Jasmine.

And Jasmine could tell. "Fine, then," she said, her joking tone gone. "Ashley, if you're coming with me, let's go. Josh, I really would like the path through the trees re-mulched as soon as possible. I asked you to do that several days ago. And there are some boards on the dock that are rotting. We need them replaced before someone puts a foot through them."

Yeah. Good reminder of his place in their social structure. He told himself to be grateful for it. "I can try to get to the dock tomorrow—you've got some extra boards in your boat-house, so it won't take long to replace a few weak ones. I'll probably get to the mulch early next week. Everyone came up this week and found a lot of stuff they want done, so I'm working through the list as quickly as I can."

"Most of the names on that list are there because *we* referred you to them. Why don't you do the boards *and* the mulch tomorrow?"

Another good reminder. So he made himself smile. "I appreciate the referrals. But the mulch is a bigger job, and nobody's going to get hurt if a path isn't mulched. So it's lower priority."

"It would be a shame if we had to find someone else to recommend to people."

Okay, there had to be an end to it. "If you can find some-one else who does work of my quality at my price, I guess they deserve your support." He stepped backward, disengaging from the conversation, then said, "Good night," and turned for the parking lot.

He was halfway to the door when he felt a warm hand catch his, and he turned to see Ashley looking tentative but determined. "Good night," she said quickly, and she brought her free hand to the back of his neck and pulled his head down. She stood on her tiptoes and pressed a quick kiss to the corner of his mouth. "Thank you."

It made no sense to let her go. He wanted to drag her out of there. No, not drag her—pick her up and carry her. But she'd been drinking, and Jasmine was . . . Jasmine was Jasmine. Always playing her games by rules only she knew. Josh wasn't interested in being her pawn anymore, and he felt a bit protective about Ashley, too. He had no idea what Jasmine was up to, but Ashley shouldn't get dragged into whatever it was.

"It was nice to meet you," he said, and he gently eased out of her grip.

She blinked and let him go. "I'm here for another week," she said. "Until next Friday. Do you think maybe—"

"This is the busy season for me," he said quickly. "Paths to mulch, you know? Very important stuff. No time for much else."

Another blink. "Okay," she said.

She sounded sad, but he bet he could kiss her into a better mood without much trouble. Except he wasn't supposed to be thinking that way. He knew better. "Good night, Ashley." He turned before she could say anything else that tempted him to do something different. He was dimly aware of people watching him, trying to figure out why the hell he was walking away from the woman behind him. It was a small town and half the bar knew who he was. They knew he'd made different decisions in similar situations in the past.

Ironic, he supposed, that he gave up on summer women right before he met one who seemed like she might be something a bit more. But he shook his head as he headed out the door and toward his pickup. Ashley was in town until Friday. Had he lost his mind, thinking there was going to be something more that developed over that time? Summer women were transient. For a while, that had been their biggest charm. But he was too old for that crap now, and he was tired of being the one getting left behind when they went back to their glamorous city lives.

"You heading out early?" he heard, and turned to see Theo standing just outside the bar door. It was the smoking area, but Josh had never seen Theo actually light up—he probably figured just being around smokers was enough of a nod to the rock 'n' roll lifestyle. "Had enough already?"

"I guess so, yeah. I'm getting too old for it maybe."

"Ninety percent of the guys in the bar would have cut off a body part to have either of those women fighting over them," Theo said philosophically.

"You want an introduction? Ashley seems nice enough, but Jasmine? Mess with Jasmine at your own risk."

"What would you do if I said yes?" Theo leaned a little closer, trying to get a better look at Josh's face in the dim light. "Not Jasmine. . . . I've already been chewed up and spat out by women like that, thanks very much. But if I asked for an introduction to Ashley . . ."

"I'd say you didn't need it. You've already met. She likes your band, remember?"

"She likes my band, but as soon as you gave her the time of day, I might as well not have existed. That's Ashley Carlsen, you know. The *movie star*. That's who you just walked away from."

"Yeah," Josh said slowly. "I think I noticed that."

Theo shook his head in amusement and mock disgust, and they stood silently for a moment before Theo headed back in to his band and Josh started for home.

He was climbing behind the wheel of his pickup as a black sedan pulled up to the bar door. It looked completely out of place in the surroundings, but he knew why it was there. He'd spent enough time in the backseat of the damn thing. Sure enough, Jasmine came staggering out of the bar, her arm looped through Ashley's. They were both dressed for city clubbing, totally over-the-top for a Vermont bar, but Josh hadn't noticed that inside. He'd just seen Ashley, a pretty girl with a sweet smile.

Now, as Jasmine's shrieking laughter stabbed his eardrums even from across the lot, he could see how ridiculous it all was. Ashley was part of another world. A glamorous land where housekeepers washed her underwear, drivers took her home from bars, and handymen spread mulch on her friends' pathways. He'd visited that world, but he'd never belonged. And he didn't want to be a visitor anymore.

He had enough to worry about. He wasn't a kid anymore, and he didn't have the energy for getting involved with something he knew was going to end badly. So he watched the car pull away and he drove home by himself.

JOSH usually got caught up on his paperwork on Sundays and then took the rest of the day off, but he wanted Jasmine McArthur off his back. And, maybe, just maybe, he wanted one more look at Ashley Carlsen. He knew it was stupid, but once she'd dropped the whole seduction routine, he'd really liked her.

Yet in his typical contrary manner, he carefully arranged to visit the McArthur place at the time he was least likely to run into anybody. Especially anybody who'd been out late the night before, drinking and carousing.

The sun was barely over the horizon as he parked off to the side of the driveway, well away from the expensive cars of the people who belonged there, and hoisted his toolbox and the replacement boards out of the truck bed. The McArthur cottage was, like many others on Lake Sullivan, on top of a low cliff overlooking the lake; he found his way to the long wooden staircase that connected the house to the waterside and made his way down.

That was when he saw her. She stood on the end of the McArthurs' dock, still and graceful as a heron, silhouetted against the rising sun. She was wearing a simple one-piece bathing suit, watching a family of loons swim past.

Josh felt like a peeping tom, invading Ashley's moment of peace and solitude. Just as he was about to turn away and find somewhere else to start his day's work, she raised her arms and gracefully dove into the water, like a mermaid returning home after too much time among the humans.

She stayed under a long time, long enough that he started worrying about submerged rocks her head might have connected with. His feet were on the gangplank when she reappeared thirty feet away from the end of the dock. She'd turned around underwater, so she was looking back toward the shore, and he still had the sense that she was returning to her own world. He could see it in his mind, the way she'd dive again and disappear with a quick flash of her tail fin.

But she didn't. She just raised an arm to wave at him, then ducked back underwater. By the time he got to the end of the dock he could see her skimming along just under the surface of the water, a long, pale line against the dark green of the lake.

She smiled as she lifted her face out of the water and looked up at him. "You're here early. Is there a mulch emergency?"

"Just trying to get the dock fixed before it's covered with people."

"Should I stay in the water, out of your way?"

"No, it's fine. One person won't be a problem."

She didn't climb out right away, though. She floated on her back, her eyes closed, as he tried not to look in her direction. He was there for a job.

He had the old boards unscrewed and stacked by the time she climbed up the ladder and wrapped a towel around herself.

"You're up early, too," he said. If he'd thought about it he'd have kept his mouth shut, but he'd been distracted by trying not to watch the towel as it edged down over her breasts. "Especially since you were drinking yesterday."

"Swimming's the best hangover cure I know," she said with a smile. "Nice cool water, and I swear the pressure of it against my skull helps squish my brains back where they're supposed to be."

"That seems medically unlikely."

She shrugged. "I don't ask questions, I just feel grateful that it works." She settled onto the diving board and leaned back, her eyes closed again, her face turned toward the sun.

He worked quietly for a couple minutes, then glanced over to find her watching him. "You know what you're doing, huh?"

He frowned. "It's not too tricky. Take out the old boards, put in the new ones. They're already cut to the right length, even."

"I wouldn't know how to do it."

"You already do." He held his cordless drill out toward her. "I'm using this as a screwdriver. I just place the board, slap in a couple screws, and it's done. You want to try?"

She didn't answer right away, then said, "Yeah, I kinda do. Is that okay?"

"Sure, if you want. There's not much to mess up."

She practically skipped across the dock, and stood so close to him he could smell the clean lake water in her hair.

"This trigger controls the drill. Push it gently for slow, or speed it up by pushing the trigger all the way in."

She took the drill, played with the trigger a little, and

then they crouched down and he held a board in place while she drove in a few screws. "That easy?" she asked, a pleased grin on her face.

"That easy."

"Can I do one all by myself?"

"Be my guest."

So he took her place on the diving board and she found a board and fit it into place. She didn't look totally natural. She dropped one screw and it fell between two slats, landing in the lake below with a soft splash, and she looked up at him with an almost comic expression of guilt.

"It's not a big deal," he reassured her. "They don't cost much, and one wood screw won't hurt the lake."

She nodded and went back to work, and when the board was attached she turned to him with a triumphant grin. "Look! I did that!"

"Nice work. Looks secure."

"Holy smokes." She was still beaming. "I can't believe how proud I am!"

"Neither can I," he admitted with a laugh. "You want to keep going, or should I take over?"

She looked tempted, then shook her head and held the drill out to him. "You'd better take over. I want to go out on top, before I mess something up."

They traded places again and Josh quickly finished the remaining boards. He was done. It was time to go. But for some reason he was reluctant to leave.

"Hey!" Ashley whispered excitedly. "Look! I saw those guys before. Are those loons?"

Josh looked out at the lake. He kept his voice low as he said, "Yeah. A nice little family, huh?"

"I saw them yesterday, too!"

"You come back next year, you'll probably see the same ones. At least the parents. They fly south for the winter, but they come back to the same lake every year."

"Yesterday it looked like . . ." Ashley frowned. "I was going to look it up on the Internet, but I got distracted. But it looked like the babies were riding on the mom's back. Do they do that?"

"Yeah. I'm not sure why. . . . They do it more when the water's cold, so maybe it's to help them stay warm? But I guess it would be good protection against predators, too."

"Predators? Who eats baby loons?"

"Turtles. Big fish. Hawks, probably."

Ashley looked toward the lake as if she were worrying about an attack.

"I've been on this lake for thirty-one years and I've never actually seen it happen," Josh said. He didn't want to ruin the poor woman's vacation with imagined loon carnage.

Ashley relaxed a little. "Did we count any of those on our list of Vermont hazards last night? We haven't gotten to 'T' yet. Maybe that should be 'turtles.'"

"Or 'S' for 'snappers.' There's some nice little turtles up here who wouldn't hurt anybody, not even a baby loon. It's the snappers you want to watch out for."

"I think 'S' should probably be reserved for 'snakes.' Anywhere snakes live, they should be the number one 'S'-related hazard."

"Fair enough," Josh agreed. He didn't mind snakes himself, but he wasn't in the mood to argue.

They watched the loons in companionable silence for a few more minutes, and then the dock vibrated a little as someone stepped onto the gangplank. They both turned.

"Well, you're up early!" Jasmine said with exaggerated

cheer. She had a glass of orange juice in her hand, and Josh knew from past experience that it would have at least champagne but more likely vodka in it. Ashley might swim to control her hangovers, but Jasmine preferred a hair of the dog approach. Just one more thing Josh wished he had no reason to know.

Ashley and Josh had been speaking quietly enough that the loons had come quite close, but with Jasmine's arrival they were heading away. Josh figured it was time for him to follow their example. "I got the boards replaced," he said, nodding at the wood beneath their feet. "And I'll be by on Wednesday, probably, for the mulch."

"Wednesday." Jasmine pronounced the word as if it had an unpleasant taste. "You're here today. Why not today?"

"Church," Josh said. He hadn't been inside a church since the last wedding he'd attended. And Jasmine would know his Sunday routine as well as he knew her hangover cures. But he didn't think she'd want to explain how she'd come by that knowledge, not with a witness. So he smiled blandly at her then nodded in Ashley's direction. "Snakes and turtles," he said. "But I think we missed a couple letters in the middle somewhere."

"Next time," she said.

He knew better, but he smiled anyway, then gathered the discarded boards and tucked them under one arm while he carried his toolbox with the other and headed off the dock. He tried not to react at all when Jasmine followed him.

When they reached the top of the stairs she said, "So you two are still being adorable, are you? With your little game?"

"We just can't help it, I guess. We were born that way, you know?"

"Well, I hope Ashley doesn't think that *our* game is still in play."

"Whose game?"

"Ashley's and mine." Jasmine looked at him and her face transformed into the first genuine smile he'd seen from her in ages. "Oh, Josh! She didn't tell you?"

Anything that made Jasmine that happy was going to make someone else sad, and Josh had a pretty good idea who the "someone else" would be in this situation. "So hopefully I can do the mulch on Wednesday. Might not be until Thursday, though."

But Jasmine wasn't so easily distracted. "I'm surprised she didn't mention it to you, with all the giggling you two have been doing together."

Josh was pretty sure he hadn't been giggling, but he was at the truck now, tossing the wood into the back and not bothering to secure his toolbox as carefully as he usually did. He wasn't going to engage with whatever Jasmine was up to, certainly not to debate whether he'd been laughing. Then he turned and saw Jasmine leaning against the driver's door. She wasn't going to let him leave until she said whatever it was. He braced himself and she smiled wickedly.

"I bet her she couldn't fuck you." Jasmine waited for a reaction, but Josh was pretty sure he managed not to give her one. Jasmine's shrug was over-casual. "She's having a bit of a tiff with her boyfriend at home, and I thought she could use a little distraction. For all your failings, Josh, you've always been a good distraction that way. So I thought you might be good for her, but she wasn't interested. I mean . . ." She ran her eyes down Josh's ragged clothes. "Not really her type, obviously. But with the bet? The girl's a competitor, I'll give her that. That's what made her come over to you in the bar."

It was just one more sleazy interaction with Jasmine. Just one more opportunity for her to poke at him, looking for holes in his armor. This wasn't anything new. There was no reason for Josh's stomach to be churning.

"I need to get going," he said, but she didn't move from her spot by his door. He could have picked her up and set her aside without any trouble, but she was a client and he was on her property. He supposed he could have gone around to the passenger side and worked his way across the cab, but it would have been awkward, especially with her laughing at him the whole time. So he just stood there and waited.

"She's a movie star, Josh. Did you honestly think she'd be interested in you without a little outside encouragement?" Jasmine smiled sweetly.

And he managed to return the expression. "No, not really. I mean, you and me? Yeah, okay, that made basic sense. But someone like Ashley? Totally out of my league. We were just talking about loons, Jasmine. Nothing for you to be jealous about."

He saw her eyes narrow and knew he'd gone too far. But he just couldn't make himself care. She had more money than God and she had a lot of influence with the Lake Sullivan summer people. She wasn't a good person to have as an enemy. But she was an even worse person to have as a friend.

"Excuse me," he said, and she stepped aside, letting him climb into the truck. He watched her in the rearview mirror as he pulled away. She wasn't moving, just standing there, staring after him. Planning her revenge, he was sure.

Damn it. He'd worked so hard to keep his cool around her, and he'd managed it for so long. And then he'd blown it with one stupid conversation.

He didn't want to think about what had made him so angry. Didn't want to think about Ashley and her stupid grin when she'd attached the board to the dock. So she'd been playing around. So she hadn't really wanted him. Big deal. He'd known she was trouble, and he'd stayed away. He'd done the right thing. He was fine. Just fine.

He wondered how long it was going to take before he started believing the lines he was telling himself.